Consumed by Fate

SHANNON MAYER

Consumed by Fate

NEW YORK TIMES BESTSELLING AUTHOR

SHANNON MAYER

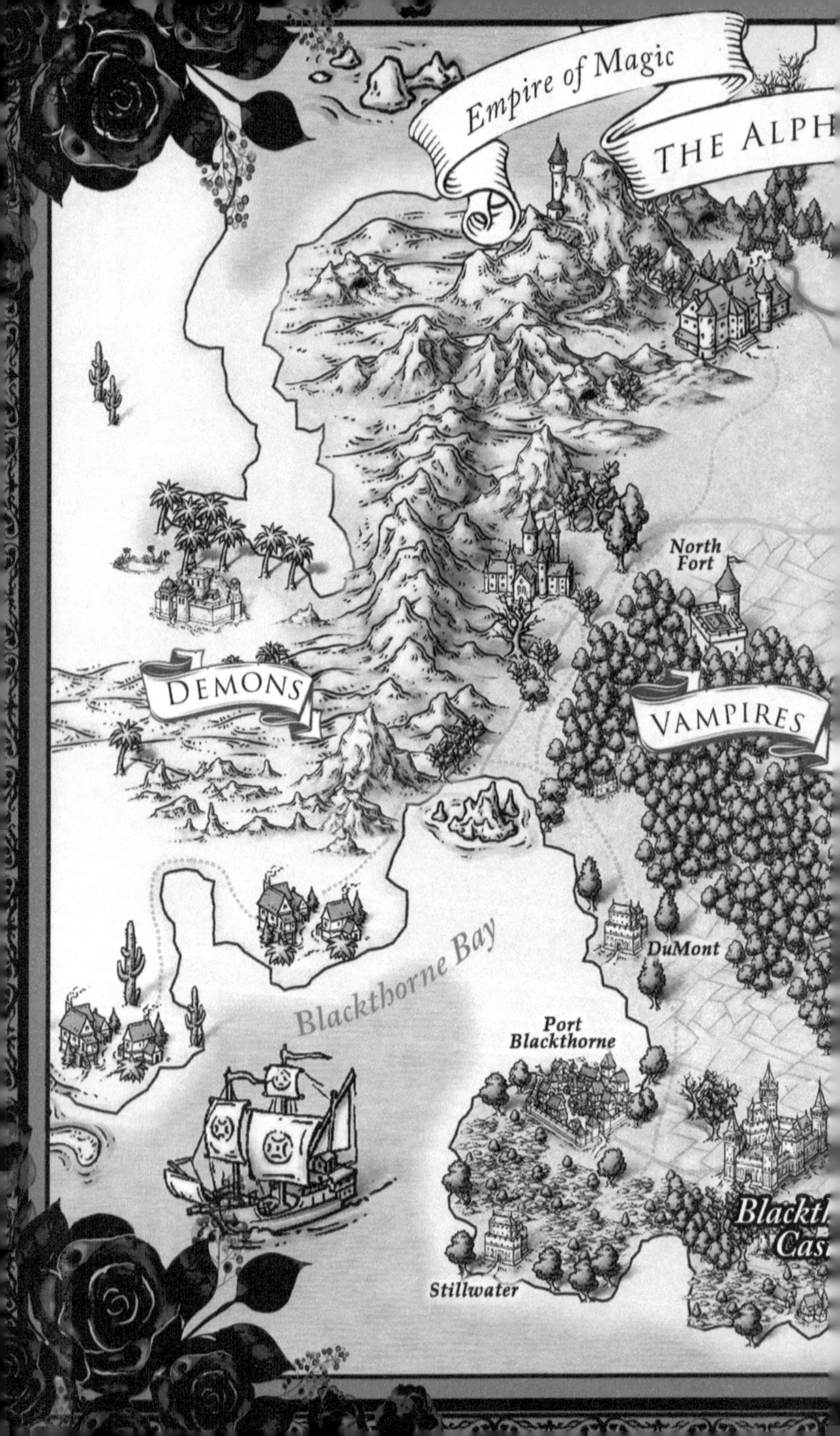

Empire of Magic
THE ALPH
DEMONS
VAMPIRES
North Fort
DuMont
Blackthorne Bay
Port Blackthorne
Stillwater
Blackt
Cas

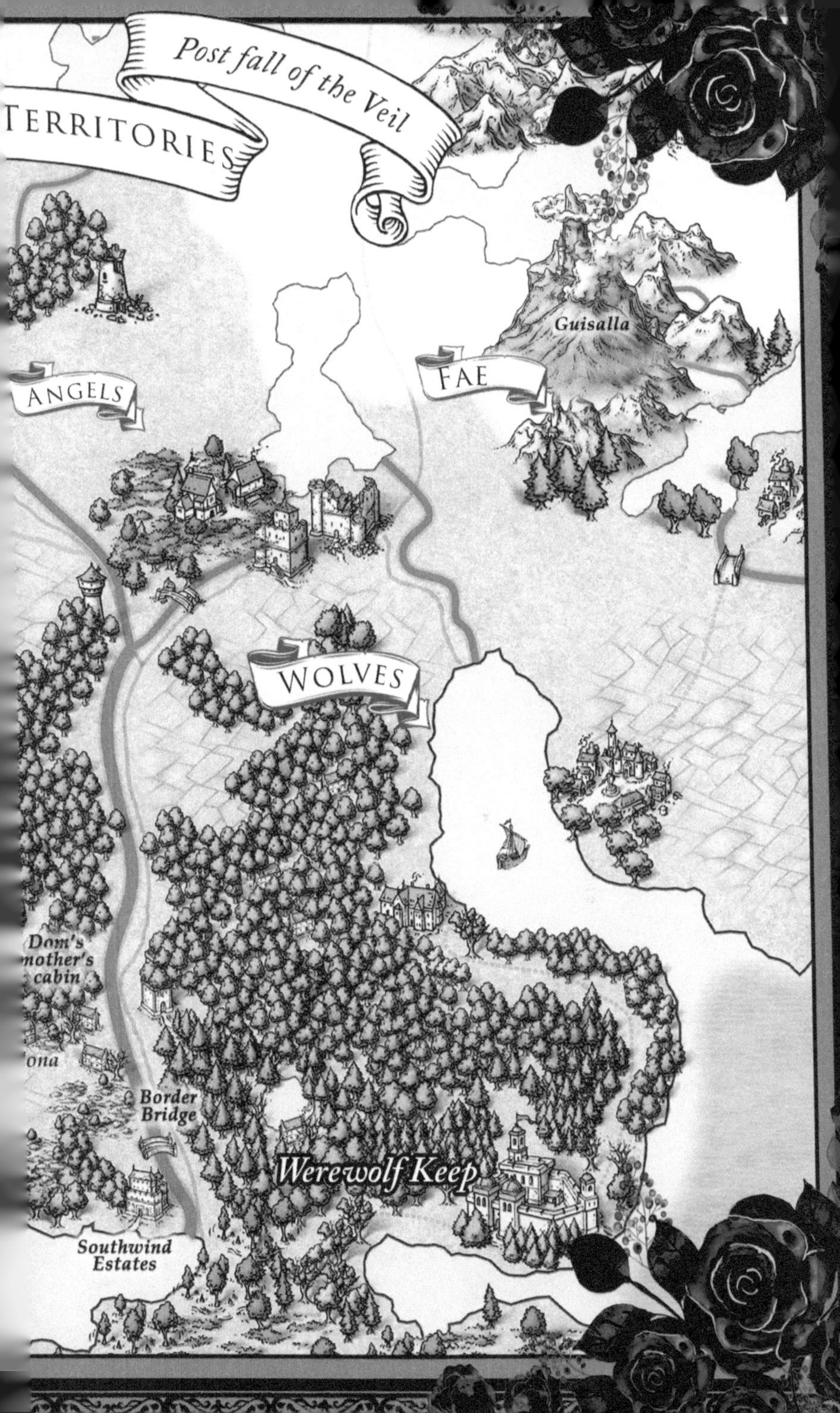

Post fall of the Veil
TERRITORIES
ANGELS
FAE
Guisalla
WOLVES
Dom's mother's cabin
ona
Border Bridge
Werewolf Keep
Southwind Estates

Prologue

Maverick

I stumbled through the dense bush, wondering if the directions I'd gotten were even real. Sure, I'd been playing poker with a demon, and I'd laid my soul on the line to get the information I wanted, but if she found out I cheated...I was fucked.

Much as I wanted to mutter under my breath, curse the winged demon bitch out, I kept my mouth shut, and sound to a minimum.

Her directions had been simple, and I could still see her brilliant red lips as she gave them.

"Go northeast to the borderlands between us and the fae. The witch's hut will appear in the fog of a summer morning, as the first kiss of autumn appears."

Mind you, that had been weeks ago, and I was fighting to get to that unseen border before summer began to wane. Even now, it was possible I was too late. The mornings weren't as balmy as they'd been when I'd escaped my master.

I ran my fingertip over the stone embedded in my right wrist, pushed deep into the flesh. Or more accurately, where the stone *had* been. The wound was small and throbbed even now, weeks after I'd dug it out.

I shoved the heavy palm fronds out of my way, stumbling in the dark. I'd traveled at night, hoping to come upon the witch's hut just as the morning rose.

My *last* hope of escaping this place.

A shudder went through me. I would get out of the Territories. I didn't care that I'd been born here, or that my mother had been born here, or that we'd been owned by the same fucking demon.

I was getting out of here, one way or another.

The sunlight sparked through the trees, long beams of light igniting the world in a shower of color. The green of leaves and bush was brighter, the birds sang loudly welcoming the day, and there wasn't a fucking droplet of mist anywhere.

"Gods." I couldn't hold it in any longer, I drove both fists into the sky and tipped my head back. "I just need to find this fucking witch!"

My words echoed through the forest, bouncing around, and then back to me along with...along with a soft laugh. A shiver ran down my spine, and my flesh reacted, hair raising along my arms.

Fucking witch, eh? The voice seemed to float through the air, as if she were not physical but sheer vapor and mist. Fog rolled up from the ground as if it were steaming hot, the air filling with moisture and condensation in a matter of seconds.

I swallowed hard and did a slow turn, realizing I had gotten her attention and that if I wasn't careful, it would be the end of me and all my plans. *Play it smart, Mav.*

"I meant no disrespect, my lady! I have been searching for you for weeks and thought that perhaps...I would never find you. Forgive me."

The mist thickened around me until I could see nothing, not even the hand I held up to my face. I blinked, moisture sliding over my skin.

"I beg a boon, my lady, I am a desperate man in need of your skills and help. There is no one else I can turn to."

Why should I help you? I remain in my veiled home safe, away from those who have slaughtered so many of my sisters. Why should I help you, human?

My mother said my father had a silver tongue like no other, and that he'd given it to me. Would it be enough to fool a witch? It was about time to find out.

I dropped to my knees and bowed my head. "My daughter Delilah...she will be sacrificed on the next full moon in the demon lands. My master, the Red Baron takes his pleasure with the girls and then tortures them, bathing in their blood. My Delilah...she is to be next."

I let my voice hitch on the last bit, cracking and dropping so that the words were barely clear.

Now, the trick of telling a good lie, is to keep as much to the truth as you can. The Red Baron *did* take girls, and rape them, and torture them for days, until he finally ended their lives. I did not, on the other hand, have a daughter.

"She..." My voice ended on a sob, and I covered my face with both hands. The witch herself had given me a way to make her want to help me.

Her sisters were dead, that's what she'd said.

Then I'd give her a *new* sister to try and save.

"She carries magic, my lady, like you. I don't know how she was blessed, but she is still young...only nine, with locks of raven and eyes full of starlight. I would die for her, my lady, but I cannot kill a demon, I cannot escape this place without help. I am a mere man. As you said, just a powerless human."

A low hiss ripped through the air, and the mist evaporated. I lifted my head. A cloaked figure stood in front of me. One hand lifted, crooking long, elegant fingers tipped with dagger-like nails. "Come with me."

She turned in a swirl. I caught a glimpse of shimmering black skirts, a flash of leather boots, and a figure so shapely it truly caught me off guard. I expected the witch to be old, shriveled, and ugly.

This...this could be an even easier job than I'd

thought. If I could seduce her too, perhaps she would give me more than a way out of this place...

Mind bursting with the possibilities, I hurried after her.

She flicked her fingers, sparks shooting out around her hands. They floated for a moment around her, like stars caught mid-air, before falling to the ground. The thick loamy earth seemed to soak up the sparks, pulling them in deep, as if thirsty for the magic.

A sudden groan split the air, like a beast bellowing early in the morning.

Right before my eyes, a structure sprouted up from the ground, as if it were grown from the seeds of magic she'd let loose. The peaked roof first, dirt flowing down off the shingles, then beams and wooden slats, doors, windows followed.

The earth heaved and shoved the house out, only settling once the door was clear of the ground. Deep green vines with brilliant red flowers worked their way up around one side of the house, smoke puffed softly from the chimney above. A light flickered inside, visible through the warped glass of the front window, but there was no knob that I could see on the door...

The witch stepped to the entrance and the door swung wide without her touching it.

"If you truly mean to save your daughter, then enter. But do not think there will not be a cost. All magic has a cost, Maverick."

I swallowed hard, fear nearly choking me. If she

could read my mind, I was done. "You...know my name?"

"I know a great deal, Maverick." She tipped her head to look back at me. Her eyes were silvery, rimmed with gold. They made me think of cat eyes, watching the mice while deciding which one it would pounce on.

I found myself bowing—in part for show, in part for real. Her presence commanded respect that I hadn't felt in a...well maybe my whole life.

A few steps later, and I was inside the witch's hut. The door clicked shut behind me and...the house rumbled as it began to sink back under the crust of the earth. I put a hand on the wall to steady myself. There was no way out if I fucked this up.

"How...did you know my name?"

She flipped off her cloak over a high-backed chair, revealing herself fully. "I've been watching you stumble around my forest, muttering under your breath."

I nodded and pulled my thoughts together. *You're a terrified father.* "My daughter, Delilah. You can help her?"

The witch stepped into the firelight, her hair silvery like her eyes, only unlike her eyes the strands leaned to a lilac tone that made me think of the flowers my mother grew. The urge to reach out and touch it had me lifting my hand. I snapped it back to my side and shook my head, fear wrapping around me.

"Your beauty makes me forget why I am here, my lady."

A laugh escaped her. "Truly, it has been a spell since I've had company. Would you prefer me to hide my true form?"

"No."

She nodded and then frowned, her expression growing serious. "Time for a bitter truth. Your daughter...to save her the cost will be high. Changing the tides of fate is no small thing." She moved across the room, the curve of her waist and breast drawing me in like a bee to honey.

Gods, how long had it been since I'd had a woman that wasn't so malnourished that her bones jabbed at me with every thrust?

Too long.

The demons took the soft, curved women for themselves and left us with nothing but wraiths.

I blew out a breath and clenched my fists. "I am willing to change those tides and pay the price." I hesitated. "For Delilah. For my daughter."

She went to a high podium where a book sat. Not a massive book in size. It could have been a simple ledger to account for her wares. Her hand hovered over it and the pages flipped on their own, a soft *shush* with each page flicking by as she moved two fingers side to side.

"Very well. A man of conviction I can work with." Her hand paused. "Here. This will be useful."

I didn't ask her the cost. I knew that a man who loved his daughter would not ask a price—he would pay anything. And so, I stayed silent as she worked.

Next, she went to a long table against the wall. She moved with ease, not slow, and not fast, as she gathered items. Like a cook, she chopped ingredients on the scarred wood surface, methodically adding them to the cauldron bubbling over the fire.

I inched my way closer, finding myself next to the podium and the ledger-like book that she'd worked from.

With her back turned, I peeked at the page she'd stopped on. To the left, the words were written in a scrawling hand—

To craft a blade of death.

To the right was another set of words in a different handwriting.

To craft power and fame.

Well fuck me up and twist my balls. Excitement shot through me. "You can truly do this?"

"I *am* doing it." She laughed softly and glanced over her shoulder at me. I made sure to be looking straight at her, instead of the book. Which was how I saw the color in her cheeks, and the way her lashes drifted as she looked me up and down. "Your mate, your daughter's mother…"

"She died of the night scourge. Three years ago. My daughter and I have been alone since then, but every day I am grateful for the child she gave me."

I bowed my head and touched two fingers between my eyes, a sign of grief and a begging for souls to pass over easily.

When I looked up, she still had her gaze fixed on me, a glimmer of tears in the corner.

Gotcha.

She went back to her work, the herbs and ingredients none that I recognized. Though when I glanced at the book, I could see what they would be.

Heart of posy.

Shells of a gryphon egg.

Sage.

Bone dust from a warrior. But it was the last set of ingredients that truly had my attention.

Powdered blood—vampire, fae, werewolf, angel, and demon.

Even I in my ignorance knew that the blood of the five races was powerful—and all together, they could become a weapon that would save me not only from the demons, but any who came at me.

I would be unstoppable.

The witch stood and put her hands to the small of her back, stretching. "Do you have a blade?"

I blinked and then touched the dagger at my side. "I do, but it's not much. Certainly not a sword or—"

"A sword is too much iron for this spell. A dagger will be just fine." She held out her hand, palm up, crooking her fingers in a wave once more.

I pulled the dagger free from the sheath and walked to her. "It was my father's blade."

Another lie. I wasn't about to tell her I stole it from the demons, after all. I needed her to think I was good and trustworthy if I wanted her help. Without it, I'd be stuck here in the Territories still trying to figure out how to make the supposedly magical dagger work. It would only be a matter of time before the demons I'd escaped found me and dragged me back to serve them.

After they'd finished torturing me, of course...

"Even better that it has a tie to you, Maverick of the desert lands. It will speak to you." She took the blade and held it to the light. "And the iron is cheap and pitted, so the magic will sink into it good and proper."

With a turn on her heel, she flipped the blade into the air where it hovered and spun slowly, end over end, until it was just above the cauldron. A snap of her fingers and it dropped into the liquid with a plunk, a bright plume of brilliant blue smoke rolling up around the handles of the cauldron.

"The power will take time to seep into the blade, Maverick." She turned to face me. "Hours. When the fire dies, the blade will be ready."

I swallowed hard as she stepped closer, already knowing where this was going. "My lady, I will gladly wait."

"Ah, but you must pay a price, Maverick." Her smile spread, showing straight teeth except for her canines, top and bottom. They each had a slight point to them, once more reminding me of the cats that stalked the sands.

I spread my hands. "What price, my lady? You know I would pay anything for my daughter's safety. To save her from the Red Baron."

She was my height so when she stepped close, we

were nose to nose. "You have a child with magic, Maverick. It came not from her mother, as I sense a lingering line of magic within you."

What the fuck? "But I am only human."

Her smile was not unkind. "Perhaps somewhere in your family line, a bastard was born, a child of a slave and master. Perhaps demon. Perhaps fae. Perhaps even witch." She lifted a hand to my cheek, her touch hot like a brand. "You are rare, Maverick. Perhaps more than you realize."

My heart was racing. *Play it right, man, play it fucking right and you will win the day.* "My lady. This...if what you are asking...is more a boon to me than to you. It is not enough for what you are doing for me. For my daughter."

Her eyes shut, long dark lashes fluttering over her near midnight skin. "A child, Maverick, as you know, is no small boon. I want a child of magic, a daughter to raise in the ways of my sisters and me. That is the payment I require, for the blade to save your daughter. Give me a child of my own."

This time, I did not hesitate. I stepped into her arms and cupped her face, breathing her in, the smell of herbs fresh around her as my lips brushed over hers, a tingle of power rippling between us, her hands slid under my shirt, drifting to my waist.

I stared into those silver and gold eyes, framed by long coils of lilac hair, and felt myself falling into her spell. As if I were looking into the stars themselves, set into the night sky.

I ran my thumbs along her jaw, feeling something shift within me.

"As you wish, my lady."

* * *

The witch lay sound asleep; the fire having burnt low hours before as she'd screamed for the pleasure I'd given her. I lay on my back, my body relaxed, satiated. The witch was...well she was a phenom, giving pleasure even as I gave it. The taste of her was still there on my lips.

She tasted like magic.

And now I had to leave her. I slipped from the bed, chasing away the desire to slide back under the covers and fuck her one more time, to take everything I could. But I needed her asleep while I made my way out.

Because I wasn't just taking the knife. That book was coming with me too.

If I was magic, if she truly thought I had something in me that was worthy of planting a child in her womb, then I would find a way to make that book work for me.

Dressing swiftly by the light of the candle, I crept first to the cauldron. The fire below was gone, not even embers were left. I could not see into the bottom. Which meant I had no choice but to trust that the boiling liquid was indeed gone, and reached in.

My fingers encountered nothing, until the bottom, my fingernails scraping along the bottom.

And I found it.

The handle of my dagger was still the same, but as I pulled it out, the blade began to glow with a soft, blue light.

Magic. I grinned and tucked it into my sheath. There was no time to waste staring at it—I was on borrowed time.

Next, I went to the ledger. I could have taken just the single page but...there was so much there.

I scooped the thin book and tucked it under my shirt.

Now I was ready to leave. And I knew just how I was going to get out.

The realization had come to me in a flash, lying in bed next to her. Her. I didn't even know her name. She never gave it.

Then again, names were powerful, especially for a witch. The last witch by all counts.

I hurried once more to the fireplace, ducking and stepping inside. The chimney was wide enough, I was pretty sure. And the smoke had to go somewhere.

I took a breath, and jumped as high as I could, snapping my hands and feet out wide, catching myself on either side of the brick chimney.

Bingo.

Moving slowly, carefully, I worked my way up to the very top. Now came the moment of truth. I put my hand up and thrust it through the dirt over my head.

My hand encountered air. Grinning, I pushed my way up, my head emerging through the thin layer of soil first, then pulling the rest of my body out.

I always did like being smarter than everyone else, and here once again, I had clearly proven I was even smarter than a witch.

I crawled out of the chimney and was up on my feet and running. I would follow the river south, as it bordered three territories. Demon. Fae. Werewolf. If I could get to the werewolves....well, my understanding was that they were the dumbest of the races. Easily fooled.

It would make getting to the mainland that much easier. I'd find a pretty girl, seduce her, get her to trust me and then bam, I was gone with the wind.

I tipped back my head and laughed. "Well done, Mav, well fucking done!"

The witch woke slowly, her body at ease with what she'd done. Already she could feel the life in her brewing, the spark of magic that Maverick had gifted her. A fair trade indeed. Her hand went to her belly, protectively. "I will keep you safe, little one. You will be the strongest witch our world has ever seen."

She rolled to her side, expecting Maverick and finding...nothing.

Her feet swung to the side of the bed, and she stood, naked and stunned. How could he be gone?

With a snap of her fingers, her dress of starlight wrapped around her, and she hurried to the cauldron. The blade was gone. Dirt was splattered all over the edges of the fireplace. She looked up, seeing a bit of light at the top of the chimney. He'd climbed all the way out?

She could forgive him, she supposed. His daughter was heavy on his mind. "Good luck, Maverick. I pray you save your daughter, even as I raise ours."

She blew a kiss up the chimney. He was clever, she'd give him that. It was a great mark that their child would be savvy, and able to problem solve as well as be a powerful witch.

She turned, a smile on her lips. So much to look forward to. So much to plan for...her smile slipped as she looked to her podium. The grimoire...her book of spells...was gone.

She ran and clasped the edges of the podium...he'd seen it, he must have seen it last night.

The only other spell that was on the page was a drought for power and fame. A laugh bubbled up in her.

"You fool. You goddess be damned fool. You think I can't spell you still?"

A tap of one foot and she raised her hands to the ceiling. The only thing that softened her was the fact that he had indeed given her a daughter. And for that...she would not destroy him...or at least not all at once, at any rate.

"A curse upon you, Maverick, for theft, for deception...your silver tongue will not save you from a long life. I curse you, Maverick of the desert, to live a life *too* long, to feel the weight of it on your shoulders, to never know safety, or peace, or rest...to feel the pressure of age even as your face remains the same." Her power flowed through her, the curse growing in strength. "Weaker... until your body becomes as useless as your black heart."

CHAPTER 1

Raven

To say my Frostbite was avoiding me would be like saying a vampire was only slightly trying to avoid going out into the sun without any protection. Although I doubted stepping into the sun could hurt worse than this. I made a mental note to ask Dominic if perhaps I should just do that—step out in broad daylight and just be done with it all.

For the past week, whenever Diana got so much as a whiff of me, she was gone. I was left with glimpses of her hair around corners, the heel of her boot, and the smell of her sorrow lingering where she'd stood a few moments before.

A pain that I'd never felt before was eating me from the inside out, like something was being torn from me, leaving a gaping hole. No amount of blood drunk touched the constant throbbing, it was like an ulcer I couldn't soothe. I'd heard of them from humans, but I'd never experienced one. No vampire would, not with our biology. Yet even breathing hurt me, and the fissures of agony were spreading with each moment that Diana stayed as far from me as she could.

My worry that took the pain even deeper...was that I wasn't just feeling *my* pain. But the fear that I was feeling Diana's too, as our mate bond deepened with the blood exchange we'd made to save her life. The thought of her hurting like this, of this being *her* suffering, was unacceptable.

She was being torn from her wolf, and it was my fault, even if we both knew it had been the only way to save her...

I had to find a way to make it better for her. I had to find a way to stop this because the thought of her going through this for much longer...I would take her hurt a thousand times over to spare her from it if I could.

Would it be best to leave? What could I do to stop this unseen wound from spreading further? Could we give her back her wolf somehow now that the shard from the Veil had calmed within her?

All those questions led me to Duchess Evangeline's door, my fist poised to knock. If anyone knew how to help Diana, it would be her—I hoped. She loved Diana as if she was her daughter.

I took a moment longer, then rapped two knuckles against the door. "Duchess, may I speak with you?"

A rustle of skirts and the softest of footsteps preceded the Duchess opening the door. No longer the proud, vibrant woman I'd always known her to be, she had aged in the last few months. Her hair was nearly all white, her skin so papery thin her veins were clearly visible under sunken cheeks. Her clothing had been taken in as she'd lost weight, but even so the cloth still hung off her frame.

I knew it had started with losing Lycan, the lover she should never have had—as forbidden as Diana and I—and with our hunting party missing for months thanks to Nefir's time-fuckery...it had left not only the Duchess, but all those who cared for Diana, believing the worst.

They'd thought Diana was gone forever; the wolf queen killed in doing her duty to her people. Killed while trying to save the world and stop Lilis.

The worst part was that Diana had come back, but not the same—her body holding a shard of the Veil, fighting to survive even as her wolf slowly perished.

I must have stood there for a good thirty seconds, staring at her as my own thoughts tumbled over one another.

"So much going on behind those eyes of yours, Raven. Come, speak with me." Evangeline's voice was a bare rasp, she stepped to the side and beckoned me in.

I crossed the threshold, into her personal space. The room was starkly bare of anything soft, or personal. A bed, a desk, no rugs...nothing else. A window barred shut to keep any sunlight out.

Guilt stabbed at me; the Duchess was having her own crisis, her grief still as raw and fresh as the day it happened, and I was going to ask her for help?

I was a dick, but I had nowhere else to turn.

"Duchess, my apologies—"

"Don't. You came to see me about Diana, and she is the child of my heart. So, sit and we will discuss." She motioned to the one chair in the room.

I moved to the chair and held it out for her as I tipped my head. "You sit, I will pace."

With a soft sigh, she held her skirts and sat down. "Fine. Pace. Tell me what I can do to help you."

I took a few steps away and did exactly that. With my hands tucked behind my back, I took three steps in one direction, spun, and went the other way, over and over.

But I couldn't find the words for a good long minute, and when I did, they weren't even the words I wanted. Because in that short time I realized there was nothing Evangeline could do, any more than Sienna could do the night before. Or Myrr the night before that. I'd gone to those I knew loved Diana, those who would do anything for her. And the answers had always been the same.

This was Diana's journey. I had to let her walk it on her own.

I didn't have it in me to hear the same message again.

I stopped in front of Evangeline and bowed my head. "I am sorry to have disturbed you, Duchess. I should just go. Forgive me."

"Raven, stay and speak..."

But I was gone, across the room and out her door, as if she were chasing me away. Because I was afraid of what she might say, if it was different than the others. Because she knew what it was to love someone taboo and she'd denied herself a life with him. They'd remained apart for the majority of their lives.

What if she told me to leave?

I was fairly sure I could live without Diana's touch, as long as I knew she was alive and well. To ensure her life though, I had to be near to her. A pleasure and a pain all wrapped up in one untidy bundle.

I didn't go first to the rooms I'd been assigned but instead found my way to Diana's rooms. The doors were closed, and no light flickered under the door, but I was certain she was there, sensing her carefully through the bond that hummed lightly between us.

Once more, I paused on the threshold of the door, hand raised only this time I did not let my knuckles fall against the wood. Instead, I placed my palm against the door and consoled myself that she was alive and well, sleeping in her own bed, safe for the night.

Breathing in the scents that were uniquely Diana as they slipped under the door to me, my racing heart and mind eased for the first time in days. This time of night had been the only time I'd been able to get close to her. I huffed a laugh at myself. As if through a thick door, and twenty feet apart were close.

"Sleep well, Frostbite," I murmured, bowed to the door and finally let myself go to my own rooms.

The fire was already crackling in the hearth, and I let out a sigh as I stepped into the sparsely furnished space. I didn't need much, but I couldn't deny that I felt a bit jealous of William at the moment. When our king and his new bride Bethany arrived, they would take the central room on the lower floor—two massive bedrooms, a bathroom with a small inground pool, a full entertainment room with billiards and darts...no expense had been spared. In short, it was fit for a king. But right now, I wouldn't mind burning off some energy swimming laps or banging the balls around.

Something...anything to take my mind off Diana.

I shut the door, and threw myself into the bed, burying my face in the pillows and wishing they were her luscious curves instead. Wishing I could just hold her and breathe her in.

My own breathing slowed and somewhere between thoughts of Diana and memories of our times together, I fell asleep, tumbling into the abyss of a dream.

The white tent fluttered around me as I stared up into the stars that speckled the desert sky. I sat up as the scent of desert flowers rolled in around me, tugging me out of the tent.

I blinked and I was outside, the oasis just as it had been when Nefir had rescued us from roasting alive under the desert sun.

The water in the distance gurgled and beckoned. Lush plants grew all around, there was a table set with food, I breathed in the scents of the desert and the inviting foods.

"This is just a dream, isn't it?"

I turned at the sound of her voice.

Diana stood only a few feet behind me in a sheer dress that rippled around her body as the desert wind tugged at it as if it would drag it off her body. Her eyes flicked to mine, uncertain, and green once more as they'd been when I'd rescued her from Edmund. I loved her frosted blue eyes...but I loved her eyes no matter their color. Her dark hair hung loose, soft curls begging to be touched.

"A dream," I said. "Yes. It's just a dream."

I stepped toward her, and she didn't back away, instead swaying into me as I cupped a hand behind her head and took her mouth with my own. While I dreamed of her every night, this was different. This felt...real.

Her lips softened beneath mine, her body pressed tight to my chest as her hands tangled in my hair, dragging me to the ground.

We fell and were suddenly back inside a tent. Distantly I knew this was a dream, but I was not complaining, nor was I in any hurry to wake up and lose this time with her—real or not.

I hooked a finger under one strap of her sheer dress and pulled slowly, tearing it from her even as it whispered across her body, making her skin pebble from the sensation. I followed the trail of the material with my other hand, stopping when I reached the curve of her breast.

She moaned and pushed upward, begging to be touched. "Please, Raven, don't stop."

"As you command," I said as I shed what little

clothing I wore and lowered myself over her. Nudging her legs apart and settling myself between them, pressing the tip of my cock against her warmth, knowing how tight and wet she would be already.

Holding myself up on my elbows, I pressed my lips against the edge of her neck, working my way along her jaw, to the bottom of her ear. A nip along the sensitive edge, and she twisted around, kissing me hard as if she'd devour me.

Sensations flooded me as our teeth nipped, and our tongues slid over one another. I growled as her fingers wrapped around my cock and squeezed, dragging her hand up and down the length of it.

"I want to taste you." She pushed me off, rolling me to the side so she straddled my waist. Sliding down my body, her pussy branded me every place it touched—belly, hip, thigh, a trail of moisture and warmth.

I slid my hands over her round ass cheeks, kneading at them as her breasts tempted my mouth.

"Frostbite, fuck..."

She dipped lower, and my hands slid up to her head as her mouth pressed against the tip of my cock. My hips jerked forward, and I fought not to pull her head down hard. Her laugh was...gods, it was music to me. "Tease," I whispered.

"Pot meet kettle." She swirled her tongue around me and slowly pulled my hard length into her mouth. She kept one hand at the base, pulsing slowly, and the other cupped my balls.

I was not going to last if she kept this up, the slow, deadly strokes of hand, lips, and tongue were unraveling me.

"Frostbite!" I arched under her, and then she was gone, and fuck, I thought I'd woken up.

Groaning, I flipped a hand over my eyes.

But she wasn't gone. She was still there, and she was not done with me yet. "From behind, Raven. I want you to fuck me from behind."

CHAPTER 2

Diana

From behind, Raven. I want you to fuck me from behind.

Heat flooded me from head to toe. "Son of a bitch!"

Thwack.

I let out a breath and lowered the bow to my side, staring at the empty center of the target.

"Fucker. He's made me a terrible shot," I muttered under my breath. The feathers at the end of my arrow were still trembling. Almost mocking me from the very outer edge of the target...

Damn Raven. Damn him for invading my dreams. It was bad enough I couldn't get him out of my head during the day when I had so much on my plate. Already exhausted from my churning thoughts and fears about the future of my people and the Territories, now I had to figure out how to fix it all on little to no sleep.

I rested my bow against a nearby tree stump and reached for the mug of strong black coffee that I'd brought out to the forest with me. Ever since I'd fed from Raven's blood, I had no appetite...for food, at any rate.

Sex and blood, though?

That was a whole other ball of fur. I craved them both, and the idea of having them together? Gods, I had to lock my knees to stay standing.

I lifted my face to the sun, letting my eyes close. For now, the warmth was still a pleasure, but even those days were numbered. Soon the sun would become my enemy, trying to roast my flesh from my bones. The cost of what I'd become. I could feel that moment coming, even if I didn't know exactly when it would happen.

My time was running out.

Just like your people when they find out what you're becoming, a little voice inside my head chimed in.

I opened my eyes, let out a snort of disgust, and took a sip of the bitter brew. Was this what my life was going to be? A constant mental litany of all the reasons I hated what I was becoming? Even who I was becoming?

I felt...weak. Where had all the righteous fury gone? The rage that had helped Sienna and I drive Lilis out of Malach's body and force her to run off and lick her wounds? I'd better get the rage back fast, or the Territories would suffer. The meeting at the ruins with all the other leaders was only days away, and that path was already fraught with countless pitfalls. No one was going to rally behind a sad sack of a queen with an identity crisis and a limp noodle handshake. I'd already seen it in the eyes of my own people. Heard the whispers of some…

"Lycan never would have allowed the demons to bring war to our shores."

"Where was she before the battle started?"

I let out a snarl as I hurled the mug against the target, where it smashed into a thousand pieces.

A low whistle sounded behind me, and I wheeled around to find Sienna standing there watching me, an assessing look on her face, her eyes not missing a thing.

"I'll tell you one thing, I'm glad I'm not that target. Whose face were you picturing there…our least favorite goddess or Raven?" she asked with a sympathetic smile.

My shoulders slumped. "I wish that I only wanted to kill Raven," I admitted, sucking my teeth in frustration, "that would make life much easier. No, the problem is, as furious as I am for him stealing my choice, I would have done the same in his shoes, given the circumstances. Now, I can't seem to forgive him, nor can I seem to stop thinking about him. It's a total mind fuck."

Sienna sighed, set down the mug in her hands, and picked up a bow. She knocked an arrow and loosed it all in a single smooth motion. Her arrow marked slightly to the right of the center. "That does sound awful. I remember the early days with your brother. The man who bought me as a slave…and still, I wanted him something fierce. It took me a long time to come to terms with the truth. Dominic bought me to protect me from those who would've mistreated me. He did it to save me, despite what it might have felt like…"

I was sure there was a lesson in there somewhere, but I wasn't in a place to hear it. I just felt so broken. Torn between the blood I was born with, and the wolf I'd become, and now back to the first?

Not messy at all.

"Don't let me stop you if you want to keep going with your target practice." Sienna set her bow down, scooped up her steaming mug from the ground, and closed the distance between us. She took a seat on the tree stump beside me, cupping her mug with her hands. "I'm just here to take advantage of the balmy weather, get some fresh air, and escape from the keep for a bit. Everyone's so tense, prepping for the trip to the ruins. It's been so long since all the heads of the different territories have been in the same room–or space I suppose."

"Yeah, well, I'm pretty sure at least Dominic and Lochlin feel that there's a good chance we may not even have to worry about the goddess." We still weren't using Lilis' name. It just wasn't worth the possibility that it would draw her eyes to us sooner than we had to. "She may get her wish without having to lift another finger if no one can agree, we all turn on one another, and no one walks out alive."

I bent to retrieve my bow and knocked another arrow. This time I shoved Raven from my thoughts and focused only on the circle in the center. If I was to lead my people in this and beg all the other leaders to work together and join the fight against Lilis, I needed to be smart. I needed to think about every move I made and stay one step ahead of both the other monarchs *and* the dark goddess. And after losing my father, fighting that bloodthirsty bitch at every turn, and grieving my dying wolf while also being torn apart by this bond with Raven, I felt woefully ill-equipped to do that.

I could almost hear Lycan's voice counseling me now.

This is where your mental toughness comes—the grit you showed from the first moment I met you. You survived against all odds as a child. Then you came to me and thrived, becoming the backbone of our people. You can do anything you put your mind to, daughter. Do not lose heart.

I sucked in a breath and let it out slowly through my mouth. Then I closed one eye and held steady, loose. This time the arrow sailed through the air in a straight line, connecting with its target, clean and true.

"There it is," Sienna said, applauding softly.

I lowered the bow again and shot her a glance. "That's about as long as I can hold it together right now," I admitted, giving in to the sudden urge to share my fears despite a lifetime of shielding them from everyone. Ever since the shard had chosen me, my bond with Sienna had deepened. If anyone could understand the pressure on me, it was her. "Something's got to give before the day of the meeting, or we can forget getting the other kings and queens to fall in line. It's already going to be hard enough to keep my people under control once they find out—" I broke off and swallowed hard. "Hell, even Kevin could tell." And it still stung that the white hell-hound had turned away from me, choosing to return to the demon realm with Gabe after the battle against Malach. It didn't bode well for my own brethren's loyalty, never mind those from other Territories..."I'm afraid the other kings and queens will be able to smell my weakness." Sienna opened her mouth, looking like she was about to argue with me, but then she stopped short and nodded.

"They're a cutthroat bunch from what I understand," she agreed. "But being what you are isn't a weakness, Diana. You and I and the others who hold the other shards...we will save the world together. You must go in with that confidence and don't let anyone take it away. I know you're going to work it out and come through to the other side of this a bad bitch, just like you were before, only stronger. Just give yourself a minute to come to terms with what's happened, though. You're not a machine. It's only been a week."

I turned my eyes to the sky. "It snowed yesterday. And today, it's like a late summer morning. Balmy and warm. Who knows what tomorrow will bring? Tornadoes that will wipe out half the land? An earthquake? A hailstorm? Time is the one thing I don't have–the one thing that none of us has. I've got to figure this out and get my shit together, or this whole world is doomed."

Her lips quirked. "Well, when you say it like that, it seems like a whole lot of pressure. Maybe we can talk through some of the things bothering you most. You mentioned being worried that your people won't accept what you're becoming. Do you know that to be true?"

I dug the point of my bow into the soft ground, creating a divot. "There were already those who opposed me, an entire faction of wolves, who never wanted an heir not of Lycan's actual blood to become their leader. There are also those who believe a woman should never have the power to lead. Things only got worse when we aligned with the Vampire Territory and my brothers came back into my life—even if the majority of people did not realize we were truly related. Once Lycan was murdered, those on my side doubled down on their loyalty, but the others...I feel like my father was the only thing keeping those dark factions from making their move to overthrow me altogether. Once they find out what I'm becoming?" I let out a harsh laugh. "It's all over."

Feeling restless, I made my way toward the target and tugged the arrows free.

"They're going to find out. Instead of worrying about it, maybe the best course of action is to rip it off like a bandage," Sienna replied, her tone, calm and measured in a way that soothed me. "What if you call a meeting with the clans before our trip? Be brutally honest and explain what happened...I think they'll respect your vulnerability. You won't win over those who already opposed you, but I do think you'll find you have the loyalty of the rest. They can't just erase your decades of loyal service to the people. You are still you—and you have still served them with a fierce loyalty."

It was sound advice, much as I was loathe to lay my secret on the line.

At the very least, I would know my fate rather than walk this tightrope of constant fear and nauseous anticipation. If there was a vote and they opted to replace me, at least I could start to plan my path forward.

And yet I could see a downside to spilling the beans.

"I have the shard inside of me. We're prophesied to reunite the shards and defeat that bitch together once we find the other girls. In order to do so, we need this alliance with the other territories. It's imperative that we're all on the same page. If I'm removed as queen, who's to say our next leader will see things the same way that I do? What if they abandon that mission altogether?"

I pressed my fingers to my temple, trying to soothe away the building headache, and the words that I'd kept inside tumbled out, laced with pain.

"My wolf is dying, Sienna. Tomorrow comes the blood moon. Normally, I would feel my wolf, the power of her, humming inside of me...I feel nothing. It's like I'm dead inside." I paused. "But I need to be sure. I want to wait one more night before I say anything. I want to take one last run and see if I can become one with the forest. Just to be sure that the vampire blood in me has won the war against my wolf. If that's...if that's the case then I'll tell my people the truth, and let the chips fall where they may. My guess is I'll be challenged for the crown. It only takes three clans to agree to a champion to represent them, and there are two who would've done it even before this."

Rustling leaves interrupted my thoughts, and Sienna and I both turned toward the sound. As I lifted my bow, instantly on high alert, a plump white rabbit darted from between the trees. I released the tension on my bowstring and lowered the bow.

"Before taking Raven's blood, I would have smelled that rabbit a mile away," I murmured, wistfully. I turned to face Sienna and held her gaze, a tiny ember of hope, still burning in my chest. "I need to ask you a question."

"Of course. We are sisters now. You can ask me anything."

"The shard made me feel as if I must choose. But I didn't get to, because Raven chose for me. If I am to be a vampire, does that mean it has to be forever? What if I fulfill my destiny, and then make *my* choice...to go back to being a werewolf?"

Her eyes widened in surprise. "And go through the changing ceremony a second time?"

"Yes."

"You would do that? After the agony...Diana, it almost killed you the first time from what I understand. It very likely would the second time."

I regarded her, unblinking. "And if I'd rather be dead than stay a bloodsucker?"

She flinched and shook her head. "I don't know the answer to your question. But, as someone who cares for you, I would advise against it. If you choose to do something so dangerous, I hope that you would at least call upon me to be by your side in hopes that I might be able to use my gift to help you through the transition."

I blew out a shaky breath and managed a half smile. "At least there's that one tiny sliver of hope. If being a vampire becomes too much to bear, I can try."

"Don't think you're not going to get pushback on this if it should come to pass. I know that there's at least one person who will protest vehemently," Sienna continued, her tone hesitant.

"That's fine, because he doesn't get a vote this time," I shot back, the ember of hope turning into the flickering flame of fury I'd been missing. I straightened and stared at her hard. "And you won't be mentioning this conversation to him or my brothers. Is that understood?"

Sienna regarded me, her head cocked to the side as her lips tipped into a wry smile. "Well, if those fools who oppose you think you don't have what it takes to be queen anymore, I pity them. But yes, *Your Majesty.* To answer your question, I understand. Now here's something *you* need to understand. A blood bond is not something that goes away if it's made with your fated mate. I won't need to tell Raven anything. If your life is on the line, he will feel it."

I sliced a hand through the air, blood boiling. "Why do people keep saying that?!" Okay, maybe other people didn't keep saying that, but Raven did. "None of us have any idea if he's my fated mate. I'm not even sure I believe such a thing exists anymore—not for me.

And if it does, part of me thinks that mine died long ago."

The boy who'd saved me from Edmund. From the moment Raven had told me that version of events, I'd known deep inside...that the boy was my mate. And he was gone.

"If that's what you want to believe, I'm not going to try to convince you otherwise. When the time is right, your heart will know the truth. Now, I will leave you to your target practice. Though I will say, your aim seems to have improved..." With that, Sienna turned and ambled away, back toward the keep.

As I watched her go, I felt a twinge of sorrow. She'd become one of my closest confidants and was my sister-in-law to boot. She'd been nothing but kind to me, had even saved my life, and I'd spoken to her like I was her queen, and she was my subject. I wanted to call after her and apologize for being such an asshole.

But that flame kept flickering, and it was all I could do not to scream.

"Is that Evangeline out there with Sal?" I asked, leaning closer to the window of the harborside breakfast shop. Sal being the water dragon who'd followed us home from our quest, the one we'd saved Maverick from. More and more, I wished we'd just fucking left him there.

"It is," Nicholas confirmed with a clipped nod. "This is the third day in a row I've seen them out there in the morning. It seems they've become fast friends, strangely."

As if to illustrate that point, the Duchess rested her hand on Sal's scaly nose and the water dragon leaned into her caress. Not so strange in my mind. It was easy to believe that the two were bonding over grief at the loss of their great loves. I'd be damned if that was going to be me joining them as a third wheel.

I knocked a knuckle on the windowsill. "Gentlemen,

we need to talk about how we're going to ensure Diana is protected at this meeting."

Nicholas and Dominic both bobbed their heads in agreement as they forked up bites of their egg and sausage pies.

"Loch should be here shortly, and we can all put our heads together and come up with a plan," Dominic said. There was a fierce light in his eyes as he continued. "I know it's been decided that no weapons will be allowed, but I can promise no harm will come to my sister so long as I'm present."

Dominic was her brother and still, I couldn't deny the surge of jealousy that roared through me. She was *mine* to protect, but because our goals were aligned, I let it pass without a word. As the head of the vampire army and their king's guard, the odds of him being allowed to attend the meeting—at least on the periphery somewhere —were much higher than mine. If I couldn't be there, I needed an ally I could trust with Diana's life. And there was no one in this world I trusted more than my old friend.

The door swung open and Lochlin strode in, a grim look on his face as he approached our table and took his seat. "I don't know what this abomination of mother nature is about, but these weather changes make me twitchy."

He took a glance around the room and noted all the eyes upon us, then he turned to me.

"Can I ask why we're not having this meeting in the keep?"

Nicholas winced, and Dominic's lips twitched. "Because as warm as it is outside, it's positively *frigid* in the keep right now."

He wasn't wrong. Diana had left early that morning, and when she came back, I was surprised that her eye color hadn't changed back to ice blue again. Her moods were as volatile as the weather, going from despair to white-hot anger on a dime. I couldn't blame her, and she wouldn't talk to me. The best thing I could do was let it run its course and stay out of her way.

Apparently, I wasn't the only one with that course of action in mind.

And they say men are stupid. "We were just talking about security at the upcoming meeting."

Lochlin huffed out a sigh. "I hate to say it, but I think we should consider having her accompanied by security in the interim as well. I don't think she should be alone outside the keep."

Adrenaline surged through my body, and my hands balled into fists.

"Has there been a threat against her?" I demanded.

"No, but something doesn't smell right. Even right after the battle with the demons, things didn't feel this tense. I have to wonder if there isn't already someone campaigning to take her place."

I took another look around the cozy room and noted

the openly hostile expressions on some of the faces that looked back at me.

He was right. Those looks were new. While there had been a small faction who had protested the alliance with the vampires despite knowing that we needed to come together to protect the Territories as a whole, those numbers seemed to be growing. And I didn't like it one bit.

"Speaking of the meeting, how are things going on that front so far?" Nicholas set his fork down and leaned back in his chair.

I grimaced, knowing that everything we were doing could be upset by a single leader throwing a fit. "We've got nearly everyone agreeing to be there and behave. Gabriel had some reservations. He's getting pushback from his people after Malach's death on our lands, but I think I've got him in hand for now. That said, the Fae are still going to take some more convincing. I think I've got an idea about how to get them on board, but I need to run it by Diana first before I pitch it to the whole team."

"Aren't you supposed to have to hide during the daytime, so you don't get a little sunburn?"

An icy calm flowed through my veins as I turned and met the gaze of the person talking. A massive bear of a man with ruddy skin and an unruly black beard glared down at me, Nicholas, and Dominic in turn, before turning his ire on Lochlin. "And *you*. Never took you for a traitor to your kind. Lycan be rolling over in his grave seeing this shit."

I moved to stand and separate this man's head from his body, but Lochlin pressed a hand on my shoulder and stood first.

"Is that the official stance of the whole Regan clan, Paddy, or just you? I'll need to note it when I report this incident to my queen."

The man called Paddy's chest deflated some as he leaned back. "Come on, Lochlin. You gotta see it." He swept his hand toward the three of us. "They goes against nature. Lycan's daughter can choose who she wants to be around, but even *you* can't think it's right for her to lead us if she chooses one of them to fuck. We should be led by one of our own, and you *know* it."

Lochlin took a step closer until the toe of his boots touched Paddy's, and their noses were only an inch apart.

"What I *know* is that you're preaching treason right now. And unless you want to be on the wrong side of a noose by day's end, I'd apologize and think before I spoke next time."

The three of us watched, tense and at the ready, as the rest of the place went silent. There were at least twenty werewolves scattered around at various tables, and only three of us, plus Lochlin, but I still liked our chances so long as we acted fast. I almost welcomed the opportunity to let my fists fly and work off some of the rage, sadness, and fear for Diana that had been my constant companion for so long now.

But Paddy blinked first, tilting his head and lowering his eyes as he took a step back, hands held up in surrender. "I'm not saying I'm going to start a war or stage some coup, Lochlin. I'm just letting you know that the hearts and minds of our people have been changing. And she's going to have to make her choice soon enough. Him or us. We can smell him on her, same as you."

He dipped his head in my direction.

Loch didn't so much as glance my way. "I'm hearing your words, Paddy. And you can be sure I'll be sharing them with the head of your clan. Now go on out of here before I allow these gentlemen to address your insults the way I would if I were in their shoes."

Paddy stepped away, not turning his back on our table until he'd reached the door. Then he let out a low whistle calling to his two companions, who rushed to join him.

"Anybody else got a problem they need to speak with me about?" Lochlin called, scanning the breakfast shop for any takers. They all averted their eyes, suddenly, much more interested in their food and drink than they had been moments before. "All right then, enjoy your meal," he said before taking a seat.

"That was pretty good," Nicholas said, giving Lochlin a clap on the shoulder. "Way to de-escalate the situation."

His grimace pulled at the scar bisecting his upper lip. "I don't know how much longer conversations like that are going to do the trick. I'll admit I've had several of them the past few days. I just hope tempers hold until after the meeting at the ruins."

He hunkered down and leaned close, keeping his voice low. "Circling back, I truly do feel that we need to *make* Diana travel with security from now on. This interaction shows just how restless our people are."

Even as he said the words, Dominic and Nicholas let out low chuckles.

Making Diana do anything was dicey on the best of days, and these certainly were not the best of days. Lochlin flicked his eyes to me, a silent request.

"I'll try to talk to her before the full moon tonight," I said, pushing my untouched plate aside.

"Maybe it should be me," Dominic shot me a sympathetic look before taking a long pull from his mug of coffee. "It's hard to hear, but I think anything you say right now is going to be met with resistance. If we want our answer to be yes, it should come from someone she doesn't feel like castrating right now."

I couldn't disagree with him, much as I hated the truth of his words. With reluctance, I dipped my head in his direction. "Fine." Fuck me, that was the only thing I could bite out without snarling.

"Do we know what her plans are for tonight?" Lochlin asked as if I weren't sitting there vibrating with irritation. In fact, if I didn't know better, the three men were deliberately ignoring me, letting me stew.

Dominic tapped the side of his mug. "I can check with Sienna to see if she's spoken to her. And if not, I'll find out as well. Given the current tensions in the community, it's probably best if she stays indoors under lockdown."

"Agree," Lochlin said, scratching, running a hand over his scruffy face. "We all saw here with Paddy today how the coming full moon makes our people more aggressive. Once they're in their wolf forms running in the night...well, things will only get worse. We need to be prepared for it."

Lockdown sounded perfect to me. Having Diana safe behind closed doors where no one could hurt her was the only way I'd get any sleep tonight. But I had already imposed my will on her one too many times. I would just have to watch as she handled this how she thought fit.

And I would be there if she needed me. It was all I could do.

I left my friends behind as I headed back to the keep with a mumbled excuse about needing to think.

My problem was thinking was all I'd been able to do —there was no action I could take that would help Diana. She didn't want my support. She didn't want my presence.

So how did I help her? How did I help carry this incredible burden she was carrying?

"One more time," I muttered as I reached the outskirts of the keep. "I have to try one more time to convince her."

Because at this point there was nothing else I could do—no dragons to slay, no quests to take on, no demons to fight.

But as I walked into the great room and saw her standing there, staring at the picture of her father above the fireplace, shoulders slumped, the last thing I wanted to do was argue with her that she should let me be at her side. But the alternative was to walk away for good and right in that moment...I could never do it.

She looked...lost standing there, as if she'd come free of whatever moored her to who she knew herself to be. Perhaps I was projecting...then again, her emotions washed through me and that was exactly what they told me.

I'm lost, drowning in this sorrow and fear with no land in sight.

I saw her stiffen as she sensed my presence, her emotions clamping down, as if she knew I was picking up on her feelings.

"Did you need me for something?" she asked without turning around.

"I was hoping we could talk for a few minutes."

She faced me then, and my heart gave a squeeze at her pale and hollowed out cheeks. "I don't have a few minutes. I have a meeting in my office that I'm already late for. Maybe tomorrow..." she trailed off, not meeting my gaze, looking past me over my left shoulder.

If I let things continue like this, tomorrow would never come. The situation was getting dangerous, and I couldn't protect her when she was icing me out.

"I'm worried about the way some of the wolves are handling recent events, and I'm hoping you'll consider staying indoors tonight. To stay clear of them." The words came out before I could stop them, knowing instantly they were a mistake. I should have let Dom handle this discussion as he'd suggested but seeing her made me forget myself.

The need to protect her overrode any other sense.

Her green eyes sparked with anger as she folded her arms over her chest. The color in her cheeks rose, pushing back the pallor of her skin.

"You make one decision for me while I was comatose, and *now* you think me *incapable* of making decisions for myself? Is that it?" she asked, cocking her head and eyeing me as if I were prey, she was considering whether or not to tear me into pieces, or let me get a running start. "I managed for a very long time before *you* came around, Raven, and I did just fine, so forgive me if I don't consult you on matters of diplomacy or my well-being."

She marched towards me and stopped a foot away, her scent instantly curling around me and squeezing tight, like a fist. How could things be so terrible between us, and I still wanted her the way I did?

"The next time you invade my dreams, beware, bloodsucker," she hissed. "Now that I know you're coming, I'll be ready for you, and not in the way you're hoping."

She shouldered past me, and I resisted the urge to watch her go. As frustrating as our all-too-brief conversation was, I couldn't deny that seeing the spark in her, the peak of color, was better than the dead stare of late. Once

I was free of the grasp of her smell, though, I actually thought about her words. Not just that she'd been dreaming about me too, but the insinuation that I'd infiltrated her dreams on purpose. I would take responsibility for the shit I'd done, but I wasn't about to let her think I was engineering some elaborate mindfuck to force myself on her.

My feet moved of their own accord as I followed her, down the hall towards her office to argue the fact that as good as I was, even I was not that good.

The door was closed when I got there, and I reached out to knock, but low voices echoed through the wooden panel. Apparently, her meeting had already begun. But it was the voice I hated most that had me seeing red.

"Thank you for agreeing to see me."

Fangs pricked at my gums as Maverick's voice echoed through the wood.

Weasley little bastard. What could he possibly have to talk to her about after what he'd done? Trading spots with her on that beach, letting her take his place as a sacrifice...fucker.

"I don't have a lot of time, Mav, so make it quick." Diana's voice held no trace of warmth which brought a grin to my face.

He cleared his throat. "Fine. Straight to the point, then. Raven might have you thinking that the reason I allowed you to take my place in Malach's grasp is because I don't care for you, but the truth is, I care *so much*. The difference between him and me is that I truly respect you as well as love you. I might not be a werewolf, but you are my queen and allowing your people to see me dissent and defy your leadership would have only made a bad situation worse."

The bloodlust lashed at my throat even as a haze of crimson distorted my vision. What. The. Actual. Fuck. She wouldn't buy what he was selling…would she?

"Look, I know I've been selfish in the past, but we're aligned in our desires, you and me. I want the Territories to remain strong and united so we can defeat the dark goddess, but how can that be when your own people aren't united?"

The haze of fury melded with a growing sense of dread. He was full of shit about the first part—he'd done what he'd done to save his own hide—but I'd always known he was a good spin doctor. It was that second part that had me suddenly fighting back a rush of bile.

"Diana, sacrifices must be made, I think we all know that. You can still have the life you want, leading these people as your father raised you to do, but from what I'm hearing, you would need to make a stand now. Show them that you aren't tied in any way to Raven and choose a mate that they will accept."

"What have you been hearing?" Diana asked. There was no anger in her voice, just solemn resignation.

"People are talking about replacing you. I've been telling them that it's not what's best. They are looking to me, as a friend of yours, Diana."

Fucking fucker. I hated that human.

"They look to you?" Diana's question was soft, and shocked. "Why?"

I could just imagine him shrugging, trying to look innocent. "I don't know. But they are, and I'm trying to help you, Diana."

Her emotions flicked to me. Uncertainty. Sadness.

Then shithead took it one step too far and I wanted to laugh. "Diana, I think the best thing you can do right now is listen to me and find a mate, I think people would look to us if–"

Us?

There was the sound of a hand on wood, as if she'd slapped the desk. "I am your queen, and *I* will decide what's best," she cut in, an edge to her tone now. "Thank you for your input, and information. I will take it into consideration. Dismissed."

"Understood." The scraping of a chair on the stone floor had me backing away from the door.

Maverick's cards were on the table now. Or at least *some* of them. He'd graduated from long-suffered annoyance to wily adversary. But he didn't know who he was fucking with. I strode down the hall, already planning how to exterminate this rat, but I couldn't seem to silence the little voice inside me that wondered...

What had he said that wasn't true?

Diana had a better chance of maintaining her position as queen longer and regaining the loyalty of her people if I was out of the picture. At least long enough to see the end of Lilis and to repair the Veil. Long term they would never accept her as queen, not as a vampire. But for a year or two? She could keep them in the dark longer if she had a mate her people respected and wanted on the throne.

A mate that was not me. A mate that had better the fuck not be Maverick.

I couldn't even think about the werewolf male she would choose to replace me, and yet I could see it was possibly the only way to help her.

Then the only question was...Was the truest, purest act of love...to leave?

CHAPTER 4

Diana

Mav's words chased me for the rest of the day, biting at me, reminding me that I had a duty to my people above all else. The same way my father's words had driven me out of the keep decades before, when I'd found Maverick being chased by the demon.

Earlier that same day, my father had told me I had to take a mate—not the first time, but it *was* the first time he'd stung me with the fact that I was shirking my duty if I didn't.

By not marrying, I was courting danger. By not having an heir I was leaving our people with an uncertainty that could drive fear into them.

No matter how much I tried to fool myself into thinking otherwise, many of my people were stuck in the dark ages. They felt that a kingdom without a king was weaker. That the lack of an alpha male in the keep was an invitation for trouble—and as far as those people were concerned that was exactly what had happened. A queen in charge had allowed Malach and his demons to the front door.

I hated that Mav and Lycan were somehow saying the same thing—that I needed a mate at my side. And that now I could see that Lycan had been right. Despite all I'd done to protect and lead my people, I was never considered on the same level as my father or his predecessors. No matter that I'd had Lycan's blessing to become queen.

No matter that I'd nearly died to become a werewolf. Not that they knew the lengths I went to in order to be one of them. No one except Lycan, Evangeline, and her maid knew what I'd been before. A few others, like Lochlin as well, held my secret close. But only those I could trust with my life.

Which is how I ended up hiding in my room. Hiding from my own people, on a night I should have been able to run free.

Maybe even the *last* night...not that my wolf was clawing to get out as she had in the past. My wolf...my girl was so quiet it was if she was already gone and my heart cracked further.

"I hate this."

I leaned on the edge of the dresser across from my bed. My room had always been my sanctuary but now it was becoming that, less and less. Trapped by the walls, trapped by decisions that hadn't been my own, trapped even by the shard.

I closed my eyes, but it wasn't Mav I saw behind my lids chastising me, offering me something I didn't want.

No, it was the curve of Raven's mouth that drew me closer as he smirked, the faint hint of fangs promising pleasure beyond anything else. Promising a safety in his arms, I'd not found anywhere else.

My eyes flew open, and I gasped as my body clenched.

"Fuck you." I snarled the words even as I ached for his touch. Ached to have him do as he wished with me. Ached to just have him hold me close and let me lower my guard for a moment.

I struggled to breathe, my body remembering clearly just how good Raven was at reading me, at meeting my physical needs before I even whispered a moan. I clutched the wooden dresser edge, cracking the wood as I focused on my breathing.

In and out, nice and slow. Keep it smooth....

Like his cock sliding into me, nice and slow..."Fuck!" I flipped the dresser, and spun, my heart pounding, out of control, sweat sliding down between my breasts as if I'd been running.

How the hell did I get past this need for him? I had the meeting with the other leaders, and I needed to be focused on the task at hand, not so fucking horny that I couldn't walk straight. And the blood moon was only making it worse...at least that was what I wanted to blame it on.

A knock on the door. "Frostbite?"

Of *course* it would be him. "Go away!"

"I heard something crash, are you okay?"

I was not okay. And it was his fault...I could punish him for it. Make him beg at my knees, making him ache the way I was aching, without release. I sucked in a breath. No, this was not a game I could win and yet I wanted to lie to myself that I could win it, that I could let him in and have him pleasure me as I'd done before and nothing else.

Frostbite. Lie to me, just for tonight.

He'd said that to me, in the oasis. When things had been different, before he'd taken what was possibly the most important decision of my life from me. When we'd just been two souls, and not a forbidden pair.

He hadn't left the door, just like every other night. He stood there. Quiet. There was no pressure to let him in...he never even knocked until tonight.

Shaking, I put my hands over my face, feeling tears prick at my eyes. Desire and fear, need and want were all tangled up.

I was being torn into pieces by my blood, my heart, and my mind. None were in alignment. And I didn't know how to change it—how to bring any of them together.

I'd moved without truly realizing it, standing on my side of the door, only the wooden planks between us.

His breathing was ragged, but I couldn't hear his heartbeat. No, I could feel it through the bond.

I wasn't the only one suffering.

I leaned my head against the door, struggling to find the right words. Lie to him, I had to lie to him and maybe then he'd go.

"I have company," I said, the three words bitter on my tongue. If he thought there was another male here then...

He huffed, and I realized he was laughing. "Sure you do."

He was laughing at me. That rage that had been so quiet woke up like a beast lunging at prey, tangling itself around my desire and it made me do something stupid.

I jerked the door open, grabbed him by the collar as he stumbled in, his stunning eyes wide as I pulled my dagger before he'd fully stepped into the room. Spinning with him still caught with my one hand, I kicked the door closed behind me, rattling it on the frame.

"Fuck you, Raven!" I had the dagger at his throat, pressing the wickedly sharp blade hard enough that a thin line of blood appeared and trickled down his neck. "You are a thorn in my side!"

He didn't yell at me; he didn't even try to get away. "Would slitting my throat make you happy? If so, then do it." He leaned into the knife, parting his flesh further. "I would die if that would please you, Frostbite."

My eyes traced the blood as it slid down to his collarbone, and then lower, into his shirt.

I couldn't help the hitch in my breath at the thought of following that line across the plains and valleys of his chest and then lower, lower...just like the dream. Just like all the dreams.

His fingers wrapped slowly around my wrist and pushed it just as slowly away. "What do you want, Frostbite?"

"Stop it. My eyes aren't even blue anymore." I couldn't look away from him, the smell of his blood, the smell of Raven consuming every fiber of my ability to think straight.

"No. But you still have the power of a winter storm in you, don't you? Your eyes could glow red, and I'd still call you Frostbite." He drew me toward him, slowly, inch by inch. "You could still cause a man to curl up and die for wanting you, and being frozen out."

And like a moth to a flame, I went with his pressure.

He dragged my hand up his chest, across the slick blood and around to the back of his neck. I dug my fingers into the strands of his hair, silken threads whispering against my skin.

Our bodies were flush to one another, his heat, the smell of him, the pressure of his cock pressing against my belly...I shuddered, my mind blank except for what I was feeling.

I should say something to stop this, I knew I should. I was furious with him, so fucking angry about...about what? I did a slow blink, as if I were dreaming. Was that it? Was this another one of the dreams that felt so real?

A part of me knew without a doubt that this was real, but that other part that ached for him whispered that I could pretend that it was a dream. I could lie to myself this time.

Lies and shadows, they'd always been there between us and I leaned on them to make this okay.

His breath was warm against my cheek, but he didn't press his lips to my skin. "Tell me what you want, Frostbite. I will serve you however you demand. Do you..." He seemed to steel himself. "Do you want me to leave the Territories?"

The question was ridiculous. "So, I can suffer alone? No. You can suffer through whatever this is right along with me."

I felt him smile as he pressed his cheek to mine. "I would suffer anything to stay close to you, my queen."

We slid toward each other at the same time, our mouths coming into contact, the heat and taste of him branding me like a fire whiskey, drowning out any good senses I had left.

One of his hands swept up under the back of my shirt, settling against the curve. His other hand dipped lower, catching me under the thigh and lifting me up so that I was against him.

He ground his hips against me and I wrapped my legs around his waist, clamping my aching center to him. Moon goddess, this was what I wanted, I wanted to get thrown to the bed and fucked until I lost consciousness, to come so hard that I saw stars and struggled to remember my name.

To escape the weight of the world for a few hours, the

weight of a crown and a path that was impossible to decipher.

A boom against the door shattered my fantasy like a bucket of ice water. "Diana, will you speak with me? Please?"

Raven held my gaze for a long moment, nostrils still flaring with desire. But Mav was right outside the door, and as irritated as I was at him for our last meeting, he'd just saved me from making a mistake I couldn't afford to make.

Struggling to breathe, I dropped to my feet and stumbled away from Raven. Then, I pointed at the window, motioning for him to go.

"Go," I hissed. Everything I'd been trying to forget rushed back to me.

Whispers of a potential coup were making their way through the territory. Civil unrest called now, when the whole world was on the brink of collapse. An internal battle would only make the job we had ahead of us more difficult. The consequences of a taboo tryst between Raven and I was too high a price to pay. No matter what I wanted.

Taboo? But are you still a werewolf?

That voice sounded a great deal like the shard.

Raven's eyebrows shot up, then he gave me a slow bow from the waist and was gone, out the window as if he'd never been here.

"Diana?"

Gathering myself, I went to the door and opened it a crack. "What do you want, Mav?"

"Are you okay?" His mismatched eyes were narrowed. "I know I might have overstepped earlier, but I'm worried for you. Have you given any thought to what I said?"

My ire flashed. "You mean about needing to find a mate so that *my own people* would believe me capable? Because apparently, I'm not capable if I don't have a dick dangling between my legs in some form or another?"

I yanked the door open wide and he moved as if to step inside. Only I'd yanked it wide so I could slam it well and good.

"Fuck!" Maverick bellowed as the door connected with his shoulder. I didn't care.

"Go away, Maverick!" I yelled. "I am trying to sleep!"

Only sleep was the last thing on my mind. The fire in me was burning hot, relit by Raven's touch, much as I hated to admit it. Something about him gave me the... what was it, energy? Desire? Some combination of the two seemed to always be tied to him.

I didn't want to call it what I truly suspected it was... he gave me strength in a way I didn't understand.

I went to the window. The massive full moon was tinged with colors that shouldn't have existed. Green, purple, and red...if there was ever a full moon to see if my wolf was truly gone, this was it.

"Are you still with me?" I whispered to my wolf, and

thought maybe...was there a distant wolf's call? Or was I hearing things I wanted to hear?

Before I changed my mind, I leapt to the edge of the window and peered at the drop. If Raven could do it, so could I.

I let go, and in a breath had landed in a crouch at the base of the keep. I took off running toward the forest. There were parts that my people avoided—like the river boundary between us and the angels.

The place I'd first found Maverick.

I cranked on the speed and struggled not to gasp at just how fast I was moving. Faster than I'd ever been as a werewolf, which only fanned the flames of my rage hotter. The wind whipped around me, dragging my hair out behind me in a streamer.

Howls erupted—my people, my friends, the clan leaders—they were unleashing their own wolves, escaping the confines of propriety for a night. Being the wolves that they were—wolves that would never be stripped from them.

I tipped back my head to howl but only a strangled scream escaped me. I pumped my arms and legs faster, as if I could escape the truth.

You already knew your wolf was gone. Again, it felt like the shard whispering to me.

"Shut up," I sobbed the words, gasping on them as if they'd choke me.

Even if it was true, just that smallest part of me had hope that there was a way back. That my wolf would be strong enough to hang on a little longer, that I'd be able to turn back into a werewolf once the war was done, the Veil healed and then...then what?

Raven gone.

My people, led by someone else.

Outcast because of what I'd had to do. Because I'd turned back into a vampire...a reality only a few people even knew. I had to hang on long enough to see them through the battles ahead. That had to be my goal.

Movement ahead and to my left drew my eye to a small clearing. A small deer with her head bent to drink from the river. The pulse in her beating a rhythm I could not ignore, and a desire I could not deny. That's when I felt it. The thrill of the hunt. But it wasn't from my wolf...it was me, and the bloodlust of a vampire I'd been denying.

She never saw me, was never afraid because there was no chance to be afraid. I leapt across the river and tackled her to the ground, my fangs sinking into her neck and stilling her as I drank deeply.

The blood was a hot rush of energy—heady relief flowed through my body, lighting every nerve-ending as I pulsed with a vitality, I hadn't felt in...well, ever.

This. This was what I'd been missing. If I was going to survive the shard and this fucking mess I was in, I had to feed.

Like a vampire.

The crack of a twig was the only warning I had

before a massive wolf slammed into me in a tangle of gnashing teeth and slashing claws.

We flipped over backwards, the limp deer tangled between us. I ended up in a crouch, on all fours, pulse pounding with adrenaline and fresh blood.

The wolf was a deep brown with a white blaze on its head and muzzle. One of the Barrach clan.

"Halt," I snarled. "I am your queen, don't you dare—"

He leapt, ignoring my command.

As if I were no longer his alpha. No longer queen.

Fury and pain shot through me as I caught him by the neck and tossed him aside, sending him through a group of saplings and into the river.

"Enough!"

But it was only a moment or two before he shook himself and rose, turning back toward me, his lips curling up over his teeth.

He wouldn't listen. Because there was no longer a connection between me and my people. My wolf was gone. And I?

I was going to die here if I didn't fight back.

CHAPTER 5

Raven

As if it wasn't bad enough being sent *out the fucking window* like some stupid teenage boy not wanting to get caught by his girlfriend's parents....now I was stuck in the lower levels of the keep, like I'd been caught by said parents and thrown in jail.

Not that the space wasn't nice. A nice space to pace and mope and throw shit as needed.

I snorted to myself as I went from one side of the room to the other. Dominic and Nicholas were playing pool on the billiards table, and Sienna sat curled up in a chair with a book in her lap and a huge orange cat draped across her shoulders like a shawl.

"You're going to have to replace that rug." Dom didn't even look up at me as he took his next shot, sinking the solid yellow he was after.

I rolled my eyes. "Then perhaps Her Majesty should have let me stay and keep an eye on her. Even with guards at the door, I don't trust that someone won't try something."

"You mean like Maverick?" Sienna turned a page of her book. "You've been here for all of fifteen minutes, and in that time, you've cursed him out under your breath more than once a minute."

I wasn't about to tell Sienna that I was cursing him out because he'd interrupted what could have been a moment for Diana and me to truly reconnect. A moment to find some healing between us, and dare I even hope, some understanding on her part? Because I knew that deep down, she understood why I'd given her my blood, but that was different than being able to look past what I'd done. To see that the decision made to bring her back to her vampiric side wasn't even a decision. That I hadn't actually known that drinking from me would send her wolf running.

None of us had.

We'd only wanted to save her. To keep her from dying and that had meant trying something without understanding the possible repercussions.

"She will come around," Nicholas said.

"You can see that?"

A shuffle and the smell of mothballs. "No, but I can." Myrr plunked herself down on the biggest chair in the room, high backed and obviously meant for a visiting dignitary.

She had a massive bowl of popcorn cradled in her arms.

Theo limped in after her, holding a wide board of charcuterie items. "Cook said to bring this down, as we're all locked up for the night."

Theo set the huge platter of food on the main table.

"That won't last." Nicholas said, softening the words with a smile. "Unless Myrr is fasting tonight?"

"Bah, rotten boy!" She threw a single popcorn at him, then seemed to regret it as she slipped from her chair, bent and picked it up, popping it into her mouth. "Waste not, want not."

Theo put his hands on his hips. "Where's Maverick? Shouldn't he be down here with us too, hiding from the beasties running wild tonight?"

That stopped my pacing. "You have a point. But maybe he'll die out there and solve one of my problems."

Dominic grunted. "Tell us how you really feel, my friend."

"She won't choose him."

We all turned to Sienna. I wanted to ask why not but didn't want to seem too eager. Nicholas caught my eye and nodded, asking the question for me.

"Why not?"

Sienna shrugged. "Because no matter how stubborn she is, she can't deny the fates that brought her and Raven together. Maverick, no matter how much she cares for him, does not stand a chance against the power of mates that truly love one another."

"You sound like you're reading that?" Theo motioned at the book in her hands.

Sienna lifted it up. *The Bonds of Fate, by Evangeline Blackthorne.* "Did you know that Evangeline wrote a book? And to find that here, not in Blackthorne castle. That I find even more interesting."

Interesting indeed..."Can I see it?"

Sienna handed it over to me, a distinct sparkle in her amber eyes. "Of course."

I shot her a questioning glance and she shrugged. "You're welcome."

I turned and headed to the massive table, ignoring the food at one end, and sitting in the shadows to read on my own.

I flipped through until I found the section that was marked by a ribbon that smelled like Sienna.

Fated Mates Across Species

It has not only anecdotal evidence, but actual written accounts that fated mates across the seven species: vampire, fae, werewolf, demon, angel, witch and human only occur at certain junctures.

Junctures where the world is in upheaval and the bonds between the six species need to be made stronger. Such events are rare, but some of note are the human world wars, one, two, and the hidden third. Other events in our own territory include the First Oracle's prophecies of destruction of our second continent, Alutheianus. The loss of so much life, drew us together as nothing else could, according to Bantheena, the First Oracle.

. . .

My jaw dropped open; my thoughts yanked away from Diana while I absorbed a truth that I had never heard so much as whispered. "What the fuck...did you know that there was a second continent? And where the fuck was this book all these years? Did Evangeline have it hidden somewhere?"

I held it up and looked at Sienna.

"Be careful how you speak to my wife," Dom growled.

I threw the book at his head, but he caught it before it could hit its mark. "I would cut my own arm off before hurting her, you know that."

The door behind us opened and the author herself stepped through.

"Duchess." I bowed from the waist, as did Nicholas and Dom.

She waved us off. "I heard some nattering on the other side of the door that included my name. What have I done now?"

Making her way to the seat next to Sienna, she lowered herself next to her one-time protégé. Sienna patted her arm. "You should feed."

"I did before I descended to the depths." She smiled and I knew without a doubt that she meant *before* Lycan's death as opposed to this place, where we were all hiding from the moon maddened wolves.

"That," I pointed at the book that Dom now held. "You wrote it?"

She held out her hand and Dominic made his way to his aunt and slid the book in front of her. "I did. I hid it here at the keep, on one of my last visits. Lycan...he hid it for me."

Her hand trembled as she placed it on the cover. "Neither he nor I thought it was worth our lives to make it available to anyone else. Fated mates across species? Taboo." Her eyes drifted to mine. "But your fated mate is not taboo, Raven. She's just angry that you made a choice for her. A choice she would have made also given the circumstances, which I believe is why she is so furious."

Her words were a strange kindness. "She doesn't want to be a vampire."

It was as if the others floated away, and I was having the conversation with Evangeline that I should have had already.

"It is because she does not remember it as anything but pain and betrayal. Her father abandoned her. Her brother tried to murder her. Her people that took her in told her that vampires were monsters—that was all she heard her whole life. Remember, she wasn't told that she'd been a vampire originally for many, many years, and the truth was kept from everyone. She was trained away from the other children, even her own adopted siblings didn't know—that is how well we masked her scent. She was well into adulthood before Lycan and I dared to tell her the truth. We kept the truth from her, and from her people."

And it must've rocked her world. "What can I do to help her, Duchess?"

Her smile was sad but still, there seemed to be some hope in her eyes. "Do not give up on her. Respect her space as she requires it, but do not leave. Do not abandon her."

Someone cleared their throat. Maybe Nicholas. "Duchess. Raven said there was something in there about another continent?"

She sighed and leaned back in her chair. "I found the last writings of the First Oracle. And in it, she spoke of the distant past, when there was a second continent. Our species were split across the two, a land bridge between them."

Her words trailed off and she flipped open the book, stopping near the back. "I transcribed it all here, so we didn't lose it. The original was written in ancient glyphs that took us years to decipher. It was the ruse that we met under, working together on a project. It was why my brother allowed me to travel back and forth. Why I...well, it does not matter now, does it?"

I might have been as engaged as the others with the story she was spinning, and in all truth, I wanted to know more but...I felt a tug on my bond with Diana.

I frowned and turned toward the door. I should have felt her above us, not to the west.

"Diana is not in the keep," I said.

I yanked the door open and was through it before anyone had a chance to ask me, or worse try and stop me. Because it was far worse than her just not being in the keep.

She was in danger—fear and rage raced through her.

I felt her fear, hunger, and frustration as clearly as if it were my own.

I raced up the stairs and out the closest exit I could find which happened to be a window. Good enough. I hit the ground running, feeling the danger around me as wolves took note of my emergence from the keep.

Bellows and screams, howls in the dark. A voice that was human—I was sure of it, and only my desire for it to be Maverick suffering somewhere let me believe it was him.

A wolf got in my way, turned wide eyes to me, and I knocked it to the side, sending it clear of my path to Diana.

Felt the teeth as the wolf bit down on her arm, breaking through her skin and digging into muscles. I ran faster. No wolf would catch me at top speed.

I would not lose her.

The world would not survive if I lost her—I would kill them all and salt the earth where their bones lay.

The trees around me changed, the sound of water reached my ears as I found her, my vision narrowed to the scene alone and nothing else.

Diana was under the wolf, sobbing, her hands buried

deep in its chest as she squeezed its heart with her bare hands.

The wolf jerked and twitched, its body convulsing.

I slid to my knees next to her and pulled the massive animal off her, already knowing it was dead. "Frostbite, look at me."

"His name is Gavin Barrach." Her green eyes were wide, dilated with the fight and the scent of blood all around us. "I was feeding and...he attacked me. I told him to stop, but he wouldn't listen! Like I wasn't even his queen."

The last words were whispered as I tugged her into my arms. She pulled away three seconds later.

"He's not dead. We have to get him to a healer."

I wasn't sure I was hearing her right. "What?"

"I didn't want to kill him. He's not himself, no one is during a full moon."

I could hear the beast's heart, a weak, sporadic thump with no rhythm, and knew she wasn't wrong. He wasn't dead.

Yet.

There was only one thing I could do. I scooped up the wolf. "I'll carry him. Let's go before anyone else sees. You cannot be seen here, Diana."

Because anyone seeing the wolf queen attacking one of her own, feeding on a deer, helped by the bastard vampire they could smell all over her? It would be the final nail in her crown. There would be no coming back from this.

"Hurry." Diana gripped my forearm. "We don't have much time."

Having someone reach through your chest and try to rip it out would do that to a heart. The problem was... that move...I'd seen William and Dominic do it on the battlefield. Hell, I'd heard that Edmund had been proficient at ripping hearts right out of chests. I was not about to tell Diana that there was a genetic component at play —that when push came to shove and she was fighting for her life, she pulled a move off that only the strongest vampires could. And against a massive, strong, male werewolf on a full moon?

It was an astonishing display of power.

"This way." She took the lead, cradling her arm as we moved as quickly and stealthily as we could. It seemed to take forever to get back to the keep, when in reality it was minutes.

The wolf in my arms was barely hanging on by a thread as we burst into the infirmary.

"Help him!" Diana yelled.

There was a single male doctor there—human—and that was it. The others were all out in the woods on the prowl like this one had been.

I laid the wolf on the table and the doctor went to work. "This is bad, Diana, the chest cavity has been mutilated, it looks like...if I didn't know better this looks like—"

"A bad attack...bear maybe?" I cut in. "Seems like this wolf got himself tangled up with the wrong opponent."

He shook his head grimly but didn't look up. "Unlikely that he'll survive. I'll give him a sedative, and that will help ease the pain—"

"Sienna could help," Diana murmured, her eyes glazed over with a mix of shock and pain. "She's a healer."

"She's also pregnant." The doctor held up a vial and a bottle, drawing a full syringe. "I do not want to put pressure on a valuable resource when we may need her for those who have a better chance of survival."

Diana's eyes narrowed. "You would gainsay me?"

He plunged the syringe into the wolf. "I am sorry. I was just offering my opinion as you seem upset."

But I knew the words for the lie they were. No one in the keep would ever have questioned her in the past, least of all one of the human doctors in her employ. She was losing respect across the board. I felt the pain of that knowledge as if it were my own, but I didn't let it show as I gave her a quick nod.

"I will get Sienna."

The doctor let out a weary sigh as he lifted the sheet to cover the wolf's face.

"Don't bother. He's gone."

CHAPTER 6

Diana

Stinging pain jolted through my scalp as I tore the brush through my tangled hair, but it only drove me to do it harder. The feeling was cathartic, in a way, and it was all that was stopping me from driving my forehead directly through my bathroom mirror.

The memory of the night before was fuzzy, likely due to shock, but Raven and I had met with Nicholas, Dominic, and Sienna right after Gavin's death. And, somehow, I'd been convinced to set up a meeting with Gavin's family. It was important to keep things as normal as possible during the lead-up to the summit with the other monarchs, but it was hard to imagine anything feeling more wrong.

Could I really walk right up to his widow and lie to her about what happened?

It's a queen's duty to act in the best interest of all of her subjects.

I could almost hear Lycan saying the words. He'd repeated them dozens of times while preparing me to step up as queen. And I couldn't deny that this was in the best interest of my people when we faced so many other dangers.

Lilis was out there somewhere, and she'd probably salivate at the thought of the chaos and division my actions could cause.

I had to deal with the other leaders and convince them to help.

My people were at the edge of a civil unrest.

But it felt awfully convenient for me to fall back on what a queen's duty was now...after what I'd done the previous night.

Killing one of my own, even in self-defense was not taken lightly even in good times.

Maybe Gavin hadn't even recognized me in his altered state of mind. Perhaps he only scented me as... other.

And the fact that I'd put myself in that position to begin with? And for what? Because I was sad that I'd lost my wolf? Because I couldn't control my hunger? Because I was the monster I'd always been told vampires were.

Tears pricked at my eyes as I murmured his name aloud for the dozenth time this morning, ensuring I would never forget it.

"Gavin Barrach."

I had failed him and the entirety of his clan. Everything from here on out was nothing but damage control.

My mind searched for some excuse, any way to get out of this, and the taste of iron flooded my tongue as the tips of my fangs dug into the soft flesh of my bottom lip.

"Fuck!" The word came out as a shout.

I stared into the mirror, my gaze fixed on the green of my irises as Mav's words replayed in my mind yet again. It wasn't as if the idea had come from nowhere. I had heard the whispers, too, that I was no longer fit to rule. And, as much as they hurt, I wasn't exactly doing a great job refuting them.

Many in Gavin's clan had not been thrilled about me being queen, but they'd done their duty and bent the knee. And whenever I had called on them, they had answered that call. Gavin himself had taken three heads in the battle against the Demons, I'd learned earlier this morning. Not my strongest supporter, but certainly not an enemy of the crown, either.

A knock at the door pulled me back to the present. "Come back later," I called.

"Open the door, Diana."

I let out a breath, recognizing the Duchess' voice. "Enter."

It would've been right to go and greet her, but I didn't have it in me at that moment. Any vitality I'd felt after drinking from the doe last night was long gone, leaving behind a bone-deep weariness I hadn't felt since my father died.

She flashed me a sad smile as she walked into the room, her hands straying to my hair as she settled wordlessly behind me. She worked on my hair, untangling it in silence for nearly a minute before speaking.

"I'm sure you're really going through it right now. Talk to me, child."

"He has children, Evangeline...I just don't get how I'm supposed to sit there and lie."

She nodded. "I understand all that, and I don't envy your position. What happened was self-defense, and that was clear, despite how you feel right now." I made a noise of dissent, and she shushed me. "But you'll have plenty of time to make it up to this man's family once we've secured the support we need. It's an ugly job, but it's one you need to do. Regardless of how your people treat you, you *are* still their queen. And, as harsh as it sounds, a queen ought not allow her faulty guilty conscience to turn one mistake into two."

A resigned calm settled over me. "That's just what my father would've said."

She cocked her head at me, making eye contact through the mirror. Her hand slipped slightly as I said it, but she flashed me a forced half-smile. "It is, I agree."

"And I do know that you're right, Duchess. It's the best thing I can do for my people now that I've gotten myself into this situation."

The carriage ride to Gavin's home passed in a haze, with Loch and Sienna tagging along to support me, but the Duchess' words had solidified something in me. My thoughts were more about how I was going to get this job done rather than *if* I was going to do it.

I forced myself mechanically to my feet as we rolled to a stop, doing my best to channel my inner queen. For my people, I could keep it together. I *had* to keep it together. I could be sympathetic, too, but nothing like this mess I was on the inside.

I just had to see them through the battle for the world, then I could step down.

Sienna dropped a comforting hand to my shoulder, and I forced my way out of the carriage, feeling more like a spectator than the person controlling my body. I slowly made my way toward the door of the adorable little cottage, but it felt like I was walking to the gallows. Blood roared in my ears as the path before me blurred.

I hadn't even reached the door when it swung open, and a woman with a babe on her hip stepped outside, her face draining of color when she saw me. There was only one reason I made house calls, and my people knew it.

"Mary, I'm so sorry...I need to speak with you, please."

"No, no. No no no no!" The whispered plea built to a primal scream, and she grasped the doorknob for purchase as her knees gave out. A smattering of footsteps sounded behind her, and two other children poked their heads through the doorway.

A tiny redhead girl, no more than nine, and a boy about the age of twelve. The boy instantly took the now squalling baby from his mother and tried to shield his sister behind his arm.

"Your Majesty...what are you doing here?" he asked, his voice barely audible over his mother's racking sobs.

The words stuck in my throat as I tried to speak until Sienna's hand slipped to my lower back, unseen by them, the warmth and energy flowing off her giving me a boost of strength.

"I'm so very sorry, Kalen, but I'm afraid your father has passed away."

The next minutes passed in a nightmarish blur as Sienna stepped in and ushered all of us back into the little cottage. I found myself sitting across from Mary while Sienna talked in low gentle tones to her children in the other room. I'd felt her healing magic washing over me from just that simple touch a short while ago, and I only hoped she was doing the same for them. It had been fleeting, as it would be for those poor young children and Gavin's widow, though...

"I knew when he didn't come home last night," Mary said softly, cupping her hands more tightly around the steaming mug of tea Sienna had prepared. "With the new babe, my wolf's been quiet, which is fine by me. Lost the taste for the hunt, for now," she admitted, rocking back and forth in her seat. "But not Gavin. He was more excited than ever. Amped up and full of energy. Gave me a bad feeling in the pit of my stomach, and I should have said so. If he hadn't gone...he'd be home with us now. If he'd just slept it off instead."

I reached out and took her trembling hand in mine, feeling every bit the traitor I was. "It wasn't your fault,

Mary. Gavin was a strong man with a stubborn heart. You and I both know if he wanted to go out, nothing you could have said would have stopped him."

"You're right about that, for certain." That got a ghost of a smile out of her before she lifted her head and met my gaze head-on. "How did it happen, Your Majesty? Do you know?"

I'd practiced it a hundred times since we'd created the story the night before, I should've known it by heart. And still, under the unbearable weight of her golden-eyed stare, the words escaped me.

I sucked in a breath and tried again. "We...we found him in the woods over near the boundary between the river and the demon realm. We can't be sure, but we're thinking possibly a bear attack."

"A bear?" Mary let out a harsh laugh. "The day Gavin is bested by a fucking bear, you could knock me over with a feather. No." She shook her head, viciously. "It had to be something else. I can't help but wonder—" she broke off and gnawed on her lower lip for a long moment until I gave her hand another squeeze.

"It's alright, you can say it."

"To be honest, my Queen, I can't help but wonder if he hadn't been challenged by another clan for his recent political stances..." Her cheeks turned pink, but she didn't look away. "I won't say I agreed with him, but I won't apologize for him either. These are strange times, and some of the people he's been hanging around with have started to question whether or not..." she trailed off and then started again, this time her expression full of golden determination. "They're wondering if you're still fit to be Queen. Do you think it's possible that one of the more loyalist leaning clans found him alone and hurt him?"

Fuck. I cleared my throat thinking that the loyalist who'd killed him was me.

"I supposed that's possible, Mary, but I can't say for sure."

"Well, you've got all those scientists and doctors. You have his body," she gestured out the window and swallowed hard. "There's got to be something you can do to try to figure it out. DNA, hair, blood samples, something."

It took all my might not to look away. The lies were coating my tongue in ash, and I didn't think I could utter another, but I managed a whole slew of them.

"I hadn't heard of your husband's recent political leanings, so we had not planned on doing an autopsy proper, given his condition when we found him. We really did think a bear was the most likely culprit based on the marks upon his body. And while I'll agree that Gavin was as strong as they come, if he was focused on spotting a kill or perhaps had been upwind of the bear, the animal could have gotten the drop on him."

"Promise me." Mary leaned in, using her grip on my hand to tug me closer, her gaze intense. "Promise me you'll at least look into it."

I nodded and pulled away. "I will." I tugged the thick

vellum envelope I'd secreted in my coat pocket and slid it across the table between us. "And this is to take care of your family in the absence of your husband. Again, I'm so sorry for your loss."

She stared at the envelope dully and didn't bother picking it up as she stood.

"I appreciate you coming personally. I–" she broke off and turned away, ragged, ugly sobs making her whole body quake and my stomach turn. I fisted my hands at my sides, tears streaming down my cheeks, her pain cutting into me.

I could be furious with Raven all I wanted. There was no more denying the truth, though...

He'd made me a vampire without my permission.

But I'd turned into a monster all on my own.

"It's about time we had a proper dinner," Myrr said, clapping her hands together with a delighted cackle as the servants set down enough platters to cover the entire center of the table from end to end.

Roast duck, creamy parsnips gleaming with melted butter, glazed carrots, braised cabbage, and an array of steaks ranging from medium-rare to near mooing, with mushroom gravy to pour over top.

It was true that, since we'd gotten back from the Demon Territory, Diana had called an end to the sit-down, shared meals at the table in the center of the keep, but we'd still had access to the kitchens and all the food inside, a fact that Theo reminded Myrr of.

"Yes," she said as she stood up to reach the steaming basket of sourdough rolls, "but it's not the same as having this smorgasbord in front of you, is it? It just makes me so happy I could weep," she declared without a single tear in her eyes, settling back into her seat and tearing into the roll as if she had a full set of teeth.

"Well, we wanted to make sure we put out a good spread now that William and Bee have come," the Duchess said with a warm small smile as she gazed upon the Vampire King and his wife.

I tried to think of the last time I'd seen Evangeline give a full, real smile and none came to mind. Not since Lycan had passed.

Maybe she was finally starting to heal a little?

Her face darkened even as I watched, the smile flickering away as quickly as it had come, as if my thoughts had touched hers, reminding her that her beloved was still dead.

As I let my gaze trail toward Diana at the head of the table, I noted that she barely looked better than her aunt. In fact, she'd hardly lifted her eyes from her plate since we'd sat down, lost in her own thoughts...

Trapped in her own guilt was more like it. A guilt I could feel between us, her emotions swirling and slamming against me. Another chasm I could not cross. I wished I could launch myself across the table and take her in my arms and remind her, as I had so many times in the past day, that this wasn't her fault. She had been the victim of a failed assassination attempt—that it was self-defense and no one would gainsay that truth. To my mind, there should have been no sweeping it under the rug or making excuses. We should have dragged Gavin's whole clan out into the sunlight and tossed his remains on the ground in front of them while demanding to know if there were others who felt the same as he did.

But cooler heads than mine had prevailed. Dom, Sienna, and Evangeline all thought that Diana's position was too precarious right now. Even if she had been acting in self-defense, it could tip her people over the edge, triggering an all-out civil war. Not to mention that there was also the matter of her killing him...as a vampire. Her scent was getting harder and harder to mask as the days rolled on.

Their reasoning had won out over my fury.

For now, we had to play it cool and keep Diana's role in Gavin Barrach's death quiet, at least until we got back from the summit at the ruins and had secured our allyship with the other heads of territories. Then we could focus on the civil unrest that was brewing amongst Diana's people.

"Have we made any headway with Cleona?" Diana murmured, eyes still lowered as she directed her question towards Loch, who sat to her left.

Sienna wrinkled up her nose. "Cleona is the fae queen? I get her and Rabia's names mixed up."

Dom grunted. "Just don't mix them up in front of them."

Loch pointed a fork at Sienna and then continued. "My sense is that she'll be there. I promised Cleona that she and Queen Rabia would not be required to be in the same room at any time and she said, I quote, 'I'll come to hear what the she-wolf has to say, but if that halo-wearing bitch even looks at me wrong, I'm out.'"

Will forked up a piece of duck. "Cleona likes me. I volunteer to act as a buffer between them if the need arises."

"Better you than me," Bee said as she swallowed a gulp of red wine and set her glass down. "I met her once when she came to visit Edmund during his reign of terror. If I had to be alone in a room with her or Edmund, I'm not sure which I'd choose."

I couldn't argue Edmund was a monster, and a good thing that he was dead, but Cleona was equally terrifying in a whole other way. The magic practically poured off her...an almost palpable energy that was unsettling, making even my skin crawl. Her amber eyes glowed with an orange light that seemed to illuminate your deepest thoughts. I'd always got the sense that, although she was slight of build, if you blinked for a second, she could have you flat on your back with both Achilles cut and your severed tongue in her hand before you even saw her move.

"I'm not afraid of her, she's a child still in her own way," Diana said flatly. "I'm only afraid of what her lack of support might do to our chances of winning this war. I'm working on a speech now, and it's going to be a balancing act. I need to appeal to the pride of the Fae, the arrogance of the Vampires, the Angels' sense of justice, and the thrill of the fight with the Demons. So long as I can keep them from infighting, I think I have a fair shot of convincing them that there is no other choice but to band together if we are to have any hope of surviving. Our proof is too strong when it comes to the dark goddess."

"I still have concerns," Dominic said as he settled back against his chair, steepling his fingers in front of his mouth. "I know we said no weapons, but–"

Diana sliced a hand through the air and finally looked up, her eyes flashing green fire. "And I meant it. It's a non-starter. There will be no weapons, or there will be no meeting—if I were one of the other leaders, I would back out immediately if I saw my host was a fucking liar." Her fork clattered to her plate. "Further, I'd appreciate it if the people around this table, at the very least, stop second-guessing me."

Dominic, bless him, didn't back down. "Allow me to finish, sister. I'm thinking as a General, protecting you being my only goal. You're thinking like a Queen, and that requires diplomacy. My job is to think as a general— and I do agree with you on the weapons front." He held up his hand. "We will be lucky if we leave there without any bloodshed as it is. If weapons were permitted, I have zero doubt that things would deteriorate rapidly. What I will recommend is bringing some reinforcements. Not just to step in and break up any potential infighting that gets out of hand, but because..." Dominic's mouth flattened into a thin line as he raised a brow, "the evil bitch goddess whose name I won't mention would surely love nothing better than to find the most powerful people in the Alpha Territories in one place at one time. I can't rationalize you being there all but defenseless. We need to protect every one of the leaders."

I tapped a finger on the table, drawing eyes to me. "If Diana shows up with an army of foot soldiers, the others will turn back, and any trust they've extended will be gone in an instant. We'll never get another opportunity to convince them," I scratched at my jaw as my thoughts churned. I was with Dom when it came to protecting my mate. Diana needed to be kept safe above anything else, but if anything got in the way of her success in this meeting, any chance she had of uniting her own people behind the cause would be gone.

This had to work. There was no other option.

"Which is why I'm not suggesting foot soldiers...or soldiers," Dominic clarified with a nod. "What if we get there hours before the others? Sienna can ride one of the Hunters and hide her in the forest. The ruins are a short distance from the shore. We could have Sal and Xephia along with some of our army at the ready in the sea. Back up only if the dark goddess makes a move."

"I can call to the Kraken as well," Sienna added, tugging a strand of auburn hair behind one ear.

The table was quiet, and I could see even Diana considering her brother's suggestion.

"I don't hate it," I said, my tone careful and measured, "but I don't believe we'll be the only ones to show up early. If we hope to arrive first, we should leave early tomorrow morning. Assuming many of the others come by air, we need to make sure that everyone is out of sight, particularly that Hunter of yours." I glanced at Diana, brows raised in question. "Your thoughts, my queen?"

Her eyes flickered at the title, as if it almost hurt her to hear it now, but, to her credit, she nodded. "I hear the sense in your words, Dominic. I agree. Despite the goddess being weakened, we don't know if she might see this as a chance too tempting to pass up. Having some safeguards in place is prudent."

She pushed back her chair and gave a wan smile to the table as she stood.

"If you'll excuse me, I'm going to spend the rest of my evening working on my speech. Loch, can you lend me your ear? I'd like to hear your thoughts on what I have so far. I'll see the rest of you in the morning."

She swept from the room with Lochlin trailing behind her as the rest of us watched in silence. She'd been gone for more than a minute before it was broken.

"So what did I miss?" Will asked, flicking a glance to everyone around the table in turn.

Theo, bless his old heart, took a crack at it and cleared his throat. "Things have been...difficult here for the wolf queen since we returned. She's not herself."

More silence.

"You know...maybe we should head down to the courtyard and do a little sparring to work off this food?" I said, tossing my napkin on the table.

I wasn't about to air out Diana's dirty laundry in

front of everyone. At first, only me, Dom, Sienna, and Nicholas had been privy to what happened last night during the blood moon. Then, we'd let Evangeline and Loch in on the news today. Will would be the last to know, at Diana's request. Maybe he would be the one to finally convince her that she'd had no choice. That I'd had no choice.

"Aye, that sounds like a plan," Dom said, shooting Will a pointed look. "Nicholas?"

"I'm in."

Bee reached beside her and took Sienna's hand. "And while you boys burn some testosterone, Sienna and I can catch up." She turned to Dominic, "Don't hurt my husband out there, or you'll have me to contend with," she added with a warning frown.

I pushed back my chair and stood as Dom, Will, and Nicholas followed suit. We were about to head for the door when I realized Maverick had also stood. In the conversation he'd been so quiet, I'd forgotten he'd been there at all. Unlike him to not air his desires when it came to what he thought Diana should or should not do.

"I think I'll join you all."

I paused and turned toward him, every muscle tensed. "I don't think you will."

"And why is that?" Maverick asked, cocking his head in mock confusion. "Are you afraid to spar with me, vampire?"

The rage was instant and all-consuming, but I refused to give him the satisfaction of seeing it. Hundreds of years of control kept me still. I was the predator, he was the prey and that had not changed.

Instead, I smiled, letting him see the fangs now protruding from my gums. "You want to spar with me, Maverick? Let's go. It's your funeral."

Dominic shot me a warning glare and then turned to face Maverick. "My brethren and I have a few things to discuss first. Give us half an hour in peace, and if you still think sparring with a vampire that would as soon feed you to the fishes given the chance is a good idea, feel free to come down and join us."

Maverick popped a wink and sidled toward the door as if he didn't have a care in the world. "Count on it. Thirty minutes, I'll be there."

I'd hated him from the first moment we'd met, perhaps even before if I was being honest with myself, and it had only gotten worse in the face of this new and perplexing bravado. My blood was pumping at the chance to take him down a peg. Maybe remove a few of his limbs while I was at it.

"If you hurt him badly, you better finish the job and hide the body because it will only make her more protective of him," Sienna said softly.

The truth of her words was like a stake to the heart, but I forced a smile. "And with that, I'll say good evening to the rest of you."

"Call me down to watch if you all start sweating and shirts come off," Myrr called after us.

Nicholas, Dom, Will, and I filed out of the room and

made our way to the armory. Once we'd stepped inside and the door was shut behind us, Will instantly turned to face me.

"Let's hear it."

I shouldered past him to the selection of weapons. "There was an...unfortunate incident last night that has thrown Diana into a tailspin."

I quickly recounted the events of the night before, as well as the fact that I'd shared my blood, and her wolf had left her.

Will grimaced. "Hell. That must've gutted her. Both to learn that she has likely lost her wolf for good, and that she killed one of her own. It's going to take some time to get past it all. I just wish this meeting wasn't upon us...that she had more time to her own healing."

"It can't be moved," Nicholas put a hand to one of the staffs. "The moons and the tides are completely messed up, and the weather has been getting crazier and more unpredictable with each passing day. Even if everyone agrees and we're able to locate all the keys quickly, we still might be too late. Something tells me that when the dark goddess emerges again, it will be in person this time, and she will come with a vengeance."

Nicholas's words felt nearly prophetic and they left no room for more banter.

By the time we all selected our weapons and grabbed a couple of spares on the off-chance Mav didn't chicken out, I was itching for a fight. The tension of the past week had me taut as a wire, and my near-miss with Diana last night had only made it worse.

"I almost feel sorry for you guys," I rolled the sword in my hand, the hilt warming to my palm. I gave a couple easy swoops with it, testing the weight.

Dom snorted. "The only thing you should be sorry about is getting your blood all over my new shirt and pissing my wife off about the stains."

"Want to bet on that, big fellow?" I shot back with a grin.

"Naturally."

Will shared a look with Nicholas, and they both nodded. "We want in on the action. I'll put a thousand on my brother. What say you, Nicholas of Southwind?"

Nick's eyes narrowed as he looked me up and down like I was a horse he was thinking about buying—or in this case, betting on. "Dom's got more experience and strategy, but Raven's got both unrequited love *and* celibacy driving him. I'll take that bet."

I blew Nicholas a kiss and then turned to face my opponent as the others took seats on the stone wall to watch.

"And what's our wager to be, Dom?"

"If I win, I want you to build a cradle for the baby. Assuming the world hasn't ended by then, of course..."

I hadn't built anything in decades. The fact that he remembered I was passing good at woodwork at one time in my life, surprised me, but I nodded. "Done. I have to think about what I want if I win. I promise I won't make it too painful, though. And if you don't agree, I'll pick something else."

"Deal."

I lifted my blunted sword, circling as he readied his own. With an opponent like Dom, it was crucial to have a plan in mind. I had a fairly even sparring record against him, which was something I doubted anyone else in the territories could say, but it always took a little extra to get over the line and actually beat him.

He dashed forward, grunting as he brought his blade down in an overhead chop. The nerves in my arm screamed as I deflected it, and the ringing of steel was still echoing through the arena as I kicked at his knee.

He lifted his leg just in time, meeting me shin-to-shin as his free hand connected with my shoulder. "Fucking hell," I said, doing my best to ignore the three different nodes of pain that'd opened on my body in the ten-second exchange. In terms of raw strength, I doubted any vampire alive could match him. But speed?

That was my domain and my best shot at whooping him soundly.

I leaped back into range, feinting toward his legs to set up a thrust aimed right at his belly. He spun around it, his blade whirling through the space I'd been a moment earlier as I ducked under it, springing up with another attack.

He brought his fist forward again, but I slipped around the blow, gripping my blade with both hands as I brought it down in a powerful overhead arc. He roared as his blade whipped into position to block.

I couldn't help but grin as I released the blade, letting it drop uselessly onto his as my hand flew directly toward his chest. My heart thrummed triumphantly in my ears as all five fingers smacked into his chest, taking a solid handful of shirt and dug my fingers into the meat of his pec.

He went still immediately, knowing what it would've meant in a real fight. "Well fought. I've never seen you go for a heart-strike before."

"Just when you think you know a guy, huh?" I said, chuckling as I clapped him on the shoulder. I'd had the move on my mind since Diana's incident in the woods, though I never would've expected to make use of it so quickly. Diana still at the forefront of my mind, I continued. "I've decided what I want for my win. Try to convince your sister to let me come to the meeting."

"Gods, man." Dom winced. "Can't you just kill me instead?"

"You've already convinced her to bring Nicholas, and Dominic," Mav called as he stepped into the courtyard. "How many other vampires do you think she needs by her side?" he added, a shitty little smile playing about his lips.

"Just one," I growled back.

"If you say so..." He crouched, picking up one of the blunted sparring swords from the ground. "So, how does this work? Do I have to wait my turn, or can I just hop right in and take on the last bout's winner?"

I frowned, staring him down. "You can't be serious."

"Why not? Worried I'll embarrass you?"

A growl tore free of my throat, unbidden, and I jabbed my blade toward the center of the ring. "You seem hellbent on your own destruction, but don't say I didn't warn you. That all of us didn't warn you."

He stepped nonchalantly toward me before dropping into a strange, low stance.

Every muscle in my body screamed for me to charge forward and skewer him right through his midsection, but I let out a breath as my eyes settled on a nervous-looking Nicholas. He gave his head the slightest shake, eyes wide, reminding me of what I already knew. As much as the bastard deserved it, Diana would lose her shit if I hurt Maverick too badly.

I had to win, but in a way that didn't seem excessive or overly harsh. I loosened my grip on my blade, then leaped forward, lashing out with a mid-paced blow at his stomach.

Mav parried, and then launched into a counterattack. His blade crashed against mine, and I couldn't help but be surprised by how hard his blows struck. Nothing compared to Dom, of course, but a comparison to the Vanators when they were super charged was far less ludicrous.

But how?

I didn't waste time thinking about it. Instead, I shot

my foot out for a kick, and he spun around it, letting his momentum carry him right into a counter. A rush of irritation coursed through me as I batted his blade aside a second time.

Let's see how you deal with this, chickenshit.

I let loose a little more power as I broke into a flurry of attacks. He barely leapt over the one at his ankle, then ducked under the one aimed at his neck. His fist shot out before I could get off a third, and I dodged around it, knowing that anything less than a flawless victory against this bastard would be a disgrace.

Maverick would crow about a win over me to anyone who would listen. And that was unacceptable.

The rush of bloodlust surged as he swung his sword again, just a heartbeat too slow. It took every ounce of self-control I had to rein it in as I brought my weapon down toward him in a two-handed chop.

His body lurched to a sudden stop, and he dropped his sword, leaping head-first toward my chest. I cursed inwardly as I felt the slice of a blade against my thigh. I had been too careless. That little motherfucker–

My knee shot upward at a speed few others could match, moving on pure instinct. I breathed out in relief as it smashed right into his chest. He dropped backward like a ton of bricks, his head bouncing off the hard packed dirt with a satisfying thunk as the dagger he'd pulled on me bounced a few yards away.

"Obnoxious bastard," I muttered, wincing as my leg began to sting from where he'd caught me.

Against the rules or not, the fucker had landed a blow on me. And with such a strange move…

I reeled, the truth of the matter striking me like an arrow straight between the eyes.

More than strange.

It had been pre-planned. I'd used the same sequence in my fight with Dom a few minutes before. He'd watched and had been waiting to bait me into doing the same with him. Tricky, and far cleverer than I'd given him credit for.

The rage in my chest burned even hotter at the thought, but I didn't have time to think on it long as he rolled to his feet and charged at me again. This time, I didn't hold back. I hit him with a closed fist directly in the jaw, relishing the sound of it cracking.

Diana's voice cut through the otherwise deadly quiet arena.

"What the fuck do you think you're doing?"

Mav stumbled toward me, and I caught him carefully by the shoulders as his jaw hung at an awkward angle, blood dripping to the ground in a steady patter. Blood that drew my eye like nothing else.

"He asked to fight," Nicholas said. "This is not anyone's fault but his own."

"Yes, well a child will ask to hold a weapon long before he is ready, that does not mean you give it to him!" I snapped back, anger at Raven, and some at myself for being distracted when Maverick was injured.

Mav tensed under my hands, a shudder rolling through him before he jerked away from me. His jaw protruded sharply to the left at a wholly unnatural angle, and I winced.

"Go to the infirmary, Maverick. I'll have Sienna meet you there."

He glared at me and then stalked off without a backward glance, his gait steady despite his injury.

I spun back toward Raven, only then noticing the blood welling from a slash against his thigh. "Are *you* injured?"

"No..." He was staring at me with something very near surprise. I realized all the men were. Surprise or horror? I felt a niggling of something closer to embarrassment on Mav's behalf rolling off them, most especially from Raven, damn that bond. And why would he be embarrassed for Maverick?

"What are you all looking at?"

It was Will who spoke. "Sister...I know you were trying to help Maverick, but you also just gravely insulted him. A male's pride can only take so many blows like that before he crumbles."

Gravely insulted? It took my mind a moment to replay the words that had flown from my lips. A child not ready to wield a weapon...no wonder Mav was pissed. I put a hand to my forehead. "Goddess bless, could things get any worse?"

"Do not invoke her to try," Dominic rumbled.

I looked to my older brother, doing my best to ignore Raven and the urge to make sure he was not injured worse than the slash across his thigh. "Continue on with your sparring, then."

"Did you come here for a reason?" Dom leaned on his sword. "Or just to make sure we were playing nice with the human?"

I took note that through all this, Raven was quiet. "I came to talk with Will about us both speaking tomorrow. I think it will be good to model unity for them all to see."

And indeed, that was why I'd told myself I'd come this way. Not the fiery rage that had snapped through me —rage that was not my own, but clearly Raven's. I'd known only one person could set him off so quickly.

And while I might not care for Mav the way I'd once thought, I didn't want to see him injured or worse, killed. He'd been a part of our journey to find the shard and hopefully save the Territories. For that I was grateful.

Will tipped his head. "Let's go then and speak about speeches."

"I will meet you in my quarters, Will. I need to make sure Mav made it to the infirmary and that Sienna can help him." I turned and wasn't surprised to feel Raven step up to my side. "I do not need an escort, Raven."

"Ah, but perhaps I do?" Raven limped a little, favoring that leg. "I plan to head over there myself...I'm feeling strangely lightheaded."

I glanced at him. "Stop it. You aren't feeling any such–"

But no...he *was* lightheaded. His face pale and his eyes seemed almost to fog over. He shook his head and stumbled, barely catching himself on the wall.

"Frostbite, something is wrong."

In a panic, I grabbed at his arms, trying to drag him upright. "Raven, what's going on? Stop this."

"I don't know..." He closed his eyes and grimaced.

Swallowing hard, his throat convulsed but that wasn't what drew my eyes.

Against his collarbone, something moved, undulating under his skin. Rippling. Feasting on his blood.

No, it couldn't be...

I pulled him to his feet and yanked his arm across my shoulders. "Dominic! Nicholas!" I didn't dare call for Will, not when this very thing had almost killed him once.

They caught up to us when we were nearly to the infirmary.

"What's happened?" Dom took Raven's other side and together we hurried him through the doors.

"He just said he was feeling lightheaded and then... Dom...there's something under his skin." I gritted my teeth, not wanting to believe I had seen what I knew I'd seen.

We got Raven inside and flat on a table, only to have his body arching up on his heels and the back of his head. I pressed his chest down, feeling his heart beating erratically and even pausing. "Don't you dare, Raven! Don't you fucking dare!"

The one male doctor in the room hurried over. "Another patient?"

I gripped Raven's hand and kept my other on his chest, the world narrowing down to his face. "Look at me, Raven. Keep your eyes on me."

His lids flickered open, but I wasn't sure he even truly saw me through the pain.

"Dom, go get Sienna." I didn't look up.

"He's already left to do so." Nicholas was beside me. "Diana, this is bad."

The male doctor fussed around. "How long has he been ill?"

"Five minutes. Less." Which made no sense, and I knew it. Unless he'd been hiding his illness from me?

The doctor flinched. "Bad indeed. Looks like a bloodworm. Or some variation of it? Never seen it come on so fast, though. As strong as he is, he should've been showing signs for months before it came to this."

"No symptoms. I felt strong." Raven's breathing was coming in shallow gasps. "Nicholas...promise me...Keep her safe."

"Don't you fucking give him orders!" I snapped. "I'm the one in charge here. You *will* make it through this, Raven!"

His smile was pained. "Yes, my queen."

I gripped his hand harder. This was not happening; it could *not* be happening.

"Fresh bloodworm eggs would come on faster than dormant ones, but even at that, to go from healthy, with no sign of being infected, to this in such a short time... strange. Almost as if they'd been altered somehow to make them react near instantly upon ingestion."

Altered...by magic? Was this the work of Lilis somehow?

"What did he eat most recently?" the doctor asked, brow furrowed.

"The feast," I whispered, horror striking me even deeper as I understood this was more than just Raven now and it was no accident. This might have been an attempt to take all the vampires out at once. I didn't know how, but once the thought hit me, I knew I was right. "Nicholas. The others, go check on them!"

The food had been consumed by Dominic, Will, Bee, Evangeline, Nicholas, and Raven. Six vampires at a single feast. And someone had slipped the deadly bloodworm eggs into the food. The only ones affected would be vampires, which made no sense if it was Lilis.

No. This was done by my own brethren. Those who didn't want me to sully the monarchy with more vampires in our midst had finally come up with a deadly solution.

I clutched Raven harder. "Don't you dare give up."

He shuddered, blood trickling from his mouth. "As you command, Frostbite."

Someone else was talking to me from the other side of the room, calling my name but I didn't look up. I couldn't look away from Raven.

I bent my head close to his. "Don't you leave me, Raven. Don't you dare leave me alone in this. I can't...I can't do this without knowing you're behind me. No matter what, I always knew you were there. It was enough to give me the strength to do the impossible."

He groaned and his fingers tangled tighter around mine. "I don't want to go, Frostbite. But I don't think I have a choice..." Blood gurgled in his throat as he struggled to breathe.

Someone took me by the shoulders and tugged me toward them. I didn't even think, I jerked away, vaguely hearing a scuffle as whoever it was stumbled.

"I see that's how it is, then."

I barely registered the snarled words, or the voice that, in the back of my mind, I knew was Mav. His injury was nothing compared to this—he would heal, and his hurt pride would heal too.

But if Raven died...my heart felt as though it were being torn in half, shrieking as each fiber was pulled apart at the thought. The shard trembled inside of me, but my hands weren't capable of healing. They were only capable of meting out death and destruction...pain and rage, and out in full force now...

Brilliant red hair came into view, and a breathless Sienna bent close to Raven.

"Diana, you need to back up. I cannot risk the worm attaching to you."

It took a second for her words to register. There weren't six vampires at that meal. There were seven. This might not have been an attack to rid me of my advisors and my lover.

This might've been another assassination attempt if someone had realized what I was now.

The ramifications had me reeling.

Had the poisoner known my wolf was gone? And if so,

how? The thought that the attack had come from inside the keep cut me to the core, from someone I trusted—but I shoved it away. All that mattered right now was Raven.

Strong, gentle hands wrapped around my upper arms and carefully pulled me backward. Dominic held me tight. "She can save him, Di. And she will. Just have trust and give her the space to work."

Shaking, I stood there and watched, unable to look away as Sienna wove her magic that connected her to the shard, through Raven's body.

I didn't close my eyes, and yet I could no longer see Raven.

The black willows surrounded me.

A pyre stacked high, flames bursting upward around a black shrouded figure.

My throat closed off as a scream built deep in my chest, trapped by my heart as it shattered. The shard spoke to me, not unkindly.

"Even if he is not your fated mate...would you lose him?"

"No. Give him back!"

"Get me a jar, quickly," Sienna snapped, waving a hand to the doctor hovering nearby. A couple silent moments passed and then a choking growl escaped Raven's lips.

I struggled against Dom's hold, but he didn't release me until Sienna stepped back, her face bathed in sweat. Dominic finally let me go, and I forced my shaking legs forward, returning to Raven's side, fearing the worst. His eyes were closed, and when I put my hand on his chest, it rose and fell in a steady rhythm.

I let out a strangled cry and bent low to rest my head on his chest.

"He will need to rest," Sienna said. "But the blood-worms were small and hadn't attached to his stomach with their hooks yet, so I was able to pull them all out quickly."

I wanted to ask her to stay, to make sure, but she was clearly exhausted by her efforts, and I could ask no more of her than had been given already.

"Thank you, sister."

"Don't thank me yet. I need you to sit down so I can check you as well."

Because I was a vampire, like my brothers...Like Raven.

A quick nod and I let her put her hands on my face, the magic of the shard suffusing me. "There were blood-worms in you."

My guts clenched.

"But?"

"The shard protected you, keeping them as eggs, which allowed me to destroy them." Sienna's golden eyes locked on mine. "But someone was trying to hurt you all."

Shaking with adrenaline and rage, I felt the pressure of my fangs against my gums. If we hoped to figure out who was behind this before we left for the summit, we needed to act now. I didn't want to leave Raven, but I had to. Someone had nearly killed the man I loved, and I'd be damned if I'd let them get away with it.

"Dominic..." I looked to my brother, seeing understanding on his face.

"We will stay with him, Di. Go. Do what you have to do."

What I had to do was find out just who the fuck had done this and make them pay.

Ten minutes later, I was sprinting the distance to the water's edge where I'd battled Gavin Barrach, with Lochlin at my side.

"We need to search, to see if there are any signs that someone else had been there during the full moon. If someone outside the keep could possibly have known what happened..."

"Diana, this is bad, if someone else saw...there will be hell to pay," Lochlin growled as we swept the area. I was trusting his nose since my own had gotten dulled under the loss of my wolf.

I shook my head, clearing it of the thoughts that pulled it in so many directions.

We swept the far side of the river first—across from where Gavin had attacked me.

"I'm hoping I'm wrong but..." I paused on the far side of the river, across from where the fight had happened. A series of branches were bent backward, deep gray fur embedded in them. Just a few strands, but enough to draw my eye. Crouching, I brushed plants aside to see the soft ground and the massive imprints there of wolf paws. My stomach lurched.

"Loch," I croaked, barely breathing as I called to him.

He hurried over to me. "Fuck. Gray wolf, paws that size...I bet Gavin was running with Teeter and his gang. Teeter is a gray when he's turned, Diana."

And he'd also been vocal about his less-than-kind thoughts regarding me being queen—right from the beginning of my reign.

"If he saw me with the deer, then he might've decided to go with the bloodworms. If I died, it would prove I was a vampire for sure, so that's a win for them. If I didn't, a secondary problem would be solved as Raven and the others would have perished. Either way, they've gained something." I brushed my hands over the size of the prints. We followed them back through the trees, heading south. "These fit the timeline for freshness."

"Scent too." Lochlin scrubbed a hand over his face. "This is a shitpile of a mess. What do you want to do?"

Indeed, it was shit. But strangely, the assassination attempt gave me a burst of strength and understanding. My time as queen was fading, there was no denying it now. Even I could see that there was no coming back from this.

"We have to assume this was an assassination attempt now. So, we triage, Loch. You take some guards over to Teeter's place and bring him in for questioning. If he's not there, head to Mary Barrach's home. It makes me ill to prod her in her time of grief, but clearly, they were running together and Teeter might have contacted Mary since Gavin's death. Hopefully, we get some answers, but if not, so be it. We can't move the summit, so no matter what, we plan to leave in the morning, unite the territories, then deal with the fallout when we return. Just make sure that we have the keep guards on the highest of alerts."

I met his eyes, saw the concern there.

"I need one more thing from you, Lochlin, maybe one of the last things I'll ask of you as your queen."

His head snapped up. "Do not say that."

"It's coming, it must—this whole situation has left me no choice and...I knew, Loch, I knew. The best thing we can do now is to be ready for it."

I found myself reaching for the bonds between Raven and me, checking on him. Assuring myself that he was still alive. Irritated but alive. A smile ghosted over my face.

"What is it that you need?"

"A list of anyone you think might be capable of leading our people. Before the end of the week, I will name my successor..."

Dreams are strange when you're dying.

I wanted to reach out and strangle the owner of that voice, recognizing Nefir, the brother of Lilis who had, yes, helped save us in the desert. But he'd also stolen weeks of our lives, leading some in the Werewolf Territory to believe that their queen had abandoned them.

A fact that I was sure added to the unrest of her people.

"Nefir." I growled his name. My body wouldn't respond, my eyes were closed, and the god was there, like a movie screen inside my head.

Hello, Raven. Fancy meeting you here. Cusp of death and all.

"Fancy is not the word I'd use for it." I bared my teeth at him. "Why are you here?"

To see if you live or die. Your life is as important as

hers, you know. He flicked his hand and Diana's image solidified beside him. *Lovely, isn't she? Especially when she sheds all those hard layers and lets you see her heart. Heart of a dragon, if you ask me.* He lifted one hand and trailed it down Diana's cheek.

I'd have lunged toward him—maybe I even tried—but there was nothing I could do, not really. My body was bound, floundering as something rippled through me.

Something. Under my skin. "Bloodworm. Did your sister do this?"

Nefir left the image of Diana and walked closer to me, as a strange sensation in my head. *Nasty little surprise, that, eh? But no. This isn't the work of Lilis. I think you and your wolf queen—check that, former wolf queen—have made some enemies here.*

He scrunched up his lips and pouted. Fucking pouted.

"Why is my life important? You said that was why you're here." I tried again to reach for him, to strangle the words out of him if I could.

Nefir snapped his fingers and the world in my head shifted and danced all around us. When it reformed, we were standing at the top of a high mountain ridge, a city full of lights below spread out to the ocean's edge.

His voice changed, no longer inside my head, but all around me. "This place is sacred, Raven. You know it, don't you?"

I did a slow turn, taking in the ocean and the smells, the place I'd been once before. A mountain I knew.

"Vesuvius. Why are we here?"

"The last time my sister threw a tantrum was here, Raven. When she was a child, she lost control. Thousands burned. My parents wanted you to see how little she values others' lives."

I turned to him. "This does not explain why I am important. I've been here, but so have many others. It means nothing."

His smile was lopsided. "According to my mother... you will either help Diana pull through her transition with the shard, or you will destroy her. Your death will do the latter for sure. But your life could do either."

My chest seemed to collapse in on itself. "And you brought me here just to show me the power of your sister?"

Nefir shrugged. "I like the view. It's as good a place as any to have a discussion about life and death, the inevitability of it all."

I stared hard at him. "From the god who can't die... The god who doesn't care whether the world crumbles."

He scooped up a handful of dirt. "Even gods can die, Raven. The question is, would the price of a god's death be worth what you would gain? Perhaps not."

This motherfucker was always talking in circles. "You said before that we couldn't defeat her."

"Defeat and death. Two different things. Or maybe, the only way to defeat her is to finally end her. But her life…her life is attached to parts of the world. As is mine." He kicked at the dirt, sending a spray down deep into the abyss of darkness.

Tied to… "She's tied to Vesuvius?"

"Oh, it's worse than that, my friend. I am a creature made of wind and the changing seasons." He smiled. "If you've noticed, I can be rather…fickle."

"Rather." My jaw ticked with the effort of holding back the rest of what I had to say. "And your sister…" I looked down into Vesuvius. She'd been a child when she'd unleashed her wrath on Pompeii.

A child who could control a volcano.

A shiver ran through me, someone was calling my name in the distance. I turned and felt a hand wrap around mine. "They are calling me back."

"Yes. That Sienna is strong, she is healing you. The bloodworm was tricky…if your mate hadn't seen it, you'd have died. Rather gruesomely too, I might add."

I didn't have time for his games, not if I was being called back. He had information and we needed it. I lunged at Nefir, grabbing him around the wrist and anchoring myself to him.

"Your sister. Just say it plainly. Does she have control of this mountain? This volcano?"

He tipped his head to the side. "If only it was just this one." He shook me off like I had no grip strength. I floated upward, Nefir's image and voice fading. "No, my fanged friend, when she regains her strength, *every* volcano will bend to her will. She is the first fire goddess. The first and the last."

"Fuck." The word ripped out of me as I gasped and tried to sit up. Hands shoved me down.

"Raven. Don't." Dominic's voice added weight to the hands pressing on me. "You need to lay still for a moment. Let Sienna double check."

My mind raced, pieces of my conversation with Nefir, the feeling of the bloodworms being ripped out of me, but more than that...I could sense Diana and she was not close to me. "Where is she?"

"Checking on something," Dom said. "She has Lochlin with her, she's safe."

I snarled and went to push his hands off, but he just held me there. I was that fucking weak. "The bloodworms?"

"Gone." Sienna appeared at my side. "But they moved quickly. The doctor said it was like nothing he'd ever seen."

"Diana is not infected?"

"She had ingested them, but the shard protected her and obliterated them as soon as they hatched. But Evangeline..."

Her eyes flicked to her husband then to the left of us. I followed her gaze to see the Duchess on a table, her face wan. "No."

"She's alive. Barely." Sienna clutched at the edge of the mattress. "If you hadn't gone down, we never would have known in time that the food was infected. Only because we were so close to the infirmary, because Diana was with you...it was a near miss."

A near miss. "And no one else? Nicholas? William? Bee?"

Sienna shook her head, her eyes going to Dom. "No. They didn't eat the cabbage, nor did Dom, so I think we've narrowed down that dish as the culprit. And Myrr and Theo are immune, as is Maverick."

My eyes shot to hers.

Maverick.

He'd been so keen on sparring with me. It made so much sense. The sudden boldness...the strength he'd tried so hard to hide and had finally decided to let show. The fact that he'd even landed a blow against me...he had to have known.

He knew I'd be weakened because he was the one who had planted the worm eggs.

"That traitorous, backstabbing motherfucker!" The roar that ripped out of me had me pushing even Dominic's hand back. "He could have killed her!"

"Easy!" Dom shoved me down. "Raven! I think you're jumping to conclusions. Why would he want to hurt Diana?"

"He didn't. He doesn't even know what she is yet. He'd been trying to kill *me,* and he was fine with the rest of our kind going down as collateral damage."

"Other things have come to light while you slept, so I'm not so sure of that..."

"What things?"

"There was another wolf present in the forest last night. We think he may have seen Diana feeding on that deer..."

"Who?" I fought to calm myself for the simple fact that, in this state, I couldn't do anything. If I couldn't push Dom off me, then I was in no state to hunt down the would-be killer.

"I'll fill you in on all the details once you're hale and hearty."

"Fine, whatever you say. And what of the Duchess? She will be okay..."

"Yes." Sienna sighed. "It's strange to say it is a blessing, but here, we can give her infusions of blood while she is unconscious. I don't think she'd fed since Lycan died. This gives us a chance to...to help bring her back to us. Not just in body, but in mind and heart...I hope. A chance anyway."

I held up both hands, lying flat on my back in a ridiculous show of surrender. "Can I sit up? I would feed as well. I need to be back on my feet, I need to be there for Diana at the meeting."

"Assuming she even agrees to let you go."

"It's your job to convince her," I shot back, grateful when Dom grunted and released me. I tried to sit up, but it was a task as my muscles trembled with the effort. Damn it...I *was* weak from that fucking bloodworm.

"This is nuts. How did your father last so long?" I muttered under my breath.

"Sheer stubbornness." Dominic sighed. "And a much

slower parasite than what you had in you. According to the doctor, the bloodworm eggs were strengthened using some sort of spell. He thinks...an old style of witch magic. Dark, but not of the goddess."

Witch magic? How many enemies did we have?

I put a hand to my head and lowered myself back to the bed, nausea and fatigue rolling over me. I had to tell Diana what I'd learned from Nefir.

"There are many players at work here. I...I would speak with Diana as soon as she is back. If she'll speak with me."

Sienna motioned at a wooden rack on the table next to me. Six vials of blood were set in it. "Drink, Raven, the best thing you can do now is feed and sleep. I am sure Diana will come to you the second she returns."

I nodded, not as sure as Sienna, but with my eyes trying to drift shut, I reached for the first vial, pushed the cork off with my thumb and tipped it back. Werewolf, the taste of fresh snow and...a tingle of something else. Fae blood? I did a double take.

A half-breed? Here?

I rolled the blood across my tongue, trying to figure out who it was, a mystery to distract myself from the fact that I'd nearly died.

One by one I downed the vials, realizing that they'd drawn from the strongest of those willing to donate. Werewolf-fae hybrid. Human tinged with magic—that was Theo, I was sure. Pale blue that tasted of the ocean. Xefia? The one that felt like sunshine going down my throat, the power behind the blood, I was certain that was Sienna. The fourth one was Diana—her blood sung through my body, refreshing me a dozen times as much as the others combined—even over the werewolf-fae hybrid.

Sienna had told me to drink them all, but I wasn't sure I wanted to drink the last.

It seemed to have the least amount of blood in it, and sluggish, a red that didn't seem to be fresh. Hell, I could almost smell the mothballs, as if the blood had been soaked in them.

"That's exactly who you think it is," Nicholas said, startling me as I stared at the half full vial in my hands. "You drink that, and you might see the future like I had done."

I looked at Nicholas. "For how long?"

"Who can say? Apparently, even Myrr only knew it was possible when it happened to me, not a certainty."

"What if it never goes away?"

His responding grin was unexpected and lopsided. "Then we can hold hands and really fuck shit up with what we see coming, can't we?"

The laugh escaped me—my worst fear had always been a vampire like Nicholas, who could see inside my head. Now, I was actually contemplating doing something almost as terrifying. Facing a future that may or may not include Diana, head on.

"It would help her," I said. "It would surely help her cause to know things ahead of time."

"It also might help save the world, dumbass." Myrr stepped into the room. "I don't know how much time I've got, hell, maybe another hundred years, maybe two minutes, but you two...you two should outlive me."

I stared at her. "Why me?"

"Because you don't want it." She said, the most sober I'd ever seen her. "You don't want it any more than Nicky does. But the world needs guidance, even if it just comes in flashes. Won't be as good as me, you can bet your sweet patoots on that!" She jabbed a finger in each of our directions. "Still, it's better than leaving the world with nothing. At least until the next of my kind comes along. And who knows when that will be?"

She sighed and plopped herself down on the end of the bed, staring at me, her eyes remarkably clear. Waiting for me to drink her blood...Waiting for me to potentially sacrifice my sanity as she had done with hers, all in the hopes that it would help Diana, and complete our mission.

And with that, I tipped back the vial of blood, drinking down a destiny that I never wanted.

How had it been more than a week since our return to the Werewolf Territory? Of watching Diana at a distance, and wondering how things went so wrong between us?

Things on the mainland and during our travels had been so good. I'd almost earned her trust back.

So fucking close...

I'd been so close to having her and everything that came along with it—and now it was as if she was under a spell and could no longer see me. For a second there, the tension between her and Raven made me think I still had a chance. That she could get over me allowing her to take my place with Malach. But even when I'd proven to be strong...strong enough to spar with the bastard and even get in my own licks, she'd pitied me.

And rescued him.

I fisted my hand more tightly around the pint of ale I was nursing and winced as my grip slipped.

It was a fucking double-edged sword being in the Territories. On one hand, the witch's curse was weakening me more quickly than ever, causing tremors and body aches as if I were as old as my true years. On the other hand, being here also made the Grimoire's spell for power and fortune stronger than ever. With the enhancements it gave me, I could actually hold my own in a fight with Raven now.

For a short time, at least.

But now I was paying the price. My whole body felt like I'd been hit by a truck, and even with Sienna's help–after she and everyone else took care of Raven first, of course–my face felt like someone had gone to town on it with a meat tenderizer. I took a long pull from my pint and let out a snarl.

After weeks of putting up with him trying to unman me at every turn–as if I had somehow done *him* wrong–I'd finally snapped. I'd let my pride take the wheel instead of using my head.

It was a mistake. I could see it clear as day now. There had been no reason to insert myself into their little bloodsuckers' sparring match. If only I'd sat back and let the worms do their work, Diana likely wouldn't have even gone out there to...what? Rescue me like a fucking child? He might have died before the others even knew what happened. Instead, I decided to take advantage of the situation and swing my dick around a bit.

Look where it had gotten me. If Raven had ever trusted me even a little, that trust was gone, and now surely even gullible Diana had me on the short list of suspects. I'd likely never be allowed into the inner circle again. Which would make my plan a whole lot harder, if not impossible.

"Motherfucker!" I smashed my open hand against the scarred wood of the bar and pinched my eyes closed as agony ricocheted through every bone in my body.

"Eh, bad day?"

I blinked up at the hulking bartender, his amber eyes seeming to search my soul.

"A lot of bad days strung together, my friend," I managed through the pain.

He grunted. "You and me both, buddy, you and me both. What a fucking mess out there. First queen ever, only months since her father passed, and look where she's taken us? Fucking shit show central, battles with demons, allying us with the fanged ones. It's unnatural, I tell you. She's a fool, and she's going to get us all killed. I knew it the second old Lycan started grooming her for the job. Alpha wolves are male for a reason. Females are too emotional to make the hard choices."

"It's been a trying time. The world is splitting at the seams." I pressed the frothy mug of ale to my lips, keeping my expression carefully blank as I looked around carefully. "You think a king would have done better than she has, all things considered?"

"I know it, man." He paused and leaned forward.

"You don't have to look around before you speak here. We're all of the same mind in this neck of the woods. Diana did it to herself, you know. She fucking aligned with the vamps? I don't care how bad the weather gets, or what goddess bitch is kicking up dust storms, that's a never for me. We've been enemies for all time for a reason." He spat to the side, a gob of black chew.

"Might as well join us hip to hip with burning trash then say we smell like spring flowers."

I held my beer up to him in a salute. "Can't fault your reasoning there. Trash indeed."

The bartender swiped a rag across the bar. "Names Teeter. Who be you?"

I held out my hand. "Maverick."

Teeter's eyes narrowed even as his hand engulfed mine. "You were with her, weren't you? On that gods' forsaken quest that brought the demons down on us?"

I didn't pull back, knowing it would be seen as a sign of weakness. Instead, I ignored the ache in my creaky joints as I tightened my hold. "I did everything I could to save her from herself and stop this madness, Teeter. But she wouldn't listen to me. She won't listen to anyone but that vampire, Raven. He's got her ear for certain."

"You tried." Teeter nodded and patted his other giant mitt over top of our joined hands. "Good man, good man. You did what you could to sway her. Can't ask more than that of a man who ain't wolf, eh? You'd never live long enough to win that argument with a know it all bitch like her! Ha!"

He let me go and went back to serving some of the other patrons. My knuckles pulsed from the intensity of his grip. It was one of the things that had made me shy from Diana the first time—so much passion in every part of her. Her eyes. Her touch. Her desire had even made me falter. Not that I'd ever said it out loud.

Still, Teeter's words rumbled through me, swirling around as if they were trying to tell me something important. Something I needed to grasp from this short interaction. And if my cursed life had taught me anything, it was to listen to my instincts.

To survive when everyone else thought I wouldn't.

Like escaping the demons.

Escaping the territories.

Surviving the storms Lilis had sent.

Letting Diana sacrifice herself to take your place with Malach on the beach that day.

My gut roiled, and I took another swig of beer.

That part couldn't have been helped, but there was no doubt it had made her see me differently.

Chickenshit.

The nickname was the kicker. The thing I'd let get under my skin the most. It was easy to be a tough guy when you were all but immortal like Raven and his kind. Before I'd found the witch's hut, I'd been nothing more than a flesh bag waiting for death or an accident to befall me. A sickness that settled in my lungs, or an errant arrow that caused a festering wound I couldn't recover from. And still, I'd prevailed. Through the torture of demons that had broken so many before me, through the curse of a witch who couldn't handle being outplayed, through the terror of being dragged into a water dragon's lair. It was me, Maverick of the desert, who had come out on top.

And I would come out on top again. I just had to use the gifts that had gotten me this far...

I looked around the bar, studying the disgruntled faces of those around me, the tiniest kernel of a brilliant new plan forming. Influencing people. That was my strength. But how to best use it? What did I want most?

A conversation with Diana from all those years ago came back to me, and I sucked in a sharp breath. The answer to all my problems was right in front of me. Saving myself from the curse. Solidifying my future–

Teeter came back and offered me another ale which I gladly took.

"On the house."

"No. I want to support you and this fine establishment. In fact..." I pushed my chair back and climbed up on top of the bar, letting my body sway as if the drink were getting to me. "Drinks all around, on me!" I lifted my beer high as the small but rowdy crowd broke out in cheers at my announcement and all the pieces clicked into place. The start of a game I knew I could win.

It was a risk. If there was a single supporter of the crown here now, I could be signing my death warrant. But despite what Raven thought of me, I'd never shied away from a little risk...

"A toast to Diana, the Queen of the wolves!" I felt the room pause, sensed the eyes narrowing, but I stayed in character, letting my smile falter, letting my sadness at losing her show through, a slosh of beer rolling over my fingers. "May she soon break the spell that bloodsucker has over her and see the light. May some brave wolf step forward to claim her. And may he lead her with a strong hand and a brave heart, root out the bloodsuckers, and take you all back to what you were always meant to be. Warriors!"

I tipped my beer back as the pub erupted around me, and Teeter grasped my calf to steady me as I fake wobbled.

"Fat chance!" a voice called. "She's been here alone for decades upon decades, turning her royal nose up at any suitor with the balls to try and mate with her. What makes you think there's even a chance she could love another?"

I let out a soft, sad laugh. "I don't think it, fine sir. I know it. She loved me once...until that vampire came along. She offered me a life with her. To lead with her at her side. I was a fool to deny her, but I would give anything to go back and do it again."

Two beefy men who had been throwing darts in the corner paused and exchanged a look. "The hell you say? And what would be different this time?" the bigger of the two demanded.

"I'd get her in line. Guide her the way a male should."

"Atta boy," Teeter pulled me down, nearly crushing

me with his thick bicep around my neck in a brotherly embrace. "She loved you, did she? Make your move then, man."

I clasped a hand on his shoulder. "If only I could, Teeter. But I'm just a human..." I let out a heavy sigh and moved to turn from him.

"And he's a damnable bloodsucker. Far worse." He gripped my shoulders and spun me around, his amber eyes searching mine with a near-fanatical light. "What if there was a way to show her just who you really are? Would you take it? A way to do all that you want and more?"

I stared up at him. "I would do anything for her and the territory she loves so much."

His pursed his lips and nodded. "You...*you* are who we've been waiting for, Maverick. Moon goddess be praised, you finally arrived."

As Teeter turned away, calling to someone named Staven, I could almost smell it.

The winds of change...the promise in the air.

The end of the past and the start of the future.

My future. As king.

I stared out the window of the moving carriage, watching as my breath thawed the frosted glass. When I'd awoken this morning, it had still been pitch dark out and the temperature had dropped nearly 40 degrees overnight. It had gone from a late summer day to one better spent by the fire with a steaming bowl of stew.

"I don't see how we're going to do it, Loch," I said, turning to face my longtime friend who sat across from me. "With three more keys to find and things progressing so rapidly. I just don't see it, we are running out of time…"

He leaned forward and took my hands in his. I realized with a start that his skin was warmer than mine. But that was the reality of things now. Werewolves ran hot, vampires ran slightly cool, and I was a vampire.

I couldn't let myself forget it again.

"I beg to differ, Diana. If there was no chance for success, old Myrr would know it. The shards would know it...If the end of us is our destiny and it can't be changed, surely it would be just cruel of the fates to lead us on this way? Remember what you told me last night yourself. We must go in with confidence."

Words I had parroted from Sienna. I let out a snort and leaned back, pulling my hands away. "You're my advisor, Lochlin. You're not supposed to throw what I say back in my face."

He grinned and shot me a wink. "I don't get paid the big money to tell you lies, my queen."

Speaking of lies...

"So tell me again exactly what Mary said to you when you went to the cottage to speak with her."

Loch had gone to find Teeter last night to no avail. Although, unmarried and without children, I supposed it wasn't so unusual for his cabin to be empty. A quick search of the pub and tavern he frequented, followed by a visit to Mary—who claimed she hadn't seen him—led me to believe Teeter was on the run. Or maybe he was just keeping his head down until he heard word as to whether I was still alive or not. He'd surely know by now as we werewolves were a nosy lot and servants talked.

"Mary is a tricky one. Hard to read..." Loch said, squinting his eyes as he thought back on the conversation. "She's clearly still in the grips of grief, so I can't be certain, but I did feel she wasn't being completely honest with me when I'd asked her if Teeter had reached out to her. She didn't meet my eyes when she spoke of it."

Regardless, with our trip looming, we had no real recourse that wouldn't stir things up even more. We'd added more guards to the keep to watch over those who remained, and I had to push it to the back of my mind until our return. Today was the most important day in my time as queen. And likely one of the last, with the way things were going.

"For what it's worth, I think it was smart to bring Raven along," Lochlin said, shrugging his wide shoulders. "If they have a problem with it, I'm sure they won't be shy about sharing it, so we might as well try. And between myself, him, Dominic, and those waiting in the wings, I feel marginally better than I did when we started planning this."

I did too, at least when it came to today's summit. I'd been irritated at my older brother for pressing in regard to Raven. I couldn't imagine he was even well enough to come on the journey, but when I'd seen him this morning before we left, his cheeks had been flushed with color, and he'd looked stronger than ever. Plus, I couldn't deny that a part of me wanted him there. Even if he couldn't speak, even if he couldn't hold my hand, I knew that I could reach out to him through our bond, and I would feel supported.

If that made me stupid? If that made me weak? So be it. I'd realized sometime in the middle of the night that there were precious few people in this world that I could truly trust, and Raven had risen to the top of the list. We might not be fated mates, but we were connected in deep ways that went beyond superficial and settled somewhere around a choice I'd made, and maybe even that he'd made. Once we got through the next few days, I was determined to find out how or why and explore it.

But that didn't mean I needed him sitting across from me for the next four hours as we traveled.

Between Mav's hurt feelings because I'd chosen Raven over him and disregarded his feelings completely, and the fact that I couldn't think straight with Raven in close proximity, I'd wound up riding with Lochlin alone. Mav wouldn't ride with Raven, Raven couldn't be trusted to ride with Mav without killing him, and I didn't want to sit with either one of them. So we'd decided on a small caravan of half-full carriages to accommodate, despite Sienna and Dom riding in ahead on her winged Hunter.

I thought of Mav now and frowned. There were still so many more questions to ask him. I didn't think he was behind the bloodworm attack, but at the same time I was questioning whether he could be trusted. Still, I'd needed to make nice in order to get him to come and hopefully influence the other kings and queens to join our cause. Witnessing the shattering of the Veil through Mav's memories and seeing the girls who'd become hosts of the shards was our biggest clue to finding the other keys. Without Maverick, we were offering only my word and Sienna's to convince them.

For the rest of the ride, I practiced my speech, both in my head and for Lochlin.

I just finished what I hoped was the final practice round under my breath and was surprised as Loch began to clap slowly. "Unless they're all stupid or even crazier than we think, they're going to unite behind this cause. Behind *you*, Diana. Your words are as convincing as any I've ever heard, which is why I want to once again plead with you not to step down as queen."

"I have no choice–they don't trust me to lead, not any longer. You'll come to see that in time too, my friend." I set down my notes and regarded him for a long moment. "I would choose you to take my place, Loch. There's no finer male in the Territory."

He dipped his head in acknowledgement of my words. "As much as I appreciate the vote of confidence, Diana, I can't lead. I am...no better than you when it comes to bloodlines."

I put my hand on his shoulder. "I know, Loch. I've known for a very long time."

His face paled and he drew back. "Fuck. You do?"

I laughed. "My father knew you were part fae, and he trusted me with your secret. I think it's why I always trusted you with mine."

Loch's head bowed. "Ah, lass..."

"There's nothing else that needs to be said, old friend. Now, did you have a chance to put together a list of names for me? Others who might do us proud as king?"

"I did," he said, reaching into his coat pocket and producing a small index card. He handed it to me, and I scanned the names, which didn't take long.

There was only one.

"Seriously?" I said, shooting him a puzzled glance.

"Their clan is loyal, and their hearts are true. That's my vote. Think on it until we return home and if you'd like me to give you a list of additional candidates, I'm happy to do it."

I folded the note card and slipped it into my pocket, resolving to do just that–I was surprised by the name and the youth behind it. The carriage rolled to a stop and a moment later there was a rap on the door.

"We're at the river, my Queen."

Loch and I stepped out onto the riverbank, and I shivered. Even colder than when we left, which was strange. Surely the sun should have warmed things some...

Footsteps sounded over my shoulders, and I turned to find the others coming to stand beside me at the river's edge. Mav stayed off to the side, his face twisted into a sulk, although at least his swollen jaw looked better. Will and Nicholas came toward us, followed by Raven...

Raven, who stood and stared at me like his world had been black and white before and he was seeing color for the first time. My hands itched to touch him, and I balled them into fists at my side.

"How did it go?" I asked Sienna as she and Dom walked toward us from the direction of the ruins. They'd arrived well before us, scouting and making sure no traps had been set for anyone.

"We've set up some seating around the table, and put out some food and drink," Sienna said, gesturing to the wooded area a hundred yards away. "My hunter, Belona, is tucked away in the trees over there. Both Sal and the Kraken are waiting in the depths of the river, ready to respond to our call if need be."

"And Xefia? Did you see her?" I asked, shooting her a questioning glance.

"A glimpse only, but you would know better than I if we should expect her to keep her word." Sienna tucked her hands behind her back.

I nodded, already knowing the answer to my own question. "She will be here." I looked to the river and nodded. "We should go inside and wait for the others."

We made a short walk down the bank of the river toward the ruins and I couldn't help but admire the ancient beauty of the massive alabaster columns with the cracked and teetering roof perched on top.

We'd barely taken a seat at the massive marble table in the center of the room when I heard voices outside.

"Someone's half a day early," Dominic murmured, instinctively lifting his hand to his empty scabbard for the hilt of a sword that wasn't there.

The sound of boots striding up the stone steps were followed by a harsh laugh that sounded vaguely familiar.

"Why am I not surprised in the least?" Gabe drawled, his voice echoing as he stepped into the mausoleum-like room. His black wings were spread behind him, and I had to admit that they were impressive, now that he was showing them off. "Good morning," he said, inclining his head in my direction as he tucked his wings away and crossed the floor to join us.

I spread a hand wide. "Gabe, I'm pretty sure you already know everyone here."

"Oh, I know everyone, alright. The question is, why the fuck are you here hours before the meeting is supposed to start?"

Raven shrugged. "We could ask you the same."

"Touché. Look, I don't mean to pick nits, but there are also only two territories represented here aside from mine. So why are there six of you?" He shook his head derisively. "Not that I care, but *I'm* not the one you have to worry about. Cleona is not going to like this."

"We're each permitted to bring an advisor, and I have good reason for the others, which you'll be apprised of once the meeting is in session, as they are witnesses to our cause," I said, keeping my tone firm but polite.

"You're not going to try to pretend *you* came alone, are you, Gabriel?" Will asked as he pushed his chair away from the table and stood, a tight smile on his lips.

"I may have brought a couple of friends, just in case."

The two men squared off, with Dom nearby on high alert, his eyes pinned on Gabe for even the slightest movement of aggression, no doubt.

"It's too early for this." I let out a weary sigh and slapped my hands on the table. "Can we all just sit down and put our dicks away, please? This is supposed to be the easy part. Surely, we're of the same mind. Gabe, you've seen it yourself, what this evil goddess can do. And the continued and increasing destruction of the Territories since the Veil has fallen is only getting worse. We need to let any petty squabbles go and move forward with a common goal, if any of us want to live through this. Can I count on your support?"

Gabe raked a hand through his snowy white hair and blew out a heavy sigh. "It's hard to know who to trust after what we saw with our own king. It feels like that she-devil could be infiltrating anyone at any time. I'll be honest, that makes me edgier than a desert cat watching a storm come across the sand."

Finally, a fear I could assuage. "What if I told you that's not the case anymore? What if I told you that she's been neutralized for now? Her own brother, Nefir, came and told me himself. We've got a little bit of time before she comes back into full power. Time to find a way to beat her at her own game."

"Well, that's a relief," Gabe said, strolling over to a side table laden with fruit and drinks. "Makes me a little less twitchy if that's the case." He popped a grape into his mouth and chewed.

"Yeah, well, don't get too excited," I added, figuring I might as well take the bull by the horns and break the news now, so he didn't think I'd tried to deceive him. "Nefir also admitted that he'd gone to visit his sister to try to convince her to cease this madness. Turns out she's been in captivity, which is why she used others to do her deeds. But he 'accidentally' freed her. Once she gets back her strength, she won't be taking over anyone else's bodies to do her dirty work. She'll be even more powerful and will be able to do it all by herself."

"Fucking hell," Gabe said, leaning a hip against the side table. "Well, I might as well put my cards on the table too then. My people are not happy. Half of them saw Malach as he was—a shell of his former self, withering away under her control. They knew their king was gone before he met his end and that was in itself, a mercy. But there are still many who blame you and your people for his death. I've got them on a tight leash right now, but it's going to be an ongoing problem until I can provide someone's head on a platter for his murder."

It wasn't a surprise at all, but I had to admit I wasn't thrilled with the news.

"They're going to have to get in line, because my own people are looking for their pound of flesh right now as well."

"Yummy...Did someone say pound of flesh?" A female voice called. We all turned to watch as Cleona, the Fae Queen, sauntered into the room. I hadn't seen her in decades, but she hadn't aged in the least. Her waist-length, blonde hair had flowers woven throughout, and she was dressed in emerald green from head to toe, giving the illusion of a very tall, very lean, wood sprite. It was only those glowing amber eyes that took away from her puckish charm.

Those amber eyes were trained on me now, and it was all I could do not to squirm.

"Good to see you again, Queen Cleona," Will said, his wide smile seeming genuine as he moved towards her, hand extended.

"William, you're looking well," she said, eyeing him from head to toe and then licking her lips.

Interesting.

Apparently, when Will said she liked him, he meant she *really* liked him. He bowed over her outstretched hand and kissed the tip of her fingers, which sent her off into a peel of giggles like a young girl. Something that she certainly was not.

"I didn't expect you all to be here waiting on me," she asked, as Will released her hand and stepped back. "Am I late?" she inquired, her white-blonde brows rising high on her forehead. She damn well knew the time frame and had arrived early too.

"We get it," Mav muttered, "Everyone's early. Can we just skip all the political gamesmanship and get this started, please? I already have a headache, and once the bloodsucker starts poking around in my brain, it's only going to get worse."

If I could have reached him, I would have slapped him right in the mouth as Cleona's head whipped towards him.

"And who is this?" she asked, the lilt in her voice disappearing, leaving behind nothing but biting derision.

I pasted on my most diplomatic smile. "This is

Maverick. He was a witness to the event that tore down the Veil."

She cocked her head and studied him like he was an organism under a microscope. "Well, tell the human to mind his tongue, unless he wants me to remove it for him."

Suddenly, her eyes lit up as she saw the tray of fruit on the other side of the room.

"Kiwi, my favorite!" she said, clapping her hands as she skipped over to the display as if she hadn't just threatened to dismember someone.

"I spoke to Rabia last night and she's agreed to attend via hologram," Loch said, tugging a small, black box from his coat pocket and setting it on the table. "I can see if she's able to start early as well, if all are in agreement?"

"Fine by me," Cleona chirped, piling a crystal plate with fresh kiwi.

Okay, so it was really happening. My hands went clammy as Loch made initial contact with Rabia and got her permission to create the connection early.

"You're going to be just fine," Raven murmured, leaning into me until our shoulders brushed. Just that simple touch sent a wave of calm flowing through me.

I'd put the time in. I'd practiced my speech, and all I had to do was be honest in my delivery. Surely, they'd see that there was no other way...

"Queen Rabia? Can you see us?" Loch asked as the

angel queen's image spilled from the top of the black box.

Unlike the vainer Fae, most Angels couldn't be bothered with trying to attain the illusion of eternal youth and beauty. They tended to age with grace. Rabia was still a stunner by any standard but wasn't fussed about the fine lines around her eyes or the fact that she wasn't as slim as she had once been.

"Yes, I can see you all," Rabia said with a tight smile as she glanced around the table. "Can you see me?"

"See you?" Cleona gasped, holding a dramatic hand to her heart. "Fucking hells, how could we miss you? What are your servants feeding you over there, Rabia... Lard straight from the can?"

The angel queen's eyes went wide for just an instant before they narrowed. "You blithering cock-gobbler, Cleona." She leaned forward, head down, then slapped her hand on the matching black box we'd sent her.

Gabe spoke for all of us as her image flickered and then disappeared, the connection gone.

"Well, shit."

CHAPTER 12

Raven

We all turned to stare at Cleona in stunned silence. Had this vain, childish fae-woman just blown our chances of saving the world with a *fat joke*?

"What?" she asked, eyes wide with mock innocence. "What did I say?"

"Try to contact her again, Loch," Diana snapped, gesturing to the hologram box.

I could feel the fury oozing from her every pore and was pretty sure that wasn't just our bond. She wasn't exactly hiding it well as her green eyes narrowed on Cleona with a laser intensity that I was glad was not pointed at me.

Luckily, Cleona was already preoccupied with her kiwis and didn't seem to notice. "I must say, this is very, very good. Almost as nice as the ones we grow on

Guisala," she said, sliding a spoon into the tender flesh and popping another bite into her mouth like she didn't have a fucking care in the world.

Nope.

Me getting mad was only going to set Diana off worse. Instead, I tried to exude cool, calm, and collected thoughts.

I tapped a finger on the table, drawing eyes to me. "If Loch can't get her back online, let's continue with the rest of us so this isn't a total waste of time. Rabia seems reasonable. I imagine she will be open to a private discussion with Diana once she's calmed down."

"Good luck." Cleona rolled her eyes. "She's always polishing that halo, getting all in a tizzy about what everyone else is doing wrong. She'll milk this melodrama for ages."

Melodrama. As if what Cleona just said hadn't possibly made it so we all ended up in early graves.

"Be that as it may," Diana drawled, "I'll contact her in a day or so and present her with the information we are about to share here today. She'll see, just as you all will, that we have little choice in this matter."

"That will have to do, because she's not picking up," Loch muttered.

Cleona shot me a "told you so," raised brow, but I didn't give her the satisfaction of a response.

Diana stood and began a restless circle of the room before finally stopping at the head of the table.

"The goddess whose name I shall not speak has sworn to destroy this earth, and everyone on it, so that she may start anew. I asked you all here today to impress how dire this threat is, and to plead with you to join in our fight against her."

For the next half hour, Diana poured her heart out. Told story after story of the carnage Lilis had wrought. Recapped the battles she had instigated between the vampires and the demons and the wolves. Told of the brutal death of King Malach and what it was like to witness it first-hand.

By the time it was over, I'd have been hard pressed to tell her no even if I was her sworn enemy. And it was only then that she pulled out the big guns, asking us all to follow her to the water's edge...

"Xefia?" she called.

All was quiet for so long that I wondered if Xefia had decided not to come after all. She'd insisted she be here, but if she'd changed her mind, I could hardly blame her. She was just a kid and had suffered a truly traumatic event. Still, not having her testimony would only make Diana's job harder...

Just as Dom and I exchanged worried glances, the water began to roil, and a moment later, a familiar swath of green hair swirled to the surface and broke through.

"Hello, Diana," Xefia said, baring her pointed teeth in a little smile.

"Thank you so much for coming, Xefia. These are my—" Diana broke off before pressing on, "colleagues,

Queen Cleona of the Fae, King Gabriel of the Demons, and King William of the Vampires. And you know my friends from our travels."

She nodded and swam closer, resting her arms and torso on the grassy bank. "Hello."

"As you are aware, we're in talks to determine the best way to stop the goddess from continuing her path of destruction. We hoped that hearing your story firsthand might illustrate just how dangerous she is, and what kind of devastation the different species face if we do not band together."

Xefia's bottom lip wobbled for a moment, and she nipped at it lightly before lifting her gaze and taking a deep breath. "It was a beautiful day," Xefia began, her eyes taking on a faraway look as if she were lost in the memory. "We were celebrating one of our elders' 300th birthday. Yesenia was her name. She was the matriarch of my people, and we had been planning the day for months. We'd spent the afternoon playing games and competing. The younger children were doing acrobatics and whoever did the greatest trick would win a string of rose-colored pearls. Faria won that morning for demonstrating the highest quadruple flip that I've ever seen... Hers was the first body that I saw shattered by a power that was not visible."

She sounded so grown up compared to just weeks before, but the air of composed maturity slipped as she let out a snuffle and a tear slid down her cheek. I could see Diana wanted to reach for her, but Xefia pressed on, her voice a broken whisper.

"We'd finished our evening feast. Lobsters, scallops, mussels, clams...Someone blew into the conch shell, a sign of the dancing and merriment to come, but I was so sleepy and content, I snuck off into a secret little cave spot that I go to sometimes when I want to be alone, to sleep the night away. The smell of blood woke me a short time later. At first, I thought maybe it was a rogue shark attack. We don't usually have any problems with them, but occasionally you get one that loses its way. I swam out in a panic only to realize that this was no shark attack. The water was so thick with blood that I couldn't see...I could hardly breathe. I kicked my way to the surface wiping my eyes clear and that's when I saw..." her throat worked as she swallowed hard, "Bodies as far as the eye could see. My friends, my family, our matriarch, the children...all dead because of the dark one's fury."

I wanted to reach out and hug the kid, but I knew she just wanted to get through her tale and return back to the shelter of the water.

"She needs to be stopped," Xefia said, lifting her gaze again and searching the faces of those around her. "She relishes the pain of others, and I will do whatever I can to return that same pain to her a hundred times over. If you agree to help Diana in her quest to unite the keys, restore the Veil, and rid the world of the evil goddess, I promise that you will have an ally and a friend in me, and all the creatures in the sea for all time."

She turned and shot Diana a grim smile before blowing her a kiss and disappearing back into the water once again.

I took a glance around and was surprised to find even Cleona's mouth was slightly downturned.

"Poor kid," Gabe rumbled, huffing out a breath as he turned his eyes from the water. "She shouldn't have had to see something like that. No one should."

"She's now the queen of her people," Diana said, "which is part of the reason I wanted to invite her here. As she said, she and those who remain are committed to the cause."

"Are there any more sad mermaids coming, or can we go back inside?" Cleona said with a shudder. "That was depressing, and it's getting colder by the minute."

Gods, she was a cold bitch.

We all headed back into the room and retook our seats, except for Diana and Nicholas, who stood behind Mav's chair. *Here we go, the real show is about to start.* If this didn't move Cleona...nothing would.

"There's one more thing I wanted to show you that is perhaps the most important piece. Maverick witnessed the moment that triggered the fall of the Veil. Nicholas of Southwind has an ability that allows him to broadcast the thoughts of others, and Maverick has offered to allow us to show you what happened that day, so you can see for yourselves."

I didn't relish Maverick getting any sort of accolades. In fact, I still wasn't sure he hadn't tried to murder us all.

But watching Nicholas put his hand on the bastard's head for a good round of brainfucking certainly didn't hurt my feelings.

As it had the first time we'd seen it months before, Maverick's memories began to play out like an ethereal movie projected from the palm of the vampire's hand. The massive rocks that made up Stonehenge came into focus, as did the faces of the orphans that surrounded them.

Sienna, her hair not yet the flaming red it was now, but still recognizable enough that Cleona tore her gaze away from the memory to flick a glance her way. Another girl, whip-thin and pale, with long, white-blonde hair, who we now knew to be Jade's sister, Opal. And then three others...one veiled in a black cloak, deep dark curls spilling from within the hood, a chubby girl with glasses and mousy brown hair, and the third one, a waif of a girl with hair that looked as though it had been dyed, as I'd never seen a natural head of hair that shade of blue.

It looked to be a peaceful and normal day, but that all changed in an instant when a dark figure flickered past the children, reappearing in the dead center of the stones. Ghostly, but there, perhaps not even fully seen and recognized by Maverick or the girls.

A moment later, a flash of blinding light followed a boom splitting the air. Countless, crystalline shards shot through the air like so much shrapnel. Maverick's view shifted as he turned toward the white-blonde haired girl who'd been thrown a dozen feet by the blast. She was motionless and caked in blood. With a curse, he dashed toward her, tossed her roughly over his shoulder, then sprinted away. The image above the table shimmered and then dissolved.

Mav slumped forward as Nicholas removed his hand, and the room went quiet until Cleona let out a gasp.

"Wow, that was amazing. Even better than the Titanic." She began to clap with glee. "Truly sensational. Do it again."

I looked over to see Gabe nodding his head in agreement. I was with them both, only my reason was twofold. Mav had finally served his last useful purpose. If I needed to kill him, there was nothing stopping me now. But also, Diana's case seemed airtight.

Surely everyone was going to sign on to support her now. All we had to do was work on Rabia, and we'd be on our way to an alliance ready to stop Lilis.

Diana stood back up, her hands on the table as she leaned forward. "Sienna and I now each hold pieces of the shard. We need to unite with the other three keys in order to restore the Veil. I ask you now to pledge your support and your allyship. We'd like each of the monarchs to go back to their Territory and request that their people be on the lookout for anyone who resembles the women we're looking for—the other three we saw in Maverick's memories. While they could be anywhere, the shards seem to be directing them to the territories— bringing them closer to us. Lochlin will be sending you all a file that contains a description as well as a time elapsed rendering of what these children might have grown up to look like, as best we can tell. If we start to spread the word, I think it's possible we could at least track down the other keys quickly and stop the goddess in her tracks before she regains full strength."

Diana looked around the room and lifted her chin.

"So now I ask you...will you pledge your support and help us restore the Veil?"

William held up a hand immediately. "You have my support and the support of my people."

Diana turned toward Gabe. He paused for a heartbeat, but then he nodded.

"We're going to have to address Malach's death, and it's going to take some politicking, but I see now that there's no way to get around this. You have my support."

Finally, we all turned to Cleona, and she lifted one slim shoulder.

"Mmm...so, it's going to be a *no* from me."

The air left the room in a collective *whoosh*.

"Wait, what?" Gabe asked, finding his voice before the rest of us. "Do you not believe that this bitch goddess is going to obliterate the world?"

"Oh, I believe it. The weather has been crazy, and I've heard what this Lilis can do."

We all collectively flinched as she used the goddesses name, and I wondered where she'd heard it, but she just kept on talking with her stupid mouth. "I just...don't care?" she said, wrinkling her pert nose. "I get why *you* guys do. But we fae have Guisala. So even if everything falls to shit, well...we're untouchable there. It's high up, largely sheltered by sheer cliffs and bolstered by magic. We control the weather there, and if anyone tries to attack from below, we can see them coming from miles away. We'll just wait it out and get on that new world program. I'm not hating the idea of a fresh start, removing the trash, if you will."

Her smile was sharp as a knife as she looked us over. My resolve to stay calm wavered as the anger snapped and grew in my chest.

"Why did you even agree to come if you knew you weren't going to help us?" Diana demanded, clearly reeling after the gut punch the Fae Queen had just delivered.

"Honestly? I wanted to see if becoming king had made Will even sexier. And I must admit, it has." She shot the Vampire king a long look beneath her lashes. "Totally worth the trip. And that little movie you played out of the human's head was," she paused and kissed her fingers. "Bravo! Now, if you'll excuse me, I've got to head back to my people. We've a party planned for tonight. Good luck with your..." she fluttered a hand through the air in a vague motion, "whatever it is that's happening to you guys. If I happen to see anyone who looks like any of those girls at Stonehenge, I'll let you know."

She was gone a moment later, her magic wrapping around her as she left us all staring after her.

"Selfish bitch," Maverick muttered under his breath.

I only wished that selfish bitch had heard him and

would have cut his tongue loose like she'd threatened earlier.

"I have to admit, I didn't see that coming," Gabe said, letting out a low whistle. "That's a massive blow. Having Cleona bow out actually might help me smooth things over with my people but losing them both is going to make our job tougher for sure."

Diana sighed and sat down gingerly, as if her body hurt, but I knew that was not the case. She was just heartsick, it rolled between us, clear as day. "I'll contact Rabia once you've got your people on board, Gabe. I think I can broker peace and get her on our side. She's a right-thinking leader with good morals, so I'm sure she'll agree to help, especially with Cleona out of the picture. The rest of us are just going to have to do the extra work and hope that none of the keys are located in Fae Territory," Diana said with a grim smile. "Who knows, maybe we'll get lucky?"

By the expression on everyone else's face that I was sure matched my own, no one had high hopes of getting lucky after the way things had been going.

"I'll get those images and descriptions of the other keys out to you all by end of day," Lochlin added, pushing back his chair to stand.

We exited the ruins a short time later, and I was just about to get into my carriage with Nicholas when Diana waved me over, and Lochlin stepped in my place.

"I think you're on deck," Loch said, patting my arm before he climbed into the other carriage.

For most of the ride back, Diana said nothing, and I just sat beside her in silence, loath to interrupt her thoughts. I hoped she could feel my support, but all I could feel was her sense of failure and impending doom.

"I don't know where to go from here," she finally murmured. "The Fae were our best shot of finding the other keys quickly with their magic." She lifted her gaze to meet mine. "Without Cleona's pledge, I don't think we're going to make it before this weather or that evil bitch does us in."

"Then we have to change her mind. Once we get back to the keep and regroup, we can put our heads together and figure out what we have that we can use to our advantage." I said. "There has to be a way."

"Too bad Will is married. I like Bee and all, but I wouldn't be above asking Will to toss Cleona a bone, if you know what I mean." Her words were so at odds with her forlorn expression, I couldn't help but bark out a laugh.

"Pragmatic *and* witty. Two of the reasons I love you."

The declaration hung between us, but I didn't back away from it. If she shot me down again, so be it. I'd long since resigned myself to the fact that being shot down by Diana for the rest of my life was a far better fate than knowing I had even the slimmest shot of having her and didn't try.

"I don't see how this could ever be a happy ending, Raven, but curse my eyes, I fucking love you too."

If only I'd had even five minutes to let those words

ring through me. To savor the moment, to grab her and kiss her. But the inside of our carriage suddenly blossomed with flickering, orange light.

We both turned toward the windows, and I let out a snarl as a giant sign, the letters made of flames, came into full view just half a mile from the keep.

BURN THE VAMPIRE QUEEN!

CHAPTER 13

Diana

I inched closer to the fireplace, seeking the warmth as I ran through the day's events for the umpteenth time. Despite countless hours of preparation, our meeting had been a near total failure. The fae queen hadn't seemed the least bit interested, and given her childish demeanor, it was hard to imagine what would change her mind. She believed so fully in her own abilities and that of her people to keep themselves safe that she saw no need for anyone else.

To make matters worse, I could no longer rely on the support of my own people. An image of those flickering flames rolled through my mind like a movie, and I shoved it aside. The opposition was clearly growing, and I needed to make a move. Quickly.

"I'm headed to bed."

Mav's sulky voice broke the silence, and I turned to see him standing from his chair with his fingers glued to his temples. "That mindfuck stuff leaves you with a hell of a hangover. My head is pounding."

"You're telling me," Nicholas chimed in, striding past him. "Using it is even worse. I only just woke up." He had gone to his rooms as soon as we returned, and his haggard expression told me that the five-hour nap had done little to reinvigorate him. The vampire slumped into an armchair across from Raven, Theo, and Myrr, eyeing the enormous leg of mutton the Oracle was digging into.

I dipped my head in farewell, still feeling conflicted as Mav exited the room. Things had been chilly between us since he'd brought his concerns to me—and his not so subtle offer—but it wasn't like he'd been entirely off base. The future of my reign was not looking good, and no matter how many scenarios I ran through, there was only one way to stabilize it.

If only I could buy myself a few months, maybe I'd be able to solidify the cross-species alliance and get us on the right path, but at the rate things were going, it was hard to imagine making it a few weeks. Still, passing the torch in the midst of this shitshow felt like I was setting the next leader up for failure...

My fingernails dug into my palm, and I let out a sigh as I turned my chair to face the room. More or less everyone of note was here besides Mav, and it'd be easier to get this over with in a single conversation. I waited for the door to shut behind him, the click my signal to dig into the unpleasant truth.

"Things have come to a head with my people, and we have no time to wait around and see how far they're willing to go. I guess I should start by telling you all—," I sucked in a long breath, steeling myself for what came next. "I'm going to be stepping down as queen, as soon as I can."

The room erupted with a dozen voices at once, with Lochlin's loudest of all, despite being the one to help me pick my heir. His eyes and voice pleaded. "Diana, wait just a little longer and see if—"

I faced him. "I won't sit around and wait for a full-on civil war to erupt, Loch. Our options are to move now, installing someone sane as my replacement, or risk letting this fester into something far worse. They're emboldened enough to poison our food. To come to my home and set the ground ablaze with threats. Who knows what comes next?"

"Then we root out the traitors and make an example of them," Raven interjected.

I shook my head. "Our people respect strength and loyalty, above all." It was a truth that Lycan had reminded me of countless times. "The loyalty of the majority of the clans will only get me so far. How long will they bend the knee to a struggling queen that can't even keep her own kingdom from infighting? Not long enough."

He opened his mouth to protest, then snapped it shut, a sour look on his face. "Treacherous bastards."

"Some are that." Evangeline's stern voice cut through

the room. "But what Diana said is true, no matter how much you may hate it. And right now, the fact that they have a vampire queen is just speculation. Rumor. There are many clans who don't believe it. Once they find out the truth…"

"They will come for me again, only this time it will be all of them," I agreed, the memories of my fight with Gavin out in the woods replaying in my mind. He'd only been a single wolf, yet I doubted that I could've beaten him without using any of my vampire strengths. The goddess only knew what would happen if they sent an assassin, or worse, a team of them.

"When?" Nicholas asked.

"Within the next few days," I said. "If I could do it sooner, I would; my position here is growing increasingly unstable. We have a lot of things to wrap up in that time."

I glanced to the side as Sienna's hand shot up, and I cocked my head.

"How do the werewolves even go about selecting a new leader? There's no one in line for the throne, right?"

"The king or queen selects their heir, though there are ways for the clan to stop such things…" I sucked in a breath, my gaze settling back on Lochlin. "Loch and I have discussed it, and I've already made my selection. We need strength and fair mindedness, in equal parts, and if it is someone they love and respect, even better." My stomach twisted at the gravity of the decision. The choice I made here could well be the difference between defeating Lilis and being wiped out along with the rest of the world. And, worse yet, it was the kind of decision I couldn't undo. Once I stepped down, I would be powerless. I just had to choose a successor and pray that things unfolded the way I hoped they would.

"And what will your role be once you resign?" Will asked, speaking up for the first time. "Will you be tied up with the training of your successor?"

"I think it makes the most sense for me to take on a role coordinating the alliance and trying to find the other keys." *If* we were able to form a full alliance, and that was a big 'if'. "We need someone with leadership experience to coordinate the search for the other keys. And for my successor, I'm hoping Loch will stay on as an advisor."

He bowed his head toward me. "I will, of course."

"The two of us have discussed it, and I'll be asking Elka to step in and take my place."

The name hung for a moment, and I waited, knowing that at least one person would know exactly who she was.

"Elka?" Sienna gasped, eyes wide. "Jordan's sister? She's so young..."

Lochlin nodded. "While that may be true, her performance in our battle against Malach earned her the respect of many. Her clan is well-liked and known to be loyal and kind. She was strong enough to withstand being possessed by Lilis—while she attacked you, Sienna, she also was able to survive the possession, unlike Malach. More importantly, she has a charisma about her. A way of getting people on her side without manipulation or artifice–she has the heart of a leader. She also has her father behind her. As much as it burns my ass, there are those who need to see a male figure in the keep. Hopefully this will assuage even those misogynistic bastards, and help her form a united Territory."

Something that, as a natural born half-vampire, half-human, zero werewolf, I had never truly been able to do. "I'd like you to set up a meeting between her and I, as soon as possible, Loch."

"Consider it done."

I shot a sympathetic glance at Sienna, who had tears dripping down her cheeks as she whispered with Bee. Jordan had been like a brother to her, and she'd done her best to form a friendship with Elka after his untimely death. It had been a rocky relationship from the start. But I could not dwell on that–we had more to consider. Something Raven wasted no time digging into.

"Next point of business that we can't forget about. We still need to find the person or persons who poisoned the food and get a bead on Teeter and his squad," Raven said, clenching a fist at his side. "They cannot be allowed to think they can come for you without consequence."

I gave him a quick nod. "I agree. If we don't set a strong precedent here, we may embolden them and put our next queen at risk, as well. For the time being, that's our number one priority. We'll give it a couple of days for tempers to cool and then get in touch with Rabia and get back to work on finding the keys once we've put the fires in our own house out. In the interim..." I glanced over at a grumpy-looking Myrr, who had stripped her mutton down to the bone. "I'd like to ask Myrr, Theo, Nicholas, and Bee to do some research into Cleona."

Bee leaned forward in her seat and nodded. "What exactly are we looking for?"

"Any and all potential weaknesses. Look into her personal life, political rivals, juicy secrets, all of it. When the stakes are this high, we can't afford to be precious about the means, so long as we meet our ends. Give me anything I can leverage against her, no matter how small."

Bee grinned; her smile fierce. Of course, she'd heard about Cleona's reaction to her husband. "I'll get right on it. That bitch won't hide so much as a fart gone bad from me."

Will grunted and Sienna covered a smile. Bee was if nothing else, unashamedly herself.

"I'll contact my mother. She has a close friend in the Fae Territory who might be able to help," Nicholas added.

"I'll take to the library and hit the history books. Maybe there's something there we can use," the Oracle said, smacking her gums as she jabbed an elbow into Theo's side. "Theo can be my assistant."

"Excellent. Keep me posted on your progress."

The fae queen's immature nature had been the cause of this grief, but I had a feeling it wouldn't be the last time she'd be difficult, and we needed all the ammo we could get. Someone so impulsive and shortsighted surely had skeletons in her closet or weaknesses she didn't want exposed. I just had to find them and jab my thumbs in deep.

"The rest of us will be focusing on Teeter and anyone with him who might've been responsible for the blood-worms and that burning sign. I want clan leaders inter-viewed, and the kitchen staff, too. Where did they purchase everything, down to the fucking salt, who prepared each piece of the meal, the whole nine yards."

"Looking forward to assisting," Raven said, a glimmer of fang flashing between his lips. "How can we be sure they don't strike again in the meantime?"

"I've already spoken with my guards. We'll be ramping up precautions significantly, for all of us. We can't afford to lose anyone in this room at such a delicate time."

Raven dipped his head in approval. "When we find the bastards, I also would like to toss my hat in for judge, jury, and executioner...or just the last, if I'm being honest."

Heat coiled in my belly at the protective rage in his eyes as he met my gaze, and it took a second to regain my composure. "We'll see about that. For now, let's agree to have a daily meeting to discuss our progress on all fronts. And, to the best of your ability, keep things discrete about my stepping down and my successor until we've spoken to Elka. We don't want to tip our hand before we've secured her as the successor to the crown."

"What of Maverick?" Dom interjected, speaking for the first time since we'd started our meeting.

"For Mav—" I paused for a long moment, considering. "Your discretion extends to him as well. I have some concerns on that front, and I need to do some thinking. For now, don't discuss my stepping down in his presence. I'll reassess in a few days."

"Good call, Frostbite," Raven said, rising from his seat. "I'm going to go get started with the interviews, assuming we're done here?"

"All good," I managed, waving him off as the true magnitude of what I'd just done fully set in.

A wave of anger rolled through me, and I spun back toward the fire to prevent it from showing on my face. Anger at Raven, at myself, at Teeter, and at my wolf, for leaving me when I needed her most. And, most of all, at Lilis, for putting me in this situation to begin with.

But I'd spent the past week wavering, and at least now, the course was finally set. Soon, I would no longer be queen of the werewolves. Given that I wasn't a wolf at all anymore, it was only right...

So why did it still feel so fucking wrong?

CHAPTER 14

Raven

I'd hoped getting some answers would make me feel a little better, but when I stepped up to the door of my quarters a few hours later, I was filled with frustration and muttering under my breath as if I were Myrr.

How the fuck could someone have slipped blood-worm eggs into the food under the noses of literally dozens of staff and not a single one of them have any clue? Especially if it was someone who didn't belong in the keep. Which brought me right back to square one...

The party responsible was unremarkable, meaning they belonged here. Meaning they were one of Diana's people. Someone she trusted.

Or *used* to trust.

"Fucking Maverick," I snarled softly. Thank gods she'd decided to leave him in the dark going forward, because nothing would convince me that he had anything but his own best interest at heart.

And anyone who didn't put my queen first in these treacherous times?

Was effectively my enemy.

I turned the knob and then stopped short as a shudder ran through me.

She was here. Not only could I smell her now that my thoughts weren't filled with ways to torture Maverick, but I could sense her, just through this door. My heart thudded against my ribs as I turned the knob, trying not to let hope get the better of me.

For all I knew, she could be pacing on the other side, ready to rip me a new one for something I'd inadvertently done...

But when I stepped inside, all those thoughts faded.

There she stood, Diana, Queen of Werewolves, dressed in nothing but a black, silk robe. The ends of the belt hung to the floor, leaving it wide open, exposing a wide swath of skin that made my cock throb.

"Diana, I—"

"Don't talk, Raven." She closed the short distance between us and reached behind me to shove the door closed, her breasts brushing my chest...the sweet smell of her hair filling my head. "I don't want to talk. My whole life has been flipped upside down. I'm doubting every decision I've ever made. I'm wondering why I was given that second chance by the sea that day only to have everything I've worked for snatched away...if all this pain and struggle and fighting to prove I belong has been for naught. I'm angry, grief-stricken, and confused." She laid a hand on my chest and searched my eyes with her own. "And when I look for my North Star, just to feel grounded for one fucking second—just to feel like I'm not completely spinning out of control?" Her hand slid up to cup my face. "The only thing I see is you." She lifted onto her tiptoes and peppered kisses along my jaw. "So can we just not talk about...any of it? Can we just be together for tonight and forget all the ugliness and uncertainty?"

"Fuck yes," I rasped, closing my hands over her silk-covered hips. Didn't she know that I would deny her nothing? Didn't she know that, through all the uncertainty, the one thing I was sure of was her? It wasn't the night to tell her. But I would damn sure show her.

I tightened my grip and hoisted her up in one smooth motion, and she instinctively straddled my waist. I knew just from the sudden rush of her lush, earthy scent that she wasn't wearing underwear, but a quick glance down confirmed it, and I let out a growl. "You're so fucking sexy, Frostbite."

She flexed her quads, lifting herself higher and plastering her breasts against my chest, leaning in to take a sharp nip at my jaw.

"Please," she whispered. Since this had been the stuff of my wet dreams for the past few months, she didn't need to ask me twice.

I covered the space of the large room in six long

strides, everything I passed evoking a new image to torture me.

Diana, seated on the edge of my low, mahogany dresser, legs spread wide as I licked her from back to belly.

Diana, bent at the waist, elbows on the zebra print chair in the corner, ass high in the air as I took her from behind.

Diana, in my rainwater shower, water sluicing down her body as I worshiped her with my tongue.

But for tonight, I went for the bed and just had to hope that she stayed long enough for seconds...or thirds.

I turned and sat on the edge of the mattress, sliding my hands from her hips to her ass and grinding her tight against my straining cock. Her robe slithered off her shoulders and down to her elbows, bearing the rest of her torso to me. I let out a long groan as her perfect, round tits came into full view, which made her chuckle.

"Is it wrong that I think it's kind of hot that you enjoy my pain?" I rasped, not waiting to hear her answer as I dipped my head low and flicked one hard nipple with the tip of my tongue. Her gasp in return as she plunged her fingers into my hair was anything but funny.

My fangs broke free of my gums, and I stiffened, remembering myself. I had to be careful, making every effort to ensure she didn't feel them against her skin. She claimed that I was her safe place, her North Star. But deep in my heart I knew one reminder of what I was—

what *we* were, now—and what I'd taken from her? And that could all go down in flames.

I shoved the thought aside, sucking her nipple into my mouth and batting it with my tongue as she speared her fingers through my hair, her breath catching. I sucked deeper and she began to rock her hips against me, grinding on my cock in a way that made me feel like a teenage boy again.

"Ah, Raven, that feels so good," she whispered. I flexed my hips against her, damning my stupid pants and the rest of my clothes. But I couldn't quite bring myself to let her go long enough to remove them.

I trailed a hand up her silky stomach and higher to cup her other breast, and she shivered. "Please, Raven, I just need to feel you inside me right now."

Any thoughts of trying to take it slow sizzled away as my brain short-circuited. I flipped her over in one smooth motion until she was flat on her back, legs dangling over the side of the mattress, robe splayed wide like a silky canvas to the most perfect painting ever created. I snapped my mouth closed, willing my fangs to retract as I stared down at her, etching the image in my mind for all eternity. Her lips parted, black hair spread across the mattress, legs falling open just enough for me to see that silky swath of pink that seemed to call to me.

I yanked my shirt over my head and tore my pants off, leaving myself naked to her gaze. Her eyes went wide as she leaned up on one elbow and reached out a hand to close her fingers over my throbbing member.

I let my head drop back as a hiss escaped my lips. Everything seemed to be in crisp hyper-focus...her lush scent filling my head, the slow drag of her soft hand as she worked me up and down, her breath coming faster and faster. I could even hear the pounding of her heart and the blood rushing in my own ears. The sight of it, her small hand stroking up and down, slow, and then faster, nearly undid me. I could come like this in thirty seconds if I let myself. Instead, I used every ounce of willpower I had and pulled away.

"Not so fast, Frostbite," I muttered, the sound a guttural facsimile of my normal voice. "I need to taste you."

Those chilly eyes seemed to shoot with flames as she let herself drop back against the mattress again. "Do your worst," she said with a feral smile.

I slowly dropped to my knees, savoring every moment as I lifted both of her legs and swung them over my shoulders, spreading her wide before my hungry gaze.

Her pussy glistened in the dim light, pink and slick and ready for my tongue, and I dove in like a man starving, lapping and licking and sucking, losing myself in her. So wet, so hot...

Dimly, I could hear her calling my name as she once again drove her fingers through my hair and clutched tight, alternately pinning me closer, melding my mouth to her clit, and then pulling away, begging for mercy, before starting the cycle all over again. She bucked and grinded, and I held her tight, a port in the storm.

When her legs tightened and I could feel her muscles trembling, I released her, sliding her further up the bed until she was spread-eagle. Then, I climbed onto the bed, wedging my shoulders between her silky thighs. Breath suspended, I slid one long finger deep inside her channel, groaning as the wet heat closed over me like a velvet glove.

"AH!"

I had to block out her cries as I flicked at her clit with the very tip of my tongue, alternating close, long licks, short flicks, and a deep thrust with my finger.

Her hips began to bounce as she whimpered my name. "Raven, please, don't stop. Don't stop, I'm gonna—"

She broke off as I plunged my finger deep one last time and sucked her clit hard. As she exploded, as she came, hard, her pussy closing over my finger, gripping and releasing, and making my cock flex and bounce in time as I imagined how that would feel around me. I held her through her climax until she shivered and twitched in the aftermath.

It wasn't until her legs went limp, and she sucked in one last shuddering breath that I gently pulled my finger back and lifted my head.

"So fucking perfect," I murmured through gritted teeth.

Don't think about what it would feel like to plunge those fangs into her thigh. Don't think about how hard she would come if you put that finger back in as you drank from her.

Someday maybe she'd be ready for that, and I would be there. But if that day never came? I took in her glowing skin, flushed cheeks, eyes glassy with desire—this would be more than any man deserved.

I climbed up higher until my body was poised over hers. As weak as she seemed, she managed to lift both hands up and run them over my shoulders and biceps, and she squeezed my muscles.

"Thank the gods clothing is a thing," she said. "I don't know how the fuck I'd keep the other ladies off of you if they knew what you looked like naked."

I bent low and touched my nose to hers. "Frostbite, one thing you never have to worry about is other women. I can't see anybody but you."

And with that, I flexed my hips and nudged at her warm, wet entrance with the thick head of my cock. She froze instantly, and I paused.

"You want me to wait?" I asked. Praying the answer was no, but ready to roll to my side if need be. She shook her head, and her eyes seemed to gleam with a fresh sheen of tears.

"No, I just...It feels like I've been waiting my whole life for this. You know what I mean?"

I knew exactly what she meant. And we both held our breath as I slowly drove my hips forward, taking her inch by inch, deeper and deeper, until my cock was seated to the hilt, leaving her to stretch and pulse around me. Her throat worked as she tipped her head back, nostrils flaring as she breathed in and out through her nose.

"It's like coming home," she whispered.

In the dim light, I could see the very tips of her fangs poking through her gums. Seeing them, wishing she would latch on to me as I thrust in and out, only made my cock stiffer. And then I was moving inside her, in and out. The hot, silky drag of her flesh working me over and over in a dizzying rhythm. I should've savored it. Slowed down and took my time, but the pressure building inside me was like an avalanche. There was no stopping it.

"Frostbite…" I hissed, squeezing my eyes closed as her nails dug into the muscles of my back, driving me over the edge. The taste of her still on my lips, the scent of her swamping my senses. She bucked and stiffened beneath me even as I came in pulsing, hot jets, unable to hold it in a second longer. "Mine!"

But it was in the moments after, as we caught our breath and came back to earth, that the bond between us shimmered with her unspoken reply.

Yours.

I rolled to my side and dragged her with me, blood humming with satisfaction and hope.

She might not have said it out loud…it might take a little more time for her to accept, but something deep inside her knew it too, as surely as I did. We were meant to be. The knowledge only lit a fire under me like never before.

If a life with Diana was even possibly part of my future, I'd tear the world apart to see it happen—Maverick's smirking face flickered through my mind.

And gods help anyone who tried to stand in my way.

CHAPTER 15

Diana

T he cold air nipped at me as I made my way down the corridor, and I found myself wishing I hadn't been forced to leave my bed.

I'd woken up in Raven's arms, with the smell of pancakes in the air, feeling better than I had in days despite how things had gone the day before. Even now, my mind was quieter than it had been—that was Raven's influence, I was sure—and I felt more certain about what I needed to do. But as I made my way to the front doors of the keep to find Sienna there waiting for me, nerves fluttered to life in my belly.

Her eyes brightened as she saw me, and she charged right up, pulling me into a hug. "Thank you," she whispered, "for inviting me to come with you."

I hugged her back, shooing away the concerned-looking guard at my left. "You're an honorary member of Clan Killian, it makes sense to bring you."

She pulled away, fishing a small badge from her pocket that bore the seal of Elka's clan. Her smile didn't reach her eyes, and I could see how much sadness she still carried with her over the death of her friend. "It was Jordan's."

I nodded, smiling sadly. "I'm very sorry for what you lost. He was well loved by his clan."

"I look forward to seeing them again. How are we getting there? I fear we will be followed," she said, keeping her voice low as we stepped outside.

"Definitely possible. Which is why we're taking loads of guards, and Elka will be meeting us in the dark willows, so we don't have to worry about anyone taking a pot-shot at us," I added, turning as our carriage rolled up to us.

My four guards squeezed in first, checking the inside of it before beckoning me in. The precautions were exhausting, and I added it to the long list of reasons to despise the wolf clans doing this to me.

I left the door part way open, watching the scenery as we rolled by. The dark willows came into view before long, their gnarled branches barely visible through the curtain of swaying, dark leaves.

Pure melancholy seemed to radiate off them.

"They're here already, just ahead," I said as they came into view. Kavan stood a head taller than Maya, and they were huddled around their nervous-looking daughter.

We hadn't told her the reason for the meeting, of

course, and I was sure the anticipation had been eating away at her.

"Spread out," I said, turning to the guards as the carriage slowed to a halt. "You can form a perimeter around us, but our conversation needs to be private."

The largest of the guards scrunched his face up and shook his head. "Your Majesty, I fear that…If I could at least—"

"You have your orders," I shot back. Kavan and Maya were honorable werewolves, down to their very bones, and I felt no need to fear assassination or subterfuge.

Not from them, anyway.

The guard frowned but dipped his head in assent. "As you wish."

They did as I asked and spread out as we piled out of the carriage, forming a wide circle around our meeting spot. Sienna and I strode toward the waiting werewolves. Kavan stepped forward to greet us, dropping into the half-bow that was customary.

"My Queen."

"It's good to see you well, Clan Killian," I said, saluting as Maya and Elka greeted me.

Movement flashed at my side, and a wave of sadness rolled over me as I saw Sienna rushing forward with tears dripping from her cheeks. Elka pulled her into a hug, with the two older wolves putting comforting hands on her shoulder.

"I'm sorry that I haven't visited as much lately. Things have been crazy." Sienna spoke through her tears.

Kavan shook his head, "There's no need for apologies, young one. We know how important you are to this world."

"There will always be a spot for you at our table whenever you have time, Ceecee," Maya agreed.

"What a place for us to meet up, too." Elka's expression was grim as she stared at the shifting willow that hung a few feet away. "I haven't visited this place since Jordan passed."

"Same." Sienna's tears were flowing even harder, now, and she pulled Elka into a second hug. She sucked in a breath, taking a moment to compose herself before pulling away to continue, "I've been meaning to ask you if we can meet up for a few hours at some point. Now that some time has passed and the wounds aren't as fresh, I'd love to share some stories about him, get to know what he was like during his time here. If you—"

Elka cut in with a trembling smile. "I'd love that."

A jolt of nerves spiked through me as the ground beneath us began to rumble, and I took a large sideways step as I saw the willow beginning to shift. It was a strange thing to watch happen, no matter how familiar it was. The ground writhed and shook as the roots pulled it along, the branches warping and rearranging as it moved.

"I won't keep you in suspense," I said, turning back to Elka as the tree slowed to a halt. "I'm sure you've heard rumors about what's been going on, both over the past months, but even more so since the battle against the demons, and—" Damn. Actually saying the words out loud felt so final... "And I've decided that I'm going to step down as Queen."

The three Killian wolves gasped in unison, and it was Kavan who spoke first. "You be sure about this, Your Majesty?"

I nodded, holding up a hand. "I've deliberated on it for a long time, and it seems to be the only option I have left." I'd briefly considered telling them about my missing wolf but decided against it. Like a fox's den holding onto the scent of its owner long after it had moved on to another part of the forest, I still smelled like them...for now. But soon enough, there would be no hiding it. Everyone would know, and new leadership needed to be firmly in place before that happened. I sucked in a breath, my gaze settling on a confused-looking Elka. "Given these trying circumstances, and how hesitant the clans were to even accept me as queen in the first place, now is the time to select my successor. That's where you come in."

Her brows furrowed. "I will do whatever it takes to help, Your Majesty, but I'm not sure I'm the one best suited to advise you in this matter. Perhaps—"

"I'm not looking for advice, Elka." I met and held her puzzled gaze. "I'm looking for a Queen."

She went still for a long moment, then her jaw dropped. "I... I'm not ready, Your Majesty. I'm not even a clan head, yet."

"I wasn't either. According to Lycan, it's better that way. You don't have the ingrained tendencies that come with age, or past grievances and long-standing feuds with other clans. You're respectful enough to hold tradition in high regard, while not being a slave to it. It's the perfect balance of old and new that I hope will satisfy both my supporters, and those who have opposed me."

Kavan frowned, his eyes stormy. "Will she not become a target?"

"I can't make any guarantees, but I'm planning to root out the worst elements in the time I have left. I don't want her to start off on the back foot, either."

"If you can pull that off, won't it be safe for you again? Why not just recommit to the throne once you've neutralized the threat?" Elka asked.

A sigh stuck in the back of my throat, and I held it in.

"The issue is larger than a few individuals, at this point. Too much has happened, and a pound of flesh is required before we can wipe the slate clean. I made my choices, and am willing to donate that pound, but not before I ensure that I'm passing the torch to someone worthy. Once you're crowned queen, I will step back completely. Given what a pillar you've been in the community, and the fact that you come from the most respected of clans, even the dissenters will fall into line."

At least, I hoped they would...

Kavan pulled back, still looking unsure as Maya began to speak. "So you wouldn't be around to teach her?"

I shook my head. "We don't want to give anyone the

idea that she's just continuing my reign. The more distance we put between us, the better."

"How will I learn to lead our people, then?" Elka shook her head slowly. "I don't feel anywhere close to ready for something like this. It feels crazy, like I've stepped into a strange dream."

Her concerns were fair, and I held up my hands. "My advisor, Lochlin, will stay around to teach you, and your father has plenty of leadership experience as well. Loch is a very, very good advisor. He will help you with anything you need."

Elka stared off into the distance, the thoughts churning behind her eyes. "What makes you think I'll be a good fit for the job? I know I did well at the battle against the Demons, but this is a huge step—being a warrior is not the same as being a leader."

"You were already doing great things in your community before that. I've seen the way you've risen in the ranks, Elka, and I know it's not just because of who your father is." The reasons that Lochlin had given me were many—her accomplishments, her choices in times of strife, even her acceptance of Jordan and then Sienna.

Sienna took a step forward, cutting in for the first time since we'd begun speaking about it. "We all see the way the soldiers act around you, even the veterans. You have something special, Elka. I agree with Diana—I know you have what it takes to do this."

She dipped her head in thanks to her adopted sister. "Thank you, Ceecee, truly, but I'm still not sure I see what you do. I'm young. Inexperienced. And female. Just as you are female."

I smiled though I could feel it trembling on the edges. "But you were not adopted into your clan as I was, you were born here, of this soil and blood."

Her hesitation was admirable. She didn't want the position. All the more reason for it to be hers.

"It's up to you, of course, and I understand that it's a huge undertaking. I just want you to know that I believe in you and that you have the backing already of William and Bethany, and perhaps more important, Myrr, the Oracle."

Her mouth had been open, I'm sure to protest, but that last name slowed her. "The Oracle?"

"I asked Lochlin for a list of recommendations," I said, "and he brought back only a single name. Just one, out of all our clans. I understand why. You loved Jordan so fiercely. You handled being possessed by a dark goddess and came out the other side stronger for it. You have the strength and resolve needed, and the heart and compassion to make judgments fair. When I took your name to the Oracle...she agreed. It is you, Elka, that the werewolf clans need."

Silence fell except for the whispers of the black willows rustling in the nonexistent wind, as if the whole world was waiting on her, holding its breath.

She never looked away from me, her eyes narrowing slightly, her back stiffening.

"I'm not afraid of the responsibility, or the risks, but

I want to be sure I can do the job justice–it is not just my family that it affects, but all the clans." She paused and nodded. "I need to take a day to discuss it in private with my parents."

I noted how she'd straightened, how her tone had changed from one of uncertainty to one I'd expect from a leader twice her age. I tipped my head. "Of course...But, given the state of affairs, that's the longest I can give you. Things are coming to a head, and we need to have everything in place as soon as possible."

Elka tipped her head. "I understand. I'll come to you tomorrow, regardless of my answer."

I sucked in a deep breath of the chilly air, feeling like a weight had been lifted off my shoulders. The bullet had been bitten, and there was no turning back now. The rest was out of my hands. All that was left to do was wait. "I look forward to hearing from you."

I turned to Kavan, leaving the matter behind for now.

"We have reason to believe that a wolf named Teeter is behind the recent upheaval. What do you know about him?"

Kavan's face darkened, his eyes narrowing. "From the pub, yeah? My men have orders to stay away from the place. Lots of rabble rousing and trouble over there— dissension is a common theme."

"He's on the run, as far as we can tell. He hasn't been seen of late. I'm hoping you can put some feelers out and let me know if you hear anything about his whereabouts." I rummaged through my pocket, producing the list I'd written the night before. "There are a few other wolves we think might be in league with him, here are their names. Try to keep things discrete."

Kavan nodded grimly. "Clan Killian'll do all it can, Your Majesty."

And I believed him. He had been among Lycan's most ardent supporters, and later became mine. Now, with his daughter considering the throne, he would view it as his job to do whatever he could to keep her safe.

"No matter what you decide," I said, turning back toward Elka, "I want to extend my gratitude toward all three of you. Loyalty such as yours is rare. Especially in times like these."

"You are too kind, my Queen," Kavan said, dipping his head low.

"We'll be on our way, then. Send a messenger right away if you hear anything." I said my goodbyes, then waved for the nearest guard to collect the rest of the men while Sienna embraced her honorary family.

Things had gone about as well as could be expected, and I was cautiously optimistic by the time the carriage pulled away a few minutes later.

"She is impressive," I said, turning toward Sienna. The meeting had only reaffirmed my impression of the girl. She'd responded well, treating the request with the seriousness it demanded without rejecting me outright.

"I was worried she was still a bit young, but just the fact that she's being so cautious with her answer makes me think she's mature beyond her years. She's as good as they come," Sienna agreed.

I eyed the guard between us, speaking carefully as I continued. "I just hope I'm not asking more of her than is fair. It's a tumultuous time…"

"She's grown. Whatever risks she might not see, her parents will surely remind her of. You asked her because you believe it's what's best for your people. Now it's up to Elka to decide if it's what's best for her."

Sienna was right. And, for now, I had to shift my focus to the more immediate concern. I cracked my knuckles, a slight rush running through me as I thought about it. Teeter and his squad had to go down if I wanted Elka to have any chance at success, and I'd do whatever it took to make that happen, even if it was the last thing I did as queen.

No.

Even if it was the last thing I did, period.

CHAPTER 16

Raven

I took a pull from my scotch, glancing over my shoulder at the sound of footsteps just behind me as I stifled a flash of irritation. Last night should've been one of the best of my life. I'd gotten to sleep with Diana in my arms. But I'd been plagued with nightmares and, in every single one of them?

I'd wound up burying my beloved.

It left me feeling unsettled and stressed all fucking day as I tried to reassure myself that these dreams weren't the same thing as a premonition. No, if Myrr's blood had given me some sort of precognition, it would be happening like it did for Myrr. At any random moment, bam! Premonition. Not some run of horrific dreams, each one more disturbing than the last.

So I'd spent my day trying to find the person or people behind that damnable burning threat in hopes of at least nipping that in the bud and finding a little bit of peace on that front, but I'd come up empty. Someone or *someones* out there would see my mate dead, and here I was, hamstrung and helpless, with no idea where to go from here...

"Mind if we join you?" Will said as he, Nicholas, and Bee strode into the massive library.

As much as I liked all three of them, company was about the last thing I was in the mood for. I greeted them, nonetheless, scooting over to make room for them in the seating area. Then, I drained the rest of my glass and gestured to the bar filled with crystal decanters against the wall.

"Help yourselves, if anyone is interested in drowning sorrows."

Will took my empty glass and made a beeline for the bar as the others sat.

"Served by the king himself. And who said I wouldn't amount to anything?" I glanced around the table as the others sat. "Any news?"

Bee frowned and shook her head. "Cleona's past is squeaky clean, as far as we can tell—that, or she knows how to wipe her footprints better than anyone I've ever known!"

"I haven't heard back from my mother's friend yet, either," Nicholas said.

I gestured toward Will as he poured us all drinks. "There's always option two." Cleona's infatuation with Will was the only thread we had to tug on so far.

Nicholas chuckled. "I doubt Bee would take very kindly to that."

"Not going to happen, so don't even ask," Bee said, crossing her arms over her chest and glaring at me.

I held up both hands in surrender. "I wasn't saying he should follow through on it, I was just saying maybe let her think there's a chance..."

Will returned with a tray balanced on one hand as he passed out drinks with the other. "When do you think you'll hear back from your mother's contact?"

Nicholas shrugged. "Impossible to say. The Fae come and go as they please, and prefer magic to technology, so it can be a challenge to track a person down. All that's left to do on our end is wait."

"The fae are definitely an interesting lot," Bee interjected. "I was in the library all day with Myrr, and I couldn't believe some of the stuff I was reading. It might be difficult to pinpoint which things are scandal-worthy enough to actually use against her, and which things are normal for them."

"What did you read?" Will asked as he took his seat close to Bee.

"Well, for one, marriages are rare, and monogamy even more so." Her face lit up, and she grabbed Will by the arm. "Oh yeah, wait until you hear about how they deal with thieves..."

Nicholas tapped me on the shoulder, pulling my attention away from them.

"Hmm?" I pulled over my scotch, throwing back a

healthy swallow as I shoved a particularly brutal night-mare about Diana from the forefront of my mind.

"Hear anything about Teeter?"

"No one has seen or heard from him. Interviewed all the staff in the keep, too. Loch spoke with anyone who might frequent that bar, along with several clan leaders, and Gavin's widow, Mary. So far, we've got nothing."

"Think they're all covering for one of their own? Or is he just doing a damn good job at hiding?"

"I'm confident in my ability to spot a liar, and I don't think any of the staff was involved." If I did, they'd have already been in a room getting mind-fucked by our own Nicholas right now. "If I had to guess, he's nowhere near the keep."

"Has anyone talked to Mav today?"

I instantly tensed at hearing his name. Diana had been quite sure he wasn't behind the poisoning, but it had been damn hard to stop myself from confronting him.

"Nope, and I was asked not to track him down," I said, my hand straying toward my glass once again.

"You really think he's involved with all this?"

"I don't have any proof, but my gut says yes. Then again, my guts fucking hate his ass, so maybe I'm biased." I pushed Maverick from my mind and focused on the things I *could* control. "Regardless, it's Teeter we have to find."

"Can't help but wonder if he isn't being harbored by some clan or other, though. Wouldn't be hard, given how much independence Diana allows them. The clan leader wouldn't even have to know, necessarily."

"It's possible. She wanted to keep things low key so as not to rile up the clans who are already against her, but I'll see what she thinks about putting up a reward for information. We're not getting anywhere being subtle."

Memories of the previous night flashed through my mind, unbidden, as I thought of going to Diana's rooms now, and I had to hide my fangs in the rim of my glass as they punched through my gums. I gritted my teeth, the arousal morphing quickly into more frustration. We were closer than ever, yet I couldn't shake the feeling that she was still holding something back.

The worst part?

I couldn't blame her. Given what I'd taken from her, no matter the reason, it was a wonder we'd even been able to get back to this point in our relationship, never mind the one I longed for. And now, it was even harder because I was spending every waking moment thinking about how to get her out of this safe and sound.

But what then?

I leaned back in my chair, pondering the question for the first time. I'd join her in her search for the remaining keys, of course, but would things continue as they were now? Or would she pull away yet again?

Nicholas' voice broke me out of the thought. "Why don't you just tell her?"

I turned, glancing down to see if he'd been touching my arm or something. "I thought I told you not to go fishing around in my head." Creepy as his powers were, they were supposed to require touch to function.

He laughed, holding up his hands in mock surrender. "I didn't read your mind. I just read your face. You aren't exactly good at hiding your feelings for her. So, explain it to me. Why don't you tell her that you were the one who saved her from Edmund when you were children? Maybe if she knew, she'd see that you were always meant to be from the very start."

"That's exactly why I won't tell her," I shot back. "The last thing I want is for her to feel like she's beholden to me because of something like that. I want her to *choose* me, not feel like she never had a choice."

I'd already done that to her once, and it had nearly ruined everything.

"Don't you think she'd resent not having all the information, though? It's a big secret to keep from her."

I was about to reply when a frantic-looking Lochlin rushed into the room.

"They've come for Diana!"

I leapt out of my chair and sprinted from the room, Nicholas and the others hot on my heels. I kicked into high gear once we got out the front door, surging past Lochlin as we moved toward the front gate of the keep. A mixture of relief and confusion washed over me as Diana came into view. She was alive, well, and surrounded by guards as she faced the five clan leaders standing before her.

My muscles tensed as one of them began to stride

forward, but I held back when her guards stopped him short.

"We're not here for battle. I'm only here to deliver this letter."

He produced a sealed envelope, stepping back wordlessly once she took it.

"Holmgang, then?" she said, her expression solemn as she tore open the envelope without ceremony.

My heart thumped heavily in my chest as Lochlin let out a low string of curses.

Her eyes flitted downward for less than a second before she stuffed it into her pocket. "I accept your challenge. We meet at noon...the clearing in the west forest."

She spun without another word, sliding past me on her way back to the keep. I followed, but she was silent until we reached the front doors.

"I don't see that I have a choice," she murmured, her expression darker than I'd seen in weeks, despite all that she'd been going through.

"Choice in what? What the fuck is a Holmgang?" I demanded.

"A physical challenge," Lochlin grunted, "for the throne."

"What?" Nicholas blurted, echoing my thoughts. "They can do that?"

"It's only happened once in the past two centuries, but yes. If at least five clans sign off on it, her hand is basically forced. She can either fight their champion, or step aside."

"She plans to step aside anyway. Why fight?"

"Because if I don't, they pick my successor." She leveled me with a fierce look. "I won't have it."

I gritted my teeth. "Alright then, can you choose a champion of your own?"

She shook her head. "It must be me. If I win, they won't be able to issue another challenge for ten years. That will give Elka a chance to settle in."

"And if you lose?"

"I won't," she said, her expression growing defiant.

"But if you did?"

Lochlin stepped between us, his expression grim. "Raven...It's a battle to the death."

The words hit me like a punch to the gut, and it took every bit of self-control I had to not charge right back through those doors and gut all five of those bastard clan leaders.

"Unacceptable. We'll find another way out of this. We can—"

"I'm doing it, Raven," Diana cut in, slicing her hand through the air to stay further argument. "It is the way of my people, and anyone who tries to stop me will be henceforth considered the enemy."

She swept into the keep, head held high, as I stood there feeling as helpless as I'd ever felt in my life.

In less than a day's time, the one I loved most in the world could well be dead.

And, this time, there wasn't a fucking thing I could do about it.

CHAPTER 17

Diana

The day dragged, the tension in the keep so taut you could have strung a highwire with it, if you'd been so inclined.

I could have stayed in my rooms, could have practiced for the upcoming fight, but I did neither. My time here as queen was rapidly fading, and I wanted to...have my own kind of goodbye.

Raven found me in the infirmary, his presence palpable as I spoke quietly to the doctor.

"I wanted to come personally to thank you again for the work you did on our visiting allies, as well as the many years of service you have performed to the highest level." I took the doctor's hand—Fallan Delogha—and gripped it gently. "I hope you know that you are deeply valued."

Fallan did a double blink and tightened his hold on

my fingers gently. "My Queen. You have more than adequately expressed this on many occasions."

I nodded. "Perhaps. But you have saved many lives."

"And there have been some I could not." He frowned, and my guts clenched as I could almost feel him thinking about Gavin. "But thank you. You have always been gracious."

I slipped away, Raven shadowing me as I made my way through the keep, greeting those who'd served faithfully, making sure I said what needed to be said.

Was I dying? No, but if Elka would take what I asked of her, my time in the keep would be short. The keep where my father had raised me. Where I'd learned what it meant to be a wolf...to be a queen.

Fuck. I put a hand to the wall as emotions threatened to overwhelm me.

"Frostbite." Raven was there in a flash. "You okay?"

He put his hand to my lower back, supporting me without being too over the top. I nodded as a guard and a maid turned down the hall toward us. The guard stiffened up and saluted.

"My Queen."

The maid...her eyes narrowed, and she sniffed as she took the next turn to her right, avoiding crossing our paths, not speaking a word to me as if, as if I were already dead to her.

Raven let out a rumbling growl that would make a werewolf proud. "Maybe she's the one who laced the food."

I shook my head and pushed myself off the wall. "Lee, do you have a message for me?"

"A visitor." Lee tipped his head. "Elka of the Killian clan has requested to meet with you."

My heart gave a double thump. She either would accept or she would not. I had done all I could to impress upon her the importance of her choice.

"Thank you. Take her to my personal quarters. I would speak with her there."

"Of course, my Queen. And, for what it's worth at this late hour...it has been an honor to serve you." He put his fist to his chest and bowed low, holding the position.

I bit my lower lip, one fang dragging across and piercing the flesh, reminding me that I was his queen for not much longer.

Walking toward him, I put my hand on his shoulder and squeezed. "You have served the crown faithfully, Lee. You have your queen's thanks, and gratitude."

A shudder went through him and when he stood back up his eyes glistened. "Thank you, Your—"

"Diana," I cut in softly. His eyes shot to mine and I smiled. "Just Diana."

He closed his eyes and nodded, one tear slipping down his cheek as he spun away from me. "I will bring her to your rooms, my Queen."

"So many still love you," Raven said softly. "Saying your goodbyes will not change that."

I wanted to lean back into him. "I know, because I love them too. They're my family."

Raven turned me to face him. His turquoise eyes were so intense, so different than the first time I'd met him and I'd thought him a clown. A fool. How well he'd hidden his strength and heart.

A wayward thought struck me. How much more bonded would I have felt to my true mate? Guilt flashed through me.

"I should go, Elka is waiting."

"Go. I will follow." He stepped back and bowed to me.

Nerves fluttered as I made my way to my rooms.

Who would I ask if Elka turned me down? Perhaps her father...but he did not have the charisma that Elka had, or the vigor of a youth who believed they could take on the world.

I didn't have to ask Raven to wait outside my rooms. He stopped a few feet away, tucked his hands in his pockets and leaned against the wall, looking for all the world like he wasn't guarding my door.

"Thank you."

"No," he said, his eyes intense even while his voice was gentle. "You never have to thank me. I am here, Diana. To whatever end comes for us and this world, I will not leave your side. Nothing but death could take me from you and even that...I'd crawl from the grave to return to you."

His words struck through the last of the fears that were buried deep—that I would be alone in the end.

Words stuck in my throat, and I turned and let myself into my rooms.

Elka stood with her back to me, looking out the same window I preferred, her hair woven around her head in a crown braid. Was it a sign? She wore a pair of clean, tawny-colored soft pants, and dark brown leather boots that rose above her knee to her mid-thigh.

Her fitted jacket was a deep green—the royal green—and had a high collar. As she turned, the etching on the left side where the clan the queen or king came from sat the mark of Clan Killian. But on the right...was my father's clan symbol. A lightning bolt across a sword.

Her eyes gave away nothing. She tipped her head ever so slightly. Not a bow. An acknowledgment from one queen to another. "Diana."

I smiled. Not my title. My name, as if we were on equal footing.

"Elka of Clan Killian. I see you have made your choice."

Her smile trembled only a little and I watched her pull herself together, locking down the emotion but still letting it shine in her eyes—gods, she was exactly who we needed.

"I have."

Elka's decision made it that much easier for me to go into

the fight, knowing that she was ready to take on the crown.

I'd made my way to the clearing with Lochlin and my guards. I'd invited Clan Killian and Elka to be there as well. The issue was more with Raven and my brothers. The talk before we left was frustrating to say the least.

"You cannot interfere. Not even if I am...in trouble," I reminded them for what had to be the tenth time.

"I don't care." Raven shrugged. "I'm not going to watch you get killed."

"Nor will I," Dominic grunted. "You are my sister, and—"

"Don't leave me out of this." Will waved a hand. "Your death would be a disservice to not only your people, but to us. We love you, Diana. We aren't going to lose you now that you are in our lives again."

If not for Will's softer words, I would have just raged at them all.

"You think she cannot fight this fight?" Evangeline's voice turned the three men around. "You think she has not prepared for this fight, or one like it, her entire life? There has always been the threat to her...a chance that someone would challenge her. Especially after Lycan—" She broke off, the grief plain on her face as she pressed on. "And when young Elka takes on the crown, she will need to be prepared for the same at any given time. Because there will always be a man, weak and fearful, that will try to take away the power of any woman he sees as a threat. Any excuse. Any reason. That has not changed, not in all my years. And you do this woman that you all love a great shame to believe that she cannot withstand a single opponent."

She snapped her hands to the table she sat at and stood up. Her anger was...well I was glad it was not directed at me. With the blood she'd been force fed after the bloodworm attack, she had regained more than her smooth dark skin and the curve of her waist. She'd been reborn somewhere in those moments between life and death. Perhaps my father had spoken to her on the other side and told her to keep fighting. Whatever the reason, she was the fiery Evangeline she'd been my whole life, and a bone-deep relief filled me now that she was back.

"Auntie," Will said, his tone low and soothing. "It's not that we don't believe she can do it. She would fear for us, too, if we were put in the same position."

The Duchess snorted. "But she would not imply that you were not capable."

"I did not," Raven said. "I have seen her fight; I know she can do this. But if they pull a stunt—"

I held up a hand, finally cutting in. "If they cheat, then we kill them all. Together."

Dominic and Will shared a glance and then they both nodded. "Agreed."

Raven's smile was all predator. "Then I shall pray that one of them fucking sneezes at the wrong moment, so I can call it a deliberate distraction."

I smiled as I stood in the clearing, dressed in my fighting leathers. Vest, pants, boots. No weapons. There were never any weapons in our Holmgangs. Just pure physicality.

My supporters spread out around half of the ring. Lochlin, Dominic, Will, Raven, Elka.

The other half...well the other half of the ring was as expected. Teeter and four of his men stood around the edge. It was the other wolves behind them that made my heart clench. So many wanted to see me dead. Faces of those I thought of as friends. Faces I never expected to see on the side of my enemies. Even Gavin's wife, Mary, stood there glaring at me, her true feelings laid bare now that my position was weakened, and she had protection.

I shook my head, not bothering to reach out to any of them. They were lost to me, and, in some ways, I couldn't blame them. Perhaps Elka would be able to reach them in time. It was the only hope I had.

"I'm surprised you would not fight me yourself." I made myself smile at Teeter, let my anger rise through me. The shard whispered through, but I pushed that power down. This had to be on my own abilities. If there was even a hint of magic or a weapon in sight, the match would be forfeit.

"I'd love to." Teeter smiled back. "But there are others better suited to the ring and the sheer brutality required. I won't risk losing the future we've longed for over pride."

I had to work to hide my frown, because I knew that Teeter was an excellent fighter. He'd been a soldier a long time and had nearly risen to the rank of General.

Nearly.

His violent tendencies got in the way of that last step, and he'd been let go from the ranks. So, what did that say about the wolf they *did* choose?

One last calm breath, and I stepped across the line into the ring. Thirty feet across sounded big, but it wasn't a lot of room. And being thrown out of it didn't stop the fight, it only restarted it back in the middle.

Now that I'd crossed to this side of the ring, I was committed, no matter who I faced.

A heavy footfall from the forest drew everyone's eyes.

An energy that was dark and violent flowed ahead of my competitor and my heart...my heart nearly stopped when I saw his face rise above the others. Bright yellow eyes, tawny hair hanging around his head like a lion's mane, his teeth were as stained as ever as he grinned across at me. Seven feet tall, and just about as wide, I knew I had the fight of my life on my hands in every sense of the word.

Cammon was the monster who'd challenged my father thirty years before. Only because of my father's generosity and desire for change had the bastard been allowed to live after a brutal fight that had nearly seen my father maimed. It had been a shifting point in the way we ruled.

Not through violence but strength of heart *and* body.

But this Cammon had taken his loss to heart. This Cammon was even bigger, badder, and stronger than before. Almost unnaturally so. His arms were the size of fucking cannons, and he cracked his knuckles as he stepped into the ring.

"I'm going to enjoy killing Lycan's little pity project."

If there had been a moment where I thought I would tremble before him, it washed away in a wave of fury. I made myself smile at him, though I suspected it was more a baring of my teeth.

"And I am going to fix the one mistake my father ever made and bury your ass."

CHAPTER 18

Diana

Cammon stood across from me, yellow eyes locked on my face, yellow teeth partially bared, a low growl rumbling through him.

There was no referee in a Holmgang, not really, but today we'd made sure there would be someone neutral present to ensure others didn't interfere. Teeter and his people would pull any trick they could, and we all knew it.

A beat of wings above us, and eyes shifted upward—but not mine. I waited, keeping my gaze locked on my opponent.

Gabe dropped down through the trees, his wings tucked tight to his body as he landed in the middle of the ring with a soft thud, positioned between Cammon and me. He straightened and held out his arms wide, as if he were a ringmaster and not a referee.

"I'll be overseeing things. If either party cheats, they

will forfeit the match for their contestant." He swept his cobalt eyes around the crowd. "Anyone interfering with the fight will also forfeit the match for their contestant."

I noted he looked hard at the men on my side, saving a special, telling glare of warning in Raven's direction, but I didn't dare take my eyes off Cammon. At this point the match was on, the only thing between me and him was Gabe.

"No time limit, this goes until it is done. The mark of the ring shall come into play only if someone is bodily thrown out. If both contestants work their way across the line, the fight continues wherever it may lead. The crowd will shift to make space as needed."

"To the death they fight, no quarter given this time!" someone shouted, a younger male by the sounds of his broken cry.

I didn't know who spoke, but they were on Cammon's side.

I let out a bark of laughter. "I look forward to holding you all to that when Cammon is on his knees, begging me to spare his life like my father did before me."

Gabe stepped out of the ring and then sliced a hand through the air. "Begin!"

Cammon and I did a slow circle.

"You'll be the one on your knees, bitch, sucking my cock and praying I fuck you before you die like a squealing pig!" His side of the ring erupted in cheers and jeers.

I loosened my body, knowing that, even if I had

retained my wolf, I was still not stronger than Cammon. Female wolves were smaller and lighter than their male counterparts. The only way to win here was by using my wits and speed. And as a re-born vampire, the latter was something I had in spades.

This motherfucker had no idea what was coming for him.

I snarled, unable to keep the sound in as I bared my teeth right back at him. And then the fight truly began.

Cammon lunged at me, one meaty hand swiping through the air where my neck had been a split second before. I ducked and slid away from him, making sure to not go too far.

Running from him would do me no good and tipping my hand at just how fast I was…I needed to hold that until the end.

"Slippery bitch," he growled, spinning to face me.

"Simple words from a simple man," Raven said from our side. "How many times did you get dropped on your head as a child?"

"Three." Someone from Cammon's side answered.

Raven laughed, Will and Dominic joined him, and the sound buoyed my nerves. Lochlin even chuckled. "He ain't known for his smarts."

"And I'm sure all that psycho 'roid rage isn't helping with the few brain cells you have left, is it?"

Cammon took a look back at Raven to give him a side eye, and it was all I needed. I shot forward, dropping low and driving a fist toward Cammon's left knee. He wasn't fast enough to fade the blow, but he lessened it by sidestepping.

I flowed with the forward momentum, spinning and kicking out at his right knee, catching it fully. It cracked under the heel of my boot and Cammon howled. I'd have cheered if I thought one good blow would do the trick, but it was going to take more than a busted kneecap to put someone his size down.

I rolled and turned as Cammon leapt through the air, his arms going around me as he tackled me to the ground. We hit hard, the wind leaving me in a *whoosh* as I took the brunt of the fall, his forehead snapping into mine with a force that drove the back of my skull into a rock below.

Fuck.

Stars burst in behind my eyelids and the sound of the crowd seemed far away as I blinked rapidly, trying to pull my shit together.

Eyes glazed with adrenaline and rage, Cammon threw one thick thigh over my hips to straddle me with barely a wince at the surely excruciating pain in his knee.

"Just like that, boys! Look at her, all dazed and confused from a single blow!" He smacked my cheek hard enough to draw blood on my lips, and I let my head bobble, unresisting.

I took long slow breaths as I lay there, gathering myself, feeling the fuel that I'd consumed earlier spinning through me. Lochlin had donated, as had Raven. The blood of my best friend and advisor sung hot. Raven's sung sweet, rolling through me with a power that he always kept in check.

Cammon kept on talking, as if he were a preacher at a podium, frothing at the mouth as he whipped up the masses with his words.

I was already through the worst of the blow, my head was ringing, for sure, but that didn't mean I was out.

"You want a show, my new King? I can give you a show!" Cammon tipped his head back and howled, as he ripped his shirt, his hands then going to his...was he going to try and rape me?

I think not, motherfucker.

Raven's panic-tinged rage came through loud and clear, and I sent him a soft soothing thought.

I got this. I got this.

Cammon pawed at the waistband of his pants.

"Just finish her!" Teeter yelled. "We don't need to be—"

I bucked my hips upward hard, while bridging off my arms at the same time. Not only did I throw Cammon off me, but we were close enough to the edge of the circle that he ended up outside, pausing the match.

"Restart," Lochlin yelled.

"He's right," Gabe confirmed. "Time for a restart."

I rolled to my feet and stood. I could already feel the knot swelling on the back of my head, but I would deal with it. No open wounds yet, so that was a bonus.

Cammon strolled back into the ring, barely limping, bare chested, and...fuck...I grimaced as he reached into his pants and gave himself a long, lazy stroke. "I like you under me, bitch, that's where you belong. I'mma fuck you into the ground in more ways than one."

Two more strokes and he pulled his hand free.

"I'd watch my words, mutt." Raven's voice was a near whisper, and probably no one else heard the edge to it, but I did. If by some chance I didn't survive this, Cammon was a dead man.

But I had no intention of losing this match.

"Jealous?" Cammon let out a low rumbling growl in Raven's direction. "I'll fuck you next, pretty boy."

"You can try." Raven's icy rage probably couldn't be heard by anyone listening to him taunt Cammon, but I could feel it under my skin, fueling me.

Lighting a dual blaze of anger in me. One of my own, and one of his. How dare this piece of shit try to humiliate me like this, while making a mockery of the whole fucking contest?

"You going to circle around me all night? Lazy cunt. Waiting for a man to do a job that you should have never had. We shoulda killed you the night you were crowned."

I had a plan, I could see the pieces in my head, coming together. I just needed to get him into position.

"Regrets..." I smiled and gave a mocking bow, sweeping my arms wide. "They will haunt you *all* this night. Every single one of those who backed you, Cammon, will regret this moment. But you...you won't regret it. You'll be dead."

He laughed.

I feinted to his right, and he lurched, stumbling from the pressure on his already busted knee. Seeing my chance, I leapt to the left, slamming a fist into his side to put him even more off balance.

He staggered back, roaring, but it was too late. My left hand rammed into the side of his neck with a squelch, burying itself deep into the flesh of the side of his neck. I gritted my teeth, squeezing down on the tendons there for a handhold, to pull myself around and onto his back.

Locking my arms around his neck and my legs around his waist, I knew that this was now a game of will. "Time to die, Cammon." I whispered in his ear, but I knew they all could hear me. I knew they all could see what was about to happen.

I closed my arms down on his windpipe with everything I had in me, and squeezed his middle, cutting off his air in two places. He bellowed—which was stupid as he only lost more air—and clawed at my arms with his dirty fucking nails, blood and flesh ripping under them.

He reached back and grabbed at my hair, but he had no flexibility to reach me, tucked as close to his back as I was.

"Do something, rip her off your back you fool!" Teeter yelled.

"Kill her!"

"Fuck her up!"

Those were my people, once. And now they were out for my blood—they wanted to see me raped and killed.

Because I was a woman—because they'd always hated that I'd led them instead of someone with a cock and balls.

Cammon spun and I kept my head tucked tight, my arms and legs clenching with everything I had. Elka came into view as we spun. Her eyes were bright, and I saw the fierce wolf in her, how hard she was fighting to hold back leaping in to help.

Because wolves fought at each other's sides, not at each other's throats.

"Hold!" She screamed, "You got him, Diana! Don't you fucking let go!"

I grinned. Gods, she was the one, if there was ever any doubt, it washed away with the fury of her words supporting me.

My brothers—they were at the very edge of the circle, their bodies tense. "Lock him down!" Dominic growled.

They all had worry etched on their faces but Raven... he was grinning. Pride shone in his eyes as I looked to him, and that feeling rolled between us.

I could almost hear his voice.

You got this, Frostbite.

Cammon, of course, took that moment to try and turn the tables. He rushed out of the ring and toward a tree. Fuck. I gritted my teeth and breathed out, trying to make myself smaller before we hit. I knew what was coming.

"Allowed!" Gabe bellowed, "Stay out of their way."

Cammon spun and slammed himself—and me—

into the tree trunk. Bark and splinters busted through my shirt, jabbing deep. Ribs cracked, shooting bolts of pain through my torso. He stumbled forward and then rushed back, slamming me against the tree again.

Pain erupted through the entire length of my body each time he went flying backward, using me as a battering ram. My bones rattled and groaned, some of them breaking.

The urge to sink my teeth into the back of his neck almost overcame me as I fought to stay latched to his back.

Four times, five, six...I couldn't let go. I refused to give in. I would not let this man destroy my family, my home, the people I loved.

"You got that bitch! One more, Cammon!" Teeter yelled.

It was time to make my move.

As Cammon started back toward the tree, as fast as ever, I let my legs unhook from around his waist.

"You got her now, she's relaxing!"

No, he fucking well didn't have me. Time to show them just how fast I was.

Ignoring the pain lashing me, I ran *backward* up the tree as he got us close, and then leapt sideways, taking Cammon's neck and head with me, putting everything I had into twisting his neck. My hand found his jaw, and I pulled for all I was worth, my body weight help-ing me.

The crack of his spine was as loud as a lightning bolt

striking a tree, and about as shocking, I think, at least for Teeter.

Cammon's head lolled loosely, and he went to his knees as I released his neck. I could have let him drop, but instead I reached over and grabbed his greasy hair, holding him steady on his knees.

His heartbeat was still going. He was alive. For the moment.

"For those who think a queen is weak. For those who thought to stage a coup, let this be a lesson to you." I turned and dragged Cammon's limp body with me. He wasn't dead yet, which made him a lot more useful for the example I was about to make of him. I pulled him all the way back to the center of the circle, ignoring the wounds in my back, ignoring the way I struggled to breathe.

I stood there and made sure to lock eyes with Teeter first, then the others on that side of the ring. Even Mary.

Then I wrapped my fingers around Cammon's windpipe, dug my fingers in deep, all the way till I could feel the edge of his spine—and then and only then did I pull, ripping his throat clean out—showing dominance in a wolf pack in every sense of the word. His flesh dripped in my hand as his body slid sideways, the sound of his heart finally stopping.

I threw Cammon's throat to the ground and stood over it.

"I will not be defied, nor will any leader who follows me. Right now, you will bend your knees to your queen, or I will consider you a traitor, and have you executed before dawn. No burial rights, no trials. But a leader as you wish to have—violent and prone to killing to prove a point."

The gasps that rumbled through the other side did not bother me.

I stood and waited.

Easily half dropped to their knees, their heads bowed. But the other half? Teeter and his gang were gone before I could tell my guards to gather them up. No surprise there.

"They are traitors to the crown," I said. "And will be marked as such."

Those on their knees were trembling.

I turned to look at Elka. "I am still queen, and, as such, I take this moment to name my successor. Elka of Clan Killian...will you step to the throne when the time comes for me to pass the crown?"

Gasps slid through the clearing.

Elka stepped into the ring and went to one knee. "My queen, I humbly accept this offer."

I nodded, the relief fleeting, already knowing what I had to ask next. "And the traitors, do you agree with me that they should all be slaughtered for their treachery?"

She lifted her head and met my gaze, the first test as soon-to-be-queen at her feet. I could only hope she understood just what I was offering her.

CHAPTER 19

Raven

"Did you know she would offer them a fair trial?"

I worked my fingers across Diana's scalp as she sat in the tub, soaking. As much as I'd feared for her life during the fight, I'd also seen the powerful, brilliant woman she was—not that any of that was a surprise to me. I'd known for a long time that she was perhaps the most amazing soul I'd ever met.

Diana made a soft mewling sound in the back of her throat as she leaned into my hands. Gods, she distracted me, and I could barely think what question I'd asked her as she answered.

"I had a strong feeling she would. Her family is very fair, and she was raised with a sense of justice that is evident in all she does. All the clans will see what I did as a leader overstepping, and what she did as a correction of that overstep. It will help her be seen as the right person for the job." Diana tipped her head to the side, laying her cheek against my arm. "You helped, you know, distracting Cammon."

I grunted, thinking of that werewolf made me want to tear holes in him adding to the damage that my Frostbite had inflicted. "I did little but be myself. He just didn't much like me. Funny, that."

Her laugh was soft and warmed me through, chasing away cobwebs of uncertainty. "You being yourself has gotten you into more than one fight."

"If you recall it has gotten me into your bed, as well." I kissed the top of her head and stepped back as she took a half-hearted swat at me. All I cared about was the fact that she was healed—courtesy of Sienna and a healthy dose of blood. I could feel her fatigue and lingering aches, but the broken ribs, cracked spine, and punctured organs were no more. The worst was done.

"Now what?" I grabbed the large, pre-warmed towel from the basket and draped it over Diana as she stood, water sluicing down her curves. My fangs and cock reacted, and I couldn't help but drag Diana out of the tub and crush her to my body as I kissed along her wet neck. "Forget I asked any questions, just let me fuck you ragged."

She tipped her hips against me and let out a soft sigh as my fingers found their way between her legs, to the silken folds that begged to be spread, begged to be worshiped.

"Raven...we have a meeting."

"I can be quick...okay, maybe not quick, but I can surely have us both satisfied in under an hour."

She let me take her weight as I slid a finger along her wet warmth, teasing. "Maybe an hour and a half."

A knock on the door had her pulling from me. "Yes?"

"A reminder, my queen, the meeting is in twenty minutes."

Diana let out a sigh and called out. "Of course. Thank you, Julia."

"Do you want help dressing?"

I nipped at Diana's neck, and she didn't swat me away this time.

"No, I'll be fine, thank you, Julia." How she kept her voice steady...I wouldn't have been able to. "Raven. You have to stop; we have to get ready."

"Is that a command?" I let my hands skim the body of my mate, knowing that there was no time for how I wanted to worship her.

"Yes." She smiled and stepped back, the towel dropping. "I have to get dressed, and you need to get control of yourself." She motioned at my crotch and I looked down.

"You don't want me to get...a hold of myself maybe? Or would you rather get a hold of me?"

Her lips quirked up, and her green eyes danced with light. "Get ready, Raven." Gods, to see her smiling, to know that the worst of her time as queen had passed, it eased my fears for her. For us.

I made myself turn and leave her to get ready in peace. If I stayed, there was no doubt we'd make the meeting start late. Making my way to the great room, I was surprised to see that I was the first one there.

No, that wasn't quite right...

"Who are you? That Lochlin fellow said he'd be right back! He couldn't hear me!"

I spun to see a hologram of Rabia, the queen of the Angels, sitting on her throne.

"Your Majesty," I bowed deeply. "Apologies, I arrived early for the meeting, not expecting anyone to have arrived already."

She huffed and waved a hand, deep silver feathers dangling from her wrist. The end of each feather was tipped with a violent red, as if freshly dipped into blood. "I'm not exactly here, am I? This technology is marvelous, but fickle, like so many things in our world." Her eyes latched onto me. "You didn't answer with your name."

"My apologies, I was startled only. My name is Raven, my home is...or was on the mainland in Seattle."

"Ah, you are the one that I heard has finally thawed the ice queen's heart?"

I grinned wide, not feeling any threat from Queen Rabia, only curiosity. The truth was, the old queen was known to see love lines between people, so it was rather nice that the bond between myself and Diana was visible to her, even without Diana here. "Is that what you call her? Funny, I nicknamed her Frostbite."

Her laughter filled the room, as she tipped her head back. "Ah, you are a charmer! So fascinating that she lost her heart to you, of all the men who sought her hand when she first took the throne."

As interesting as that was, and as much as I wished to ask more about Diana's early years as heir, we were joined by an out of breath Lochlin. "Your Majesty, can you hear me now?"

"Yes, yes, I've been chatting with Raven here. I must tell Diana that I approve. I always love to see fated mates find one another." Her smile was genuine, but it was Lochlin who choked.

"Fated...holy fuck. Pardon my language." He bowed but tipped his head to look at me, the question still hanging between us.

There was naught that I could do but shrug. "She doesn't know, don't tell her."

Rabia clapped her hands. "Oh, we won't interfere, will we, Lochlin?"

He about choked again as Diana swept into the room, wearing a deep red gown that dipped dangerously low and had me staring hard. Very rarely did she let her body be on display, as she felt she always had to prove herself, particularly to the men.

"Rabia, thank you for coming. I am deeply sorry for what happened at the last meeting." Diana stopped just shy of the other queen and dipped into a curtsy, sweeping her skirts wide.

"Why do you curtsy to me, ice queen?" Rabia

tapped her chin with one gnarled finger. "But more, why do you apologize for the little tart who did the damage? You did not set her up to behave that way."

Diana nodded. "To answer both, I curtsy to a queen I respect. And I apologize because the disrespect happened at the meeting I had invited you to attend."

Rabia sighed.

As they'd spoken, the others filed into the room. Gabe was still present, as was Will and Bethany, Dominic and Sienna, and of course, Myrr. Theo was not with her, seeing as he was not actually part of this discussion, despite his time with us thus far. The last to enter was Elka. Rabia looked toward the young werewolf. "And who is this?"

"Princess Elka, please meet Queen Rabia of the Winged Seraphs."

Rabia laughed. "You remembered! We weren't always angels, any more than the demons are demons, eh cousin?" She winked, fucking *winked* at Gabe. "Well met, young Elka. So, you are the successor to the throne?"

Elka dipped into a curtsy, spreading her skirts wide and dropping far lower than Diana had. "Yes, Your Majesty. Your wisdom and grace precede you. I am deeply honored to meet you and look forward to working with you in the future."

Rabia clapped her hands again. "I like her, Diana. Very much. Well chosen!"

Myrr grunted. "Well obviously, I knew she was the right one too!"

My lips quirked. Was Myrr *jealous*?

"We need to discuss why we are all here," Diana said. "Much as I would love to visit, we have a problem that none of us can solve on our own."

"Cleona is the problem," Rabia said, "And one that we must solve. I read all the paperwork that Lochlin here sent to me. After discussing with my advisors and consulting the stones, we agree. We must all combine our skills and strengths if we are to save our world, and the human's."

Diana let out a breath, but it was Bethany that spoke up.

"Perhaps we can slip some mushrooms into her food before we speak to her next? Something hallucinogenic perhaps?"

Sienna choked on a laugh. "She is allergic to mushrooms! You know that!"

Bethany blinked her big blue eyes a few times, looking cagey. "Are you sure?"

Rabia nodded. "Ah, you must be William's young bride? You noticed that Cleona is...taken with your husband?"

Bethany's eyes flashed blue fire. "She can get taken right off the edge of a cliff for all I care. Her successor cannot be as bad as her!"

Diana walked slowly back and forth in front of where Rabia's hologram was set up. "We don't know who

Cleona's successor is. No one does. We need to find a way to convince her to help us."

Bethany huffed. "I'd rather that volcano she sits on top of busted its cap."

I blinked a few times. "What did you say?"

"That the volcano blows its lid right under Cleona's ass!" Bethany snapped. "She's been sending him dirty pictures of her tits!"

William grimaced. "I've not seen any of them, love, and even if I did, I don't care about her. I love you."

I waved my hands, getting their attention. "She's sitting on a volcano. You're sure? One thousand percent sure, Bee?"

Bethany frowned. "Yes. It's in all the topography of the Territories. The only mountain here that's considered a volcano is the one that Cleona's castle sits on."

Her words rattled through me, and it was my turn to pace. I had to tell them about my visit with Nefir when I was dying, when the bloodworms had almost taken me.

"Raven? What is it?" Diana put her hand on my arm, no doubt feeling my agitation through the mate bond.

"Let me gather my thoughts."

"Ah, just spit them out!" Myrr snapped. "It's late and I want a hot toddy and a donut before bed."

I turned so I faced them all. "Do you know who Nefir is? All of you?"

Rabia and Elka shook their heads, so I quickly filled them in on his connection to the dark goddess, never using her name.

"When I was...dying from the bloodworm, Nefir visited me in my dreams. I didn't mention it before because Diana had a lot on her plate already, and I wanted to wait until things here stabilized before adding more wood to the dumpster fire." Diana sucked in a sharp breath; I pressed on. "But in the dream, Nefir took me to a high mountain and the short version is, the dark goddess isn't just a dark goddess...she's a fire goddess. And when her full powers return to her, she will call all the fire to the surface. Every mountain with any connection to lava will blow. She'll burn the world down for whatever vengeance she's enacting. And that will include Cleona's Mount Guisala. Of all of us, she is actually the least safe if the dark goddess regains all her powers."

The silence only lasted for a few seconds before someone started to laugh. I spun to see Rabia giggling, slapping her leg as if we were playing poker and she'd just won her hand. "Oh, this is too rich! Too rich! That little brat will have to come crawling back!"

"But why would she believe us?" Elka asked. "What proof have we?"

A question that would have to wait as glass shattering and a ball of flame shooting through the window interrupted the meeting.

"Get down!" I leapt for Diana, pulling her out of the way of the fireball as it went straight for her.

The fireball sailed over us, bouncing off the far wall and landing in an armchair. It had been aimed at me.

The cold tile against my back grounded me. "That was too close."

Raven helped me up and we rushed to the now-smashed window. Brisk air battered at the heavy curtains that were ablaze, sparks skittering as they flapped in the wind. Dom made quick work of yanking them free of their rods and stomping out the flames even as Gabe and Nicholas managed the roaring blaze that had once been an armchair.

I stared out into the moonlit night to see three hundred or more werewolves on horseback, torches held high in one hand, swords in the other. Off to the side, a dozen or more of the keep's night guards stood, most tied up, a few flat on the ground, obviously injured...Two holding the ropes that bound the others.

More traitors who had worked against me. My gut clenched with fury and disgust, but I forced myself to take a calming breath as I turned toward the hologram.

"Rabia, we've got a bit of situation here..."

"I can see that," she said, eyes wide. "Now that I know we've got my cousin by the balls so to speak, I'm content to move forward as allies. Reach out when your business there is handled and we can talk details."

Her image flickered away, and I muttered a silent prayer of thanks for small favors as I turned to stare out the window again.

"Fuckers," Raven snarled. "I interviewed all the interior staff after the poisoning incident, but only made it partway through the massive list of soldiers and guards."

"It's not your fault, Raven," I murmured through numb lips. "The movement has been growing faster every day. Like someone has been pouring fuel—"

"There she is! The Queen of the Werewolves," a booming voice from the center of the mass of people called. A familiar voice... "We only brought a small force, *Your Majesty*, but trust that there are others. At least as many to the east and to the west, flanking us, awaiting a signal, if you try to send out soldiers."

By the time I searched out the speaker, I already knew who I'd find, and I couldn't say I was surprised. But still, a last bit of my heart broke away, whatever final piece I'd still hoped for a friendship with the man who'd been my friend so long ago.

"Hello, Maverick."

Raven's entire body tensed beside me as Maverick dug his heels into his mount, nudging the animal forward to cut a path to the front of the crowd.

"I like how you're hiding in the middle of the pack when you're not sure if you're going to be ambushed, because you're a chicken shit," Raven called, fangs gleaming in the moonlight as his lips parted in a chilling smile. "You might be a weak, pathetic excuse for a man, but at least you're consistent."

"The Holmgang is complete, Maverick," I added. "I won fair and square, and Elka will be crowned queen in the coming days. There is no reason for any of this. You're starting a war...risking lives, tearing my people apart, when I've already surrendered my position."

"Sorry, Diana," Maverick replied, not looking sorry at all. "It's too late for that. At first, I thought you'd grown, and I was stunned. How could such an easily manipulated woman who couldn't wait to spread her legs for a stranger with a few kind words have become Queen? For a minute there, I almost thought you were worthy of my affections...that I could rule with you by my side. And then I saw you with that abomination and realized you were still the same old Diana. Letting her soft heart and wet pussy be her guide—"

It was only Dom and Will's quick hands that stopped Raven from leaping out the window, and even that was a close thing. It took both of them to hold him as he roared and strained to get free.

Me, on the other hand? I was surprised to find myself growing colder and calmer with every word the wormy bastard spoke. The shard throbbed and pulsed, like a living, breathing promise inside me.

I would have his head before this was over.

It wasn't a question of *if* anymore. It was only a question of *when*.

"If he won't listen, I'll at least try to talk some sense into the rest of them," Elka murmured as she shouldered her way between me and Raven to face the crowd of dissenters, head held high. "You've had a lot to say this night, human. But I wish to speak to *my* people now. I see many faces from the crowd at the Holmgang. Please know that I'm committing every one of them to memory, as you've taken my generous offer of a fair trial and thrown it back in my face with this treasonous coup. And at the behest of a human, no less?" She shook her head slowly, letting out a bitter laugh. "You all, who were up in arms because our queen was adopted into her clan. That's rich. What it shows me is that you're all hypocrites."

Despite my ice-cold fury, I couldn't deny the wash of pride that flowed through me at Elka's bold words. She was proving my choice right every time she opened her mouth.

But the good feelings didn't last long as Mav's lips twisted into a leer so different from the simpering, regretful sap who had spent the past months begging my forgiveness.

"Oh, did you guys not get the memo?" he asked, leading his horse into a tight circle as he shot a wave over his shoulder to the wolves behind him. "Diana, maybe ask your bloodsucker boyfriend, why don't you? I nearly bested him sparring the other day. If you hadn't interfered—" Raven barked a mirthless laugh, and Maverick broke off with a snarl. "Fuck you, Raven! I'm no longer just some pathetic human for you supernatural creatures to use and abuse at your whim like you've done for the entirety of my family's recorded existence. I've always been smarter than you, but now I'm faster and stronger too. And moreover, I understand these people. I *am* these people. They want a strong, male alpha to lead them." He raised his fist high. "And upon the full moon, after my turning ceremony, I will *be* that alpha. Tonight, we take the keep. Tomorrow, we take the crown!"

The men and women around broke into cheers, whoops, and howls that made my stomach burn with bile. I wished I could say it didn't hurt, but it was like a kick straight to the belly. This faithless bastard would have the honor of a wolf taking residence inside him while mine had been stripped from me, along with my crown? His silver tongue had manipulated them into believing his bullshit, to the point that they would make him...one of them?

What was this torture?

"He's always been slick, I'll give him that," Myrr

muttered from behind me as she craned to see Mav working the crowd.

"I should've killed him when I had the chance."

"We needed him, Raven," I reminded him softly. "Without him we'd never have found Jade or the shard."

Once I realized he'd never truly changed, it had been that very thought that had saved me from deep regret. As much as I hated him now, he'd been part of our journey and we were that much closer to defeating Lilis because of it.

But I'd brought him here, regardless of my reasons. And, as I watched his supporters—*my* people—celebrate his impassioned speech, I couldn't help but feel a twinge of pity for them. I'd fallen victim to him once myself, long ago. All it took was a scared, lonely soul and that silver-tongued bastard telling you what you wanted to hear, and boom. He had you in the palm of his hand.

"Fuck this," Elka muttered under her breath. "As your future queen, hear me now!" she shouted, pausing as the cheers died down. "This can go one of two ways. Either you cease this madness and turn on your de facto leader who's been nothing but trouble since he's arrived." She scanned the faces out on the ground slowly, methodically, and even I had to admit it was intimidating. "Or you can bet against me. But if you bet against me, know this. You'll forever be my enemy. And I swear on my brother Jordan's soul, I will rain hellfire upon each and every one of you if it takes me a thousand years to finish the job. There is nowhere you can hide that I won't find you. Mark me."

The silence was complete, the stillness absolute, as if even the woodland creatures and birds awaited some reply. And then it happened. A movement, out of the corner of my eye. Ranata Grayson, a few yards from Maverick, lowered her sword and turned to her husband.

"I know how you feel, Dougal. But the girl...she's something special. And she's one of ours, born into a clan proper like. We are on the cusp of a civil war. There's no turning back once brothers and sisters start killing one another. Maybe we need to reconsider..."

Mav yanked on the reins, sending his horse rearing up onto its back legs before galloping over towards the Grayson clan. Dougal put his arm in front of his wife and pushed her behind him, a fierce scowl on his bearded face as he pointed the sword tip directly at Mav's chest.

"My wife wants me and mine to walk away, so we walk away. I recommend you don't try to stop us."

Other clans in the crowd began to shift from foot to foot, looking around anxiously, and then raising their gazes to Maverick.

"Make a move," I muttered under my breath, "make one move, and you lose them all."

But Mav was quick-witted if he was anything good at all, and he recognized his predicament in the nick of time. He had their loyalty...until he came for one of their own, which I, unfortunately, was not. And maybe I'd never truly been. I would nurse that heartache later. For now, I needed to be glad as the crowd started to thin and the hundreds before me slowly thinned out by a third as the Vargas and Ferral clans joined the Graysons.

"Don't try to stop them," Maverick called to the others, as if he'd made the decision as opposed to having the decision made for him. "A man who lets a woman lead him around by the nose is no loss to me. Just like in poker, we let the weak hands fold. We're left with nothing but aces now."

He turned back to face us again, his smile wavering before returning full force.

"As I said before, Diana. This is a fraction of those who oppose you. Our numbers here have dwindled, so you live for one more day. But make no mistake, after the fourth full moon tomorrow, we'll be back with the rest, and stronger than ever. And once we're done dismantling you and yours, we'll make sure that this Territory is led by a male alpha who is committed to bringing back the days of old." He turned toward his still-impressive crowd and raised a fist once again. "Down with the Queen!"

The wolves around him echoed his cry as he wheeled around and kicked his horse into a canter. We all watched as his army followed.

It was Gabe who finally broke the silence. "I never fucking liked that guy."

"Same." It was the echo of several others, including Myrr, and I couldn't help but let out a snort.

"And again, I remind you that we needed him to find Jade. But now..." I turned to face the others—my friends, my family, my soon-to-be queen, and my...Raven—and smiled. "Now, he's fucked."

"What's the plan, Frostbite?" Raven asked, already flexing and ready for action.

"We can win the war, sister," Will chimed in. "Say the word. My army can be here in twenty-four hours and will squash them like bugs."

Dom nodded in agreement, but I held up a staying hand. "No need for all that. Like Ranata said, a civil war is ugly. It leaves a stain on its people...a sob that echoes for centuries."

"What then?" Elka asked, eyes blazing with fury. "We have to do something."

And we would. It would be my last act as queen, and I found myself nearly trembling in anticipation. Maverick would become a werewolf over my dead body... or his.

"It's simple," I said with a shrug. "We cut the head off the snake before its venom comes in."

CHAPTER 21

Raven

The long grass rustled as I crawled another inch forward. A light rain misted above, crackling against the bonfire that raged just a dozen yards upwind of us. We'd taken precautions by dousing ourselves in wolf-scent, but the wet earth and woodsmoke were like gifts from the gods, further concealing our presence from those sharp-nosed fuckers.

I paused, peeking through the grass as I gave Dom a moment to catch up.

Teeter and his crew danced and shouted all around the fire, half ritual and half premature celebration. It was still early evening, but the ale flowed freely in anticipation of that night's full moon. There were only about thirty or so wolves in this area, immediately in front of the cottage Maverick was holed up in, just as Gabe had promised. Despite the demons typically trying to keep things neutral, he had done us a solid by running a quick recon mission, following Maverick and the others off the grounds of the keep the night before at Diana's request.

It was a brilliant play out of her, because, while they'd had a contingent of soldiers watching their six on their way out, they hadn't even glanced at the night skies. They'd just led Gabe straight to their camp, a clearing deep in the eastern part of the forest. Even better, while there were dozens of makeshift shelters and tents about a half mile further into the forest, it seemed that Maverick had stayed true to form and greatly exaggerated the size of his unseen forces. Gabe had clocked only a couple hundred in camp, including the thirty-odd "guards" howling and causing a ruckus around the fire.

Hopefully, once we cut the head off the snake as Diana said, the movement would fizzle and die. But if not, I liked our odds, even if Will didn't call his army. Diana had a good number of supporters herself, not to mention those who now backed Elka. Plus, we had Sienna, who could call on her Hunter, if it came to that.

The two queens had chosen scalpel over warhammer...for now. But it gave me comfort knowing we had options.

"They're completely distracted and already starting to come unglued. We've got to make our move," Dom murmured. "We have an hour or so before the moon shows its face. And as much as there's no one I'd rather fight beside than you, we do *not* want to get caught out here once that happens."

He was right. Soon, every werewolf in the kingdom

would shift and go feral, and we'd find it almost impossible to escape, never mind being able to kidnap their human leader before his changing ceremony.

We moved in silent sync toward a cluster of trees and then paused to examine the cottage that was our target. While the front door was in plain view of the men by the fire, the back was completely unguarded, just as Gabe had promised.

I tugged the rope and long piece of cloth from my bag, tossing both over my shoulder as we crept toward the house. Then, I raised three fingers, locking eyes with Dom as I ticked them off.

3, 2, 1–

Pushing the door open, eyes darting all around as I strode silently into the home. A rustic kitchen opened before us, and we crept, painfully slowly, over to the hallway.

A quick glance at Dom to make sure he was with me. I was still surprised after all these years at how quietly he could move. His massive frame was built for anything but stealth, but the countless decades of training made him almost impossible to hear, even with my enhanced senses.

I held in a breath as I turned the corner, ready for anything that came our way, but the hall was empty, too. I scanned the three closed doors, sucking in a quiet whiff of the still air. A quick wave of bloodlust rolled through me as Maverick's odor pricked at my senses, but I tamped it down.

His scent was the most prominent, which meant there likely weren't any wolves in the room with him, and I breathed a sigh of relief. Thanks to Gabe and his scouting ahead of time, this was going to go down without a hitch.

I jabbed my finger at the middle door, and we both closed in. This time, it was Dom who did the counting.

No stealth here.

Dom just hurled his massive shoulder into the wood as I launched myself at a stunned Maverick, who sat in front of a crackling fire.

He opened his mouth to yell, but I shoved the balled-up strip of cloth into his mouth before he'd even registered what was happening.

He struggled at first, but I let my fangs snap free of my gums and leaned closer. "Elka and Diana want to interrogate you first, but just give me a reason, Maverick," I growled.

His narrow, defiant eyes locked onto mine. Then, to my everlasting disappointment, he nodded and went still.

Dom's hand was nothing more than a flash as he sent a brutal karate chop to the back of the man's neck, sending Maverick instantly into dreamland.

I looked at Dom, who just shrugged.

"They just said don't kill him yet. They didn't say anything about hurting him. No point in wasting energy if he decides to start struggling again."

"See, this is why I like going to battle with you. I miss this."

I bent to bind Mav's wrists together with the rope, and then tossed him over my shoulder like the faithless sack of shit he was.

"That's a wrap. Let's head out."

But the words were barely out of my mouth when Dom's arm shot out to keep me in place.

The high-pitched creak of a rusty hinge cut through the air, and I held my breath as footsteps clomped through the hall. Dom glided toward the door, dropping into a fighting stance as the sound grew closer.

My muscles tensed as the footsteps came to a stop, the last sound coming from just outside of the door. "Mav? You good?"

Movement erupted on my shoulder all at once as Maverick began to flail wildly, screaming as much as the gag allowed, and my heartbeat thrummed heavily in my ears.

Dom sprang through the door before the visitor could step into the room, slamming his elbow into the other man's jaw with a sickening thud. The werewolf dropped like a ton of bricks, his skull bouncing off the wood floor.

Dom and I leapt over the fallen man, dashing toward the back door. I had to strain to hear behind us as we ran and was satisfied by the lack of sound when we reached the trees.

A perfect escape?

A deafening howl split the air as if in answer, and I

broke into a full-on sprint. "The time for stealth is done. Let's fucking go!"

* * *

Maverick glared at me through beady slits as I circled his chair. "This is pointless, you know. We might have had some softies in the mix, but all that's left are rabid supporters who blame Diana for every bad thing that's ever happened to them in their miserable lives. They'll come for me...and for her. Only a short while until—"

Maverick cut off with a grunt as I yanked the rope at his wrists with everything I had, relishing the touch of white that crept into his hands as it tightened. Diana had been clear. She hoped to find out where Maverick's magic had come from and to learn of any other plans he might have put in motion. Elka had been even more clear, demanding the names of all those who had betrayed Diana beyond redemption. Maverick was to be spared until those ends were met, but as soon as Nicholas had relieved him of all his secrets...

"He's good to go," I said, nodding at Nicholas as he approached.

Maverick shrank back at the sight of him, but the young vampire paid him no heed, dropping a hand to his shoulder.

Diana took a step forward, eyes bright with anticipation as Maverick went stock still, head rolling back.

"I need to know what this magic is that he possesses,"

she whispered, watching Maverick's face like a hawk. "Show me, Nicholas."

An image sprang into existence as if from nothing, etched into the air like a too-realistic hologram. Fog rolled up from the ground, stopping abruptly at the edge of the memory as Maverick's inner thoughts were laid bare. A dense, misty forest, with mushrooms the size of bushes. A witch with a hut born from a seed.

It was almost a live-action dream, a deft skimming of the past, like a movie at double speed. We all watched in growing horror and disgust as he pleaded with the witch whose name he did not know. Watched him deceive her and earn her pity. Watched him fuck her and rob her blind, taking what seemed to be her most valued possession.

And the longer it went on, the more unbearable my rage became. I could see my own Diana in this poor woman. My own Diana, and the soft heart this mother-fucker had destroyed—

"It's—" Nicholas sucked in a breath, unsteady on his feet as the image flickered and faded. "He's fighting it, and it's taxing..."

"What did the grimoire and the dagger do for him?" Diana encouraged even as Maverick shook his head furiously.

The image flickered back into view, only this time, Maverick was older, looking much the same as he did now. He was seated at a table, staring down at his hand that trembled and shook. He gulped down something from a medicine bottle and, finding it empty, hurled it against the wall where it shattered into a thousand pieces.

"That *bitch* thinks she's outsmarted me. I *will* find a way to end the curse and grow my power. I just have to—"

The real-life version of Maverick began to jerk and twitch, eyes rolling back in his head even as Nicholas staggered backward.

"A moment," he managed, his voice raspy as he dropped to the stone floor of the great room.

Maverick continued seizing until I shot a hand out and clapped him hard in the cheek. Then, he stopped and stared at me in mulish silence.

"You're making this much harder than it needs to be," I muttered. "Let the man do his job and we can all move on."

Well, maybe not *all* of us...

"It's a rather chilling power..." Elka murmured, studying the clearly exhausted Nicholas with concern. "I've never seen anything like it."

"It's taking a toll on both of them," Sienna said. "Should I—?" She broke off and shot Diana a questioning glance.

"Yes. Let's give Nicholas a short break while Sienna tends to him. As for Maverick, he doesn't deserve your gift. If he doesn't survive the interrogation, so be it."

Diana waved the rest of us away, leaving Sienna with Nicholas and Dom keeping watch over Maverick.

"I guess we now know the source of Mav's longevity."

Gabe turned to Diana. "I know you were in possession of the dagger at one point, but what about the grimoire? In all your travels with him, have any of you ever seen evidence of it?"

"I still have the dagger." Diana's hand went to the sheath at her hip. "That's how I was able to drive the dark goddess back. But the grimoire..."

She turned to me and eyed me thoughtfully. "I don't recall ever seeing it."

I shook my head. "If he's had it with him this whole time, he hid it well."

"We are running short on time," Diana said, her anxious gaze shifting to the sky above and then to Elka, who had begun to pace with restless energy.

"The moon is upon us," she confirmed with a nod. "We've got five minutes or less."

Gabe's silvery brows rose high on his forehead as he stared at her. "Shouldn't you be locked up somewhere then?"

"Diana's scientists created a dagger that allows the wearer to control whether they shift during the full moon. She gave it to me since she..." Elka trailed off, shooting Diana an apologetic glance, but Diana just shrugged.

"Since I no longer need it."

I spoke up then, the ticking of the grandfather clock in

the corner of the room seeming louder with every passing second. "If we want more information, now is the time to get it, before the wolves go off the rails out there. If Nick can't continue, I'm happy to extract it the old-fashioned way..." I cracked my knuckles and let my fangs poke free.

"Nicholas?" Diana turned to face the vampire, who was now on his feet looking a little steadier.

The vampire murmured his thanks to Sienna, and then dipped his head. "Ready for another round."

A quiet Maverick grew animated again, fighting against his restraints. "Look, whatever he's doing is worsening my condition. I'll do anything if he agrees to stop probing," he managed, sliding the few inches away that his restraints would allow. "How about a deal? You ask, and I'll answer. Simple. The bloodsucker can verify the truth without going so deep, yes?"

A weary Nicholas turned to Diana, and she dipped her head in assent.

"Just know that I do this for Nicholas's comfort, not for yours. Let's give it a try, shall we? Question one: whatever malady she cursed you with, it's worsening, yes?"

"Yes. When I'm on the mainland, it's not so bad, but I also can't access the magic. Here, I have more power, but the curse is taking over more rapidly." His voice broke as he looked out the window and then turned his pleading gaze on Diana. "I've tried everything to get it to stop, Di—"

"Enough!" Her lip curled in disgust. "Stick to the facts." She shot a look to Nicholas, who nodded.

"He's telling the truth," Nicholas said after a short moment of contact with our prisoner's shoulder.

Diana stared Maverick down, her cold gaze drilling into him. "Have you ever cared for anyone but yourself at all, Maverick? What of Opal?"

He averted his gaze, staring into the dark stone of the keep's wall for a long moment before answering. "I wanted to return to the Territories so I could use the magic in my possession without suffering the full effects of the curse. I thought the shard might have power, they glowed and danced when they went into the girls, I could see the magic. So, I took Opal with me and decided to wait..."

Diana let out a low gasp. "Until she died so you could take it. Did you even try to help her at all?"

"You make it sound so terrible." Anger flickered in his eyes, and he let out a grunt. "I didn't kill her, did I? There was no helping her, anyway. It was clear the shard was too strong for her."

Nicholas laid his hand on Maverick and again nodded. "All true."

"So now the plan is to have Teeter and the others complete the changing ceremony, correct?"

"It is...it was."

"Not a lie."

Diana let out a dry laugh. "Should've taken my offer all those years ago when you had the chance. Because I can guarantee you it won't be happening now." She opened her mouth to ask another question, but Nicholas held out an arm, cutting her off with a frown.

"Something...is amiss." He closed his eyes and gripped Maverick more tightly. An image flickered into view as Maverick bucked and twisted, trying to wrestle his arm away. Maverick standing over Gavin Barrach's dead wolf, dagger in one hand, an open book in the other, even as Gavin's widow Mary and the others of her clan circled around him.

My muscles tensed as Diana's face contorted in horror.

"We need better restraints!"

I spun around just in time to see Maverick's body twist and contort, but it was too late. He exploded into a mountain of dark brown fur before my very eyes, a guttural roar tearing free of his throat.

I looked up, preparing to end it in a single heart strike, when I stopped short. Where even *was* his heart? Maverick's wolf was *massive,* three times the size of the largest I'd ever seen, with thick sable fur stretched taut over bulging, oversized muscles. Purple, vein-like lines snaked out from his blood-red eyes, which seemed to glow with unholy power.

And, crazier yet?

The white blaze on his head and muzzle.

He was Gavin. Gavin *was* Maverick. Even their scent was the same...only the two had melded into a ghoulish mix of magic and might. He'd transformed himself into a true *monster*. A zombie wolf, whose size and strength put all others to shame.

The creature lunged for Nicholas, but Elka's wolf threw itself between them, taking the brunt of a brutal blow that sent her spinning across the room to smack against the wall with a whimper. I had to admire her bravery—befitting of a queen—but she was no match for the monster before us.

As if by tacit agreement, Dom, Will, and I formed a circle around him even as Diana and Gabe dropped low into fighting stance. As Maverick took a glance around and sized us up, I realized something else. He looked confused, maybe a bit disoriented, but the man was still in there...

He tossed back his head and let out a howl that shook the rafters. Then, he leapt twenty feet in the air, clear over us, and took a running dive through the freshly replaced picture window he'd thrown a fireball into the day before. We all stared out the open window, stunned. It wasn't until a few seconds later, when the lights overhead went dark and the low hum of the heating units quieted, that Dom broke the silence.

"He cut the fucking power."

That's when it all truly clicked into place. Maverick's wolf had the ability to reason. The separation that typically made werewolves unpredictable in their animal state —especially during the full moon, *especially* the first few times shifting—didn't exist in this abomination. He was the most lethal combination of brains *and* brawn. That was why so many of Diana's brethren had followed him.

He was the apex predator.

The Alpha.

Once he truly got his wolf legs under him? He would be a killing machine. And wasn't that a kick in the dick.

Will cleared his throat and shot his sister a questioning look.

"So...maybe it's time to call in that army now?"

I stared out the window, still in shock at what we'd all just witnessed, but knowing there was little time for any of us to process those feelings. There were decisions to be made, and time was of the essence.

"Even if we had comms and could contact your soldiers, Will, I'm afraid there isn't time for them to mobilize and make it here to be of any help. We've got to assume that as soon as they shift back and regroup, they will come for us. I would expect us to be at war before noon tomorrow."

I turned as Sienna made her way over to Elka, who was in her wolf form, struggling to get to her feet from where Mav had flung her.

"Dom, Sienna. Bring Elka to the infirmary and make sure she's alright. Then, have the doctor keep her sedated until the moon passes so she doesn't further injure herself. There are flashlights and lanterns in the storage room down the hall." I turned to the other two vampires in the room as I made my way around the perimeter and lit some candles. "Will and Nicholas, please check on Lochlin."

While Elka would be able to shift back to human at will due to the dagger, Loch was a different story. He'd planned to spend the night in quarantine, and I could only hope that Maverick's wolf hadn't had the where-withal to rip off the dungeon doors and take Loch on his way out.

It seemed unlikely that he'd had the time, but I'd already gravely underestimated the bastard once today, and it had proven to be catastrophic. It was a mistake I wouldn't make again.

"Do you want me and Gabe to follow him?" Raven said, moving to my side and laying a comforting hand on my hip. "I can cover the ground, Gabe the sky?"

A chorus of wild howls and frantic yips rang through the night, and I shook my head slowly. The tides and weather had already taken such a toll on these lands as to have our third full moon in less than a month. The inconsistencies of the cycle seemed to make the wolves even less predictable than usual. It was a dangerous brew.

"No. As much as I loathe letting him get away, to follow him now would be a suicide mission."

"Even with hops like that, he'd be hard pressed to catch me in the sky," Gabe reasoned with a shrug.

"It's not just him. It's all of them. Accidents happen on full moons even when times are good. Tensions are high, my people are restless, moreover, we have no idea what Mav is truly capable of yet...Besides, half the demons already hate me and mine for what happened to Malach. The last thing I need is to tell them their new king was shot out of the sky by a fireball." I shook my head again, this time, surer than ever. "I won't consider a recon mission until dawn's first light. Even then, my instinct tells me to let them bring the battle to us. I'd rather defend the keep and land I know best than fight this war on their terms."

"Maybe I can use a bit of magic to help shore up some of your defenses? Boobytrap some entrances?" Theo said, creating flames with his fingertips as he hobbled closer.

"And if not, he can act as our little human candle, can't he?" Myrr cackled as she pulled up by his side. "If anyone wants to read in bed later, Theo's your guy."

"I appreciate anything you can do to help, Theo," I said, managing a smile. It was fleeting, though, as I looked around the room at the smashed chair, the broken glass...the people staring at me, just waiting for my instruction. "If ever I doubted it was time to step aside, I doubt it no more. If I'd have just let Raven and Dom take him out before he shifted, none of this would've happened. It would all be over..."

I let out a snarl and plowed my fist directly into the

stone wall behind me, feeling no satisfaction as it cracked and spiderwebbed outward, reminding me of my vampire strength.

I could sense Raven just behind me and it took everything I had not to lean back into him. To let him comfort me when I needed it most. Instead, I turned and let out a bitter laugh.

"Mav might be a fucking sociopathic lunatic, but he was right about one thing. I was pathetic. I let him in. In my desperation to find my true, fated mate, I opened the door that led to every bit of this."

"As much as Lycan prepared you for battle and diplomacy and the ways of a monarchy, he didn't prepare you for life." I turned to see Evangeline stepping into the room. "I apologize for the interruption, but the lights went out and, when I came to see what happened, I overheard...I don't mean to pry." She glanced around the space and jerked back with a start. "What did I miss?"

My mind was firmly on her words from moments before and I waved a distracted hand at the broken window. "Maverick turned into some sort of magically enhanced super-wolf. It's a problem, but we're going to deal with it. What were you saying about my father, though?"

She frowned with one last look around the trashed room and then nodded. "I understand that you'd feel responsible for this, but I think it's high time for the whole truth..."

I stared at her in confusion.

"The truth about what?"

A regretful smile touched her lips as she continued. "When he took you in, your father feared for your safety. It caused him to keep you sheltered to the ways of the world and of men for far too long. Then, when it came time to consider handing over the throne, he demanded you find one and take him to be yours forever. It was foolish of him, and I know he regretted that dearly after the pain Maverick caused you. You don't think he knew, but he knew."

I was already shaking my head before she even finished. It was nice to hear that my father had regretted pressuring me to find a mate, but Lycan hadn't been the one to fall for Maverick's charm. "While I wish I could lay the blame elsewhere, dear Aunt, it lies only with me. I—"

"No! There are many at fault here, me included, and there is much more to this story, child. And until you hear it, I don't think you can truly grasp how little of your fate was within your control." She turned and focused her laser sharp gaze on Raven, who seemed frozen in place.

Myrr sucked her teeth and gave him a hard poke to the solar plexus with a sharp elbow.

"Speak up, boy'o. Her mind needs to be clear if she is to succeed. She has already chosen to be with you. You're indelibly tied. It would only give her comfort to know the truth."

Raven's muscular throat worked as he stared down at the ancient Oracle.

"You're sure?"

She shrugged with a raspy laugh. "As sure as I ever am."

"Someone better start telling me something," I hissed, a band of panic beginning to close around my chest like a fist, "or I'm going to start swinging now and asking questions later."

"The boy who saved you in the water that day when Edmund tried to kill you?" I held my breath, and he held my gaze. "It was me."

I heard the words, but they didn't penetrate as blood rushed to my head and my vision flickered.

"It's not possible. I...I don't understand. I was told he was dead. I was told..."

"I know, and that's because of me. The Duchess wanted to protect me—"

"As you are trying to protect me now, Raven," she interjected, crossing her arms over her chest. "But I don't need protection. Diana...look at me," she pleaded. I did, and the emotion in her eyes was nearly my undoing. "I loved you like a daughter, and still do, to this day. I couldn't risk anyone knowing it was Raven who helped you, or he'd have been hunted to the ends of the earth and gutted like a pig. Your brother was the evilest man I'd ever seen. An ocean between them would not have stopped him. No one could know the truth while Edmund still lived."

"He's been dead for months now," I managed, still drowning in a wave of emotions I couldn't even begin to untangle. I wheeled on Raven and stared at him. "How can this be? Surely, I'd have remembered your face..."

Raven's jaw clenched as he took a step back, giving me space. "You were so young, and in shock yourself, I—"

His words were cut short as Dom, Sienna, Nicholas, and Will came sailing back into the room at the same time.

"Elka is fine now and resting comfortably, and Loch is right as rain," Sienna said, slowing to a stop as she did a quick survey of our faces. "What did we just walk in on?"

"Diana just found out Raven is her fated mate," Myrr said, clapping her gnarled hands together in glee.

Sienna winced and shot a look at Dom, who let out a string of curses.

Raven stepped forward and gave Nicholas an apologetic glance. "Man...I know you're beat, and I hate to ask, but I think it would help if she could see..."

"Are you kidding me?" Nick shot back. "When you first found out what I could do you looked at me like I was worse than a serial killer," he flexed his fingers with a sudden grin. "I wouldn't miss this chance for the world. Give it here, big guy."

Raven's mouth slanted into a scowl, but he stepped forward and presented his hand. As Nicholas closed his eyes, I almost closed mine too, knowing that what I would see would change everything.

A cool summer morning. The ocean, so bright and blue, it almost hurt to look upon. Two children, an older boy and a young girl with black hair and green eyes. Me, before I'd become a wolf and they'd turned ice blue...I was being held under the water.

The boy turned and I saw his face.

Edmund.

A second boy let out a whoop and launched himself at Edmund, even as I kicked and splashed. Taking him down at the knees. Dragging him to the sand and swinging. Over and over, even as I rose to the surface, coughing and spitting.

It was only then that a dark figure emerged, a woman, darting from the trees in the distance.

The image faded, and Nicholas released Raven to swipe at the tears running down his own face. "That was beautiful," he said simply. "You can see he loved you, even then..."

"Excuse me a moment, I seem to have something in my eye," Gabe muttered, stalking out of the room.

But I barely noticed because inside my head my thoughts were spinning over one another.

Evangeline stepped forward and took my hand in hers, squeezing tightly.

What did this mean in the context of my life? What did it mean for me and Raven? He'd kept this from me for far too long, and yet, the look on his face that day... The bravery it took as a young boy to stand against a prince to save me, with no regard for his own life?

"Lies were told to protect many, and I'm sorry for that," Evangeline murmured, pulling me from my thoughts. "I made mistakes and missteps along the way. Lycan too. But everything we did, we did with the best intentions, with hearts full of love...The same way you embraced your adopted father. The same way you embraced your new people. The same way you embraced a stranger in need of help. You did nothing wrong, child, besides refusing to forgive yourself after all these years. It's time to let go of the things you could never control."

I closed my eyes and swayed in place. Images of my father flashed through my mind. The two of us fishing by the harbor. Him laughing as I wrestled with my first slippery catch as it tried to get away. Him poring over history books beside me in the library, teaching me the ways of his—our—people. The Duchess had committed a terrible crime faking my death and sending me away. But she did it out of love, and something beautiful had come of it. I'd had a beautiful life because of it. Hell, I'd been a fucking queen for a time because of it.

She'd done the same for Raven. Saving him and saving him for...me. To give me the one thing she could not give herself. The mate of her heart.

Her soft heart only made her stronger in my eyes. Maybe it was time to give myself the same grace...And maybe even extend that same grace to another.

To my fated mate.

My soft heart swelled with joy as the reality of it finally began to set in.

"Raven? I'd like to speak to you alone in my chambers," I said, ignoring the curious glances as I swept from the room.

Let them wonder. For now, there was only one person I wanted to know my heart...

CHAPTER 23

Raven

In the few minutes it took me to shower quickly and make my way down the hall to Diana's quarters, a million thoughts ran through my head. I'd been put on the spot by more than one person, but as irritated as I was with all of them, I knew they were right. It was long past time that Diana knew the truth. It hadn't made it any easier for her to hear, though.

But towards the end, when she looked at me and asked me to meet her, there'd been a softness in her eyes I hadn't seen before. Maybe it was wishful thinking, but was it too much to hope that she'd finally resigned herself to the truth? That, while she didn't *have* to be with me, her life would be better if we were together? That, thoughts of me and what we could've had would hound her for all her days if we were apart? And now that she did know the truth, would she embrace it the way I did, or mourn it as she had the loss of her wolf?

Only one way to find out.

I rapped at her door softly, and she called for me to come in. When I stepped inside, I found her standing in the natural rock pool filled with water that took up the center of the room.

Her hair hung free down her back, and she was buck naked. I stared, motionless, as my hands flexed at my sides. Gods, she was beautiful...

"Care for a swim?" she asked, softly, stepping closer until the water only lapped at her hips. "It'd be like we came full circle, only this time, instead of you dragging me out, I'm dragging you in with me."

I made quick work of my clothing, kicking it into a pile in the corner, and then stepping into the cool water. My pulse was like a drumbeat pounding in my head as I padded toward her. When I was just close enough to reach for her, she shook her head and nimbly stepped around me to press me back until I leaned against a large moss-covered boulder. Then, she dropped to her knees before me.

"Diana," I rasped, caressing her face as she held my gaze. "Come back up here, I want to—"

"Ah ah!" She pushed my hand away and laughed. "I'm still queen for at least another day, so give me one more moment, and then you can have it your way."

With that, she tipped her head and flicked out her tongue as she leaned closer and nipped lightly at the swollen head of my cock.

I grunted and grasped at the moss-covered rock for

purchase. Her tongue was molten hot as she sucked me in, and then I could think no more. All I could do was feel as she drew me deeper, so deep that I could sense the tender flesh at the back of her throat. And then she moaned, and the rumble shot straight through me.

"Fucking hell," I ground out, sliding one hand into her hair for a long moment. I let her have her way, moving slowly at first, but then more quickly, she sucked me in and expelled me out, until her lips were barely touching me before drawing me deep again.

She was toying with me, and I fucking loved it. Soon, though, the need to flex my hips and pull her tighter, urge her faster, overtook me, and I fought it tooth and nail.

Let her take her fill, man.

But it was like she could read my mind as she set me free with a pop. I could feel the heat of her gaze burning into me as I looked down.

"Your turn, then, Mr. Impatient. Tell me what you want," she whispered, and I could feel it. Using both hands to work my cock in a dizzying, sure rhythm, with her mouth just inches away, her warm breath washing over me. I could see the gleam of her fangs just peeking out from her upper lip, and the words broke free before I could stop them.

"I want you to take my blood while I come, and then I want to do the same to you."

I looked away, biting back a curse under my breath. It

was too soon for such declarations. She'd barely gotten her head around—

"Yesss!" she hissed, cutting off my train of thought, even as she leaned closer to my thigh, her grip tightening. The strike was fast and sure as her fangs sank deep into my upper thigh.

The sensation was an electric shock that rocked me back on my heels, and I gripped a stone even harder to keep from toppling into the water. Our entire history flashed through my mind as she sucked hard and strong, taking my blood, filling me with a need so deep I could barely keep myself from howling with it.

"Yes, love," I encouraged her, flexing my thigh muscles and arching into her bite. "Take what you need."

She moaned, and I looked down to see a tiny droplet of blood trickle from the corner of her mouth. The sight was my undoing. She must have sensed it because her hand began to move more quickly in long, strong strokes.

"Yeah, that's it, Frostbite. Work that cock. Up and down, harder, harder. Keep sucking. Fuck yeah!"

I growled her name, my fingers tightening in her hair as my balls drew tight, and I started to come. She leaned into it, pressing her chest against my cock as I spurted my hot seed onto her beautiful breasts. It felt like it went on forever...waves of pleasure crashing into one another, and then the sensation of her pleasure doubling down on mine as she shuddered and rocked, coming herself from the overload of sensations, the hot rush of blood in her mouth, the sight of me taking my pleasure.

"I need you inside me, Raven!"

In a flash, I swept her up into my arms, flipping her around and seating her on the rock. Her legs wrapped around my hips instantly, and I didn't wait, just thinking about what was to come.

"Now you," she whispered, "drink from me."

She tipped her head back, exposing her long, graceful neck for the taking. It was like a dream come true, a lifetime in the making. I didn't hesitate, striking in two spots at once as I let my fangs sink into her buttery flesh and impaled her on my cock, already rock hard once again and weeping to get inside her.

The taste of her alone would have done it. I squeezed my eyes shut and tried to savor it as best I could, like honey and magic and heat in life all wrapped up into one. The power of it flowed through me, and I gripped her tighter as I pistoned my hips, working my cock in and out of her tight pussy over and over again.

The low keening in the back of her throat built up to a full scream as she came apart in my arms. I held on to her tight and flexed back before jutting in all the way, planting myself to the root and then rocking gently forward and back as she found her climax. She clamped so tight around me that I had to release her neck to let out a bark of pleasure as her own orgasm brought forth mine, and I exploded inside her in a hot rush.

I was still lost in the final throws when her legs slid away from me, and she slumped back against the mossy stone with a gasp.

"Ah, Raven, oh god, I love you, I love you. I have always loved you," she whispered, reaching up weakly and pulling my face closer to hers to lap up a spot of blood on my lip before kissing me deeply, tongue to tongue.

She loved me.

Diana, Queen of Werewolves, my Frostbite and fated mate, loved me.

It was then that I knew we would win this war. We had to, because I wanted a lifetime with this woman within my grasp...

And there was no fucking way in the world I was letting it slip through my fingers.

CHAPTER 24

Raven

The morning was not far away, but the darkness of night still held tight. I slipped from the bed, reluctantly. I left Diana to sleep though, knowing she needed it now more than ever. Much as I would have liked to remain with her, I'd promised Dominic and Lochlin I'd do a perimeter sweep of the keep with them.

Dressed, I paused at the door, a strange feeling washing over me. I blinked and saw Diana in full battle gear, her fangs exposed, fury written across her face.

"If they think they are taking Raven, I will show them just what they are up against."

I blinked and shook my head, my heart pounding. What the actual fuck was that?

Forcing my feet to move, I opened the door and slid through. The hallway was quiet, though I could pick up slight movement at the far end. I assumed it was a guard, by the soft clink of armor.

I moved in that direction, to be sure. We'd set guards up at both ends of the hall to Diana's rooms to give us time if anyone burst in.

"Soldier."

The guard straightened and shot me a look. "Sir. Is the queen sleeping still?"

I noted that he didn't give me the side eye as so many of the wolves did. They thought I was stealing her away. They still didn't fully understand that she'd been on loan to them —that she'd always been destined to come back to me.

"Yes. Let her sleep. I will check in with Lochlin and help him do another sweep over the grounds." I clapped him on the shoulder and gave him a squeeze. "If anyone shows up that shouldn't, make some noise. She would not like it if you died on her behalf."

His grin was a sudden flash of white. "I would be honored to fight at my queen's side, but I hope that it does not come to that. The way she fucked up Cammon...epic. Legendary. There will be bards singing that for a thousand years. The Queen slays the Giant."

A shiver slid through me and I grinned. "I cannot wait to hear it."

I slid past him and made my way through the nearly silent keep, down the main stairs, and to the Great Room. Lochlin and Dominic were already there, waiting on me.

"Took your time," Lochlin raised an eyebrow.

"Spoke with the guard, made sure he was awake." I stretched my shoulders back, feeling my spine crack, thinking about the vision of Diana I'd had.

I wasn't about to tell them about that. Because for all I knew, it could have just been my imagination, and not because finally sharing blood with my fated mate had stirred up the future sight Myrr had supposedly gifted me with...Right?

Right.

"We'll start on the east side," Lochlin said. "Case the sun decides to make an early appearance." He motioned at me and Dominic, "Can't have you two getting an unscheduled tan."

Dominic shook his head. "I've no plans of that. Did it once, lived to tell the tale."

I touched the dagger at my side. "I'm covered. I've still got the dagger that protects me from the sun."

Lochlin clapped his hands together. "Excellent, let's go boys. See what we can see. We had the guards clear out the area where the mob was and secure the perimeter so there won't be any additional contamination of the scene. I want scents. I want tracks. I want whatever we can gather so we know exactly who we are dealing with. Every fucking name is going to be nailed to the wall before we are done."

"Agreed," Dominic growled. "We can't leave any of them to fester into another rebellion."

I kept my mouth shut on that topic. Not because I

didn't think it was possible, but because another vision smacked me in the face. Diana again, only this time she was not alone. Elka stood with her, as did Dominic, Lochlin, and William. Dominic and Lochlin were wearing the same clothes that they were in now, only they were torn and ripped, covered in blood. The sun was only just coming through the upper windows.

I was not in the scene and Diana's face...fury and fear warred in her green eyes.

"What do you mean they took him hostage?"

I stumbled and Dominic shot a hand to steady me. "Seriously, did you not get enough blood?"

Clearing my throat I pulled away. "No, I'm fine. Sorry."

Dominic's eyes didn't leave me. He knew me too well. "What's going on?"

I ran a hand through my hair. "Fuck, if I figure it out, I'll tell you, how about that?"

"Fair."

We were at the eastern side of the keep only a minute later, and Lochlin led us out.

He squinted and took a long deep breath. "There weren't many on this side, I don't think. Maybe five or six."

We spread out and combed the ground. I marked hoof prints with unusual shapes, two that had broken hoof walls which gave distinct patterns. Bits of clothing, even things like coins that had fallen out of pockets. We bagged it all individually in the clear plastic bags that Lochlin gave us.

Slowly we made our way to the south side of the keep where there was less evidence, but there was a body. A guard had taken an arrow to his left eye on the parapet above and fallen over.

"Shit, that's Brandt," Lochlin muttered and then let out a low rumbling growl. "He'd barely taken on the guard mantle. He just turned eighteen."

It was more of the same on the western side. Dead guards, a little evidence. But it was the northern side, facing the deep forest where the rebels had come from, and it was where much of the evidence sat. More bits of cloth, leather, items that had fallen from pockets, even a few strands of hair, both horse and werewolf. All of it would be used to condemn those who followed Maverick.

There was no coming back from what he had incited them to. All because they refused to follow a queen who'd proven herself time and time again.

We had a stack of clear plastic bags in under thirty minutes. The sun was getting closer to rising, though that was not what had my attention.

I couldn't help but look to the forest over and over, instead of keeping my eyes on the task at hand. Because *they* would be coming from that direction.

Would it be Maverick, though? I didn't think so. It didn't feel like him. It felt like his big, thuggish friend, Teeter.

I put a hand to my head and closed my eyes. Was this how Myrr saw things?

Fuck me with a cactus, no wonder she was the way she was—scattered and saying the craziest things. I could see things coming. Could feel them.

And I knew in my gut I had to let it happen. This was the path that I was on—the path that Diana was on.

"Dominic," I grimaced. "You aren't going to like it. But something's going to happen while we are out here. You can't fight it; you have to let it happen."

Lochlin and Dominic turned to me at the same time.

"What?" Dominic stared hard at me. "What are you talking about?"

Lochlin opened his mouth, and I *knew* that he was going to call the guards.

I held my hand out to stop him. "Don't. People will die, and that's not what Diana would want."

Dominic's eyes narrowed. "This is from that fucking blood you drank from Myrr days ago, isn't it? Some sort of premonition?"

I might have done more than nod, but the sound of hundreds of feet, their bodies racing from the shadows of the trees, the harsh breathing.

I couldn't help it, I still put up something of a fight even though I knew I had to go with them. Hell, I landed some blows, watched as Lochlin and Dominic were hit with a smoke bomb of some sort and a thick rolled parchment was thrown at their feet.

"Bind him!"

Ropes were tossed around me, and yanked tight, and I was pulled to the ground and *dragged* from the keep, feet first. "Fuck. I didn't see that coming."

The words popped out of me and then I started to laugh, I couldn't help it. Because I'd heard Myrr say that *exact* same thing, with the same note of surprise.

The laughter rolled through me, until I was baying like a gods damned hyena. I couldn't stop. Tears rolled down my cheeks as my chest heaved and I howled.

"Shut the fuck up!" Someone kicked me in the belly, knocking the wind out of me.

I struggled a moment to catch my breath. "Thanks, I'm not sure I could have stopped on my own."

"Do you ever shut up?" Teeter loomed over me. "You're going to fucking die, and you're laughing?"

I grunted. "I'm not Maverick, I'm certainly not going to go out crying like a baby."

Another boot landed in my low back, sending a sharp pain up and down my spine that stole my breath in a whole other way.

We'd traveled only another few minutes before they hoisted me up onto a horse. "You leave a ransom note?"

Teeter glared at me as he tied me face down on the horse, my hands and feet attached by a rope run under the horse's belly.

"Maybe."

"Oh, I know you did." I winked at him. "You're going to ask Diana to hand over Elka?"

Teeter's eyes widened and a sharp spike of fear rolled off him. "How the fuck did you know that?"

I grinned, making sure my fangs were visible, thinking about how Myrr would react. I leaned into it. "Oh, trust me, I know a hell of a lot more than you pups even realize. You got any cookies on you or some sort of snack? If this is going to be a long trip, I might get peckish."

If I'd sworn at him, demanded that he release me, told him I was going to kill him, I don't think that would have fazed him.

But asking for a cookie?

He stepped back, a trickle of sweat rolling down his face. "Let's go."

Rattled...fuck, I'd rattled him by thinking like Myrr. That had not been on my bingo card this morning.

We rode for a good hour, and in that time whatever brief sense of certainty I'd had about the future had fled, no matter how hard I concentrated. I couldn't tell you if someone was going to sneeze, never mind if I was going to survive this. It had been the potent elixir of Myrr's lingering blood along with the fresh from the vein infusion I'd taken from Diana that had offered me the window of insight, but it was gone now.

The choice to hand myself over without ever seeing how it all ended might haunt me, but at least I'd had one last night with Diana. If I was going to die, then I had that to think about as my life fled—the feel of her skin, the touch of her hands to my body, the love in her eyes. Love. She'd said it over and over. She loved me. Not because I was her fated mate, just for me. Raven. The man I'd become after the boy I'd been saved her.

"Cut him down."

Maverick's voice snapped me out of my reliving of my night with Diana.

The ropes that tied me to the horse were cut, but the rest remained as I was yanked off my mount and dropped to the ground. I blinked up at Maverick.

"Hello, chickenshit."

Maverick smiled; his teeth were...bigger than before. But not white. More yellow. As if the giant wolf connected to him was consuming him already.

"Shit for brains. They said you barely fought? I'd really hoped you would have done more, we had a special surprise for you."

He pulled out a wooden long-handled weapon with a metal prong at the end. He shoved the prong against my chest and there was a click, like a lock being opened. Electricity rocked through me, darkness and stars burst across my vision and my teeth clacked shut as the pain lit up every nerve ended in my body.

I couldn't breathe.

Couldn't think.

The prongs were yanked back. "We need him alive, boss. At least until those bitches pay the ransom."

"He'll survive," Maverick all but purred. "And I've waited a long time for this moment. To have him here, at my feet. Seeing just how fucking weak he is. How fucking weak all bloodsuckers are."

The crowd gave a growling roar, but it wasn't as loud as I expected. Smaller numbers than before. But that made sense. Many had backed away from Maverick when Elka had made her declaration as future queen. The werewolves weren't stupid.

My muscles were still spasming from the bolt of electricity even if my head was reconnected to my thoughts. I should have kept my mouth shut. Should have just let him have his fun. But if Maverick was going to light me up like a human Christmas tree, I might as well earn it.

I spat to one side and let out a low moan. "You going to let them take the fall for you? Like you let that girl Opal die while you waited to steal her power?"

The prongs slammed back into me and my teeth cracked hard against one another. Longer this time. My heart *really* wasn't a fan of the treatment as it stuttered and slammed inside my chest.

Darkness once more, then light finally. I blinked as breath came whooshing back into me. I didn't think this would kill me. But to be fair, electricity was connected to fire...heat and power. Maybe I shouldn't be pissing them off quite so much. Even if I knew I had to be here, I should probably contain myself.

Teeter came into view next to Maverick. "Boss man. Let it be. He's dead either way. But you gotta wait, or we've got nothing to bargain with."

I blinked up at Teeter, and my words were a bit

slurred, as if I'd been drinking. "I knew you secretly loved me. But I'm a one-woman guy."

Teeter snarled down at me, grabbed the prongs and slammed them into me himself.

So much for containing myself.

Before the darkness took me fully, one last thought whipped through my mind, and down the bond to my mate.

I trust you with not only my heart, but my life, Diana.

The click of the door hadn't woken me, but I was unsurprised to find myself alone in the early morning darkness. Raven had to meet with Loch and Dom so they could check the grounds for the evidence we needed to nail Maverick and his followers to the wall.

But despite not waking to Raven by my side, I'd slept more deeply than I had in...perhaps my whole life.

Finding out all that had been done to keep both of us safe and alive so we had a chance to meet one day...that we were meant to be and I could finally embrace my feelings for him without guilt? It had soothed the ragged edges of my heart and soul in ways that I hadn't even known I needed.

I burrowed deeper into the blankets, breathing in the smell of my mate, wishing we were somewhere far away, just the two of us.

But it wasn't to be, at least not yet.

I had my own meeting scheduled. The ceremony to crown Elka as queen was tomorrow, and I wanted to give her as much help and information as I could before then. Because once I handed the reins over, I had to step back and put some distance between us. As much as I wanted to be with her and give her guidance for as long as she needed, if our people were to support her fully, she needed to do it alone.

With a sigh, I flipped my legs out of bed and stretched, my body aching in the most pleasurable of ways.

I dressed swiftly, and took a quick second to marvel at how much had changed.

No more binding of my breasts. No more trying to fit into a world dominated by alpha males. Fuck that. I would forever mourn the loss of my wolf, but I was a vampire now. And I would own every inch of me, proud of exactly who I was.

Only thirty minutes at most after Raven left, I was out the door and headed toward the floor above mine, to Elka's rooms. The sun wouldn't be up for some time yet, but even so, we both had items that would keep us safe from its rays. While I wasn't fully sure that I would cook out there with my part human, former werewolf blood, there was no point in tempting fate, either.

She opened the door right away, dressed, her hair braided back from her face on one side. The room was lit up inside, pushing back the dark of the early morning.

"Diana." She tipped her head, but I saw her catch herself from curtseying.

I tipped my head back. I was still queen, so I didn't have to curtsey or bow. Not yet.

"Good morning, Elka. I thought we could go over the ceremony this morning, and what the first few days will look like after you're crowned."

"Of course." She opened the door wider, and I stepped through.

We'd not been working on her memorization for long, not even an hour, when someone banged hard on the door.

"Diana!"

I shot to my feet and flung the door open. Lochlin stood there breathing hard, his face covered in filth, blood running down his cheek. "We were ambushed. They took Raven."

He pushed something into my hand, but, even as he did, I was reaching for the bond to Raven, feeling him moving north, towards the forest. He wasn't afraid. He was strangely calm.

Panic clawed at me, but I tamped it down. "How long?"

"The smoke bomb took ten minutes to clear. We couldn't find our way out of it." Dominic stood behind Lochlin. "Diana. I think...Raven knew it was going to happen, and he let it."

I looked at the rolled paper in my hand that Loch had

given me. Unfurling it, I recognized Maverick's scrawling print.

Elka will marry me and we will rule together, or your bloodsucker dies. Meet me where you first found me so we can negotiate terms.

Come alone.

Elka read over my shoulder and let out a snort. "Is he out of his fucking mind? Does he think we'd believe that he'd leave Raven alive even if I agreed to marry his stupid ass?"

Lochlin's rage-filled eyes swept past me and rested on Elka. "Princess, you are not marrying that piece of shit, not for any reason."

I didn't disagree with either of them. "I will go. Lochlin, get me one of the daggers—"

"They took them," he said. "The room was ransacked, all the daggers, in fact, all the pieces of tech we had to help the vampires with the sun are gone."

I was moving, headed back to my room, readjusting my plan. I didn't need the light of day. I could sense Raven, I could find him. "Then I will go now. There is time before the sun rises—"

Dominic grabbed my arm. "Maybe an hour, at best, Diana."

"Then I'd better haul ass," I pulled away from him. "Don't try to stop me, Dominic. You would do this for Sienna. And don't follow me. I won't risk his life because your ego can't handle being left out."

He tipped his head in my direction and held up his

hands in surrender, and, before long, I was in my room, whipping through my gear. I pulled on a couple pieces of leather armor, the bracers I liked, and two short swords. Fuck the shield, I was going in on full offense.

Turning, I let my fangs drop as I faced my brother and Lochlin in the doorway.

"If they think they are taking Raven, I will show them just what they are up against."

Lochlin stepped out of the way, but I turned and went to the window. It was faster.

"Wait!" Elka yelled.

I turned and she tossed something to me. A vial of blood. I looked to her, and she nodded. "Kill them, Diana. Don't leave anyone behind to fuck us over again."

I tucked the vial into my breast pocket. "Consider it done, my Queen."

With that I leapt from the window, landing lightly and then I was off. I could have taken a horse, but I was faster on foot. And I didn't have time to waste.

The woods I knew so well whipped around me in a blur of darkness and foliage as I locked onto Raven's signature in my head. I was getting closer, and now...pain ripped through him.

I stumbled as the first wave washed over me. Not that I felt the pain the same as he did, but I could sense just how bad it was. Like nothing he'd ever felt.

And the rage that followed blinded me.

I was sprinting again by the time Raven's voice whispered through me.

Diana, I trust you to save me. I trust you with not only my heart, but my life.

I redoubled my speed. He was hurt, dying maybe. The sun was coming up and I had to get to him.

"This way!" A whispered voice cut through the otherwise silent forest, and I skidded to a halt, whirling.

Mary, Gavin's widow, looked up at me from the fallen tree she'd been hiding behind. Her cheeks were red, as if she'd been crying, and her clothes were dirty and torn.

I crouched down. "What happened?"

She swallowed a sob, turning to the side. "It's horrible, Your Majesty. That human...he's gone mad with power since getting my husband's wolf. I know I sided against you, but—"

I waved off the concern, heart thumping heavy in my chest as another burst of agony ripped through my bond with Raven. "It's in the past. How many men does Mav have with him? Is he planning to ambush me?"

"It was just him when I left. I think he wants to face you alone. The things he's doing to the bloodsucker..." She shuddered. "Horrifying."

I cursed, striding back in the direction I'd been moving. "Get to the keep."

She caught me by the shoulder, jabbing her finger to the side. "You'll come up behind him if you go around this way. I'll show you."

I shook my head. "Just explain. I don't want you here when the fighting breaks out."

She opened her mouth as if to protest but nodded. "I understand. Just keep moving until you reach that boulder, then take a right."

"Ask for Loch once you get to the keep. He'll make sure you aren't harmed." Then I dashed off in the direction she'd indicated.

I hadn't expected her to defect, but it did make a lot of sense. Mav had gotten this far on charisma and subterfuge, but now he felt strong enough to throw that to the wayside and show everyone his true colors.

A decision that was about to result in his downfall.

I gritted my teeth through another round of pain, shifting my focus to stealth as I neared the boulder she'd indicated. With a little luck, I'd be able to catch him off guard and take him down before he had time to use Raven against me.

Raven appeared a heartbeat later, thirty feet ahead of me, his body crumpled.

Which was the only excuse I had for not seeing the trap.

A snare caught me as I took my next step, yanking me high into the air. The same wrap-around snare we'd used to great effect in so many of our conflicts with the other magical species.

The ropes shot around my upper body, binding my arms and legs tight.

"You see, boys? Predictable, just like I said." Maverick came into view as I was lowered to the ground. The clan heads who'd sided with him lurked off to the side, but my focus was on the two people stepping up from behind him.

That bastard Teeter, who'd started all of this, and a disappointed-looking Mary. She shook her head at me.

"Why?" Had she learned the truth of her husband's fate? I could hardly even blame her if she had. Self-defense or not, his blood was on my hands.

"I'm sorry it had to happen this way, Diana. The fault lies with the clans who've tolerated this for so long more than with you. A queen is meant to be her husband's helper, not a ruler in her own right. And when we allow that to be subverted, what can we expect but chaos?"

I opened my mouth to reply but was unable to find the words. She had truly bought into all this?

Mav grinned, patting her condescendingly on the shoulder. "You did well, Mary. Your husband would be proud." He glanced to his other side, gesturing for Teeter.

I struggled uselessly as Teeter and one of the clan heads dropped long pole snares over my neck, as if I were a wild animal. The nooses were tightened to a point where I could barely swallow. I reached for the well of power inside me but found it just out of reach.

Maverick strode forward and put his filthy fucking finger in my mouth to lift my lip. "See that? I told you! Those are fangs, boys. She's not even a werewolf anymore."

"You sure, boss?" Teeter stepped a little closer, but he seemed wary.

I, on the other hand, knew both Raven and I were fucked if I didn't make my move.

Maverick snorted. "I'll still marry that little princess of yours. Solidify the clans and make this place stronger than ever. Better than you could have ever made it. Because you are weak, ruled by your emotions and letting your pussy lead you astray."

The clan leaders broke into a fit of laughter.

I could feel Raven coming around, so I sent a push of energy his way, in the hopes that it would speed up the process.

"Love isn't weak, Maverick." I could only whisper around the nooses. "Love is the strongest thing in this world. Love is what allowed my father to raise me, even though I was not his daughter by blood. Love is what gave my brothers the strength to stop Edmund. Love, Maverick, is something you've never known. And its why you'll always be weak and afraid."

The nooses didn't tighten, if anything they loosened.

Maverick's eyes burned with fury, but he faked a laugh. "Of course a woman would think love is strong."

"Sun is rising," Teeter said. "If she really is a vamp, then she'll burn up next to him."

"Stand her closer to her piece of shit lover." Maverick grinned as he strode toward me.

I struggled and fought as an amused Teeter dragged me sideways, wishing more than ever that I still had my wolf. In my current form, the bonds were simply too tight. "Not so uppity now, are you?" he spat, yanking me the rest of the way to Raven's side.

Mav chuckled, turning to face the clan heads. "This is what a *real* alpha does with bloodsuckers, even if your last queen was more interested in bedding them."

"Already talking like you're one of us?" I grunted, the ropes burning at my wrist as I tugged with everything I had.

"One of *them*."

I ignored him, my heart thumping even faster as I realized how bad Raven's condition really was. His shirt was soaked in blood, and his head was lolling to the side, wobbling as if he was in a daze.

"Raven? They're going to burn us," I spat, craning my neck out to try biting at the bonds at my wrist. The taste of iron pricked at my tongue as my teeth found flesh, but the ropes remained unsevered.

Not quite.

"It's almost romantic, the way these two are about to die," Mav mused. "You know, I would've married you, if you'd only behaved. I guess I'll have to settle for that little bitch you want to take your place."

I cursed as I glanced to the side, seeing the first pinpricks of light peeking over the horizon. *Now or never.* The noose stung on my neck as I coiled and tightened every muscle in my body, then roared, releasing them all at once.

In many ways, it was a pathetic display, sending me

only a few inches closer to Raven despite the exertion. But a few inches was all I'd needed.

Mav scrambled forward as I stretched my hand upward, pressing my bloody wrist right to Raven's mouth.

Raven's fangs snapped forward in the blink of an eye, taking a long pull of blood that sent his eyes shooting open. "Frostbite?"

"We need to move!" I shouted, wincing as Mav surged into my peripheral.

Raven shot sideways in a blur, slamming head-first into his chest with a roar. His arms still hung uselessly at his side, but they writhed and twitched, as if the flesh and muscle were re-knitting before my eyes.

Mav cursed, his face alight with rage as he hurtled back, the word morphing into a roar as he shifted in a fraction of a second. He skidded to a halt, breaking into a full-on charge before Raven could free me from my bonds.

Fuck fuck fuck.

I reached for my magic as the clan heads strode forward, shifting one by one. If I could just access the same state as I had in the fight with the possessed Malach, we'd at least stand a fighting chance. I imagined unleashing it on them, trying to suppress the wave of guilt that washed over me. Even if they were my people, surely they deserved it for what they'd done, right?

But it was a truth my heart couldn't accept, regardless

of what my brain tried to tell it. The magic retreated from my touch, too wispy and ethereal to grab onto.

Mav snapped forward with his enormous jaws, but Raven dodged at the last moment, his shirt tearing as he slammed a freshly-healed fist into the wolf's side.

The enormous beast let out a growl, but it hadn't done any real damage. Mav's wolf was larger than any bear, and he was built like a fucking tank. How could anyone even *damage* him with their bare hands, forget actually beating him?

My attention shifted to the approaching clan heads. "You say men should rule, yet you're spineless enough to interrupt his duel? If Mav is the alpha because strength is what matters, then surely, he doesn't need your help with a lone, injured man."

The one in front growled at me, but slowed to a halt, and the others did the same just behind him. Teeter and Mary hung back even further, not even taking to their wolf forms. I growled as she met my gaze, and she lowered her eyes.

Mav sprang forward once again but caught a kick to the lower jaw. Rather than retreating from the massive enemy, Raven advanced, slipping just past every attack and following up with a punch of his own.

Mav's teeth snapped as he sprang forward, moving even more quickly than before, and my heart skipped a beat as he threw his weight abruptly sideways, slamming shoulder-first into the vampire.

Raven grunted as his back smashed into a tree just

behind him, barely recovering in time to duck under Mav's follow-up swipe. The tree snapped in half like a twig from the force of the blow, crashing to the forest floor, but Raven had been doing more than dodging.

He let out a triumphant roar as his arm snapped forward, crashing right toward the monster's chest.

Was he going for a fucking heart strike?

Mav's body began contorting, and my jaw dropped as he shifted all the way back to human form a fraction of a second before Raven's hand would've slammed into his heart. Whatever magic Mav had, it had allowed him to circumvent *years* of training. I doubted that even Loch could do it that quickly.

Not that it had done him much good.

Raven's hand smashed through the now-human Mav's shoulder with a sickening crunch, burying itself up to the wrist. He tore it free, cracking Mav across the jaw with a left hook before he could call on his wolf.

Mav scrambled backward, fur sprouting from his skin as he tried to shift once again, but Raven's leg caught him across the forehead before he could. He tried again and again, but Raven was simply too fast, staying on him and knocking him back to human form every time he started to shift.

A burning pain at my cheek pulled my attention away, and my eyes snapped toward the sun. "The daggers!" If we didn't get them in another minute or two, it'd cook us alive.

By the time I looked back to Raven, it was already

too late. Mary had shifted, and her small, reddish wolf sprang into action, springing through the air with her jaws open toward Raven's back. He spun in time to bat her aside, but Mav's wolf roared back to life in the momentary lapse, smashing into Raven from the other side with a massive paw.

Pure rage washed away everything else as he shot backward, and I let out a scream. The shard's power flowed through me all at once, and the ropes dissolved into dust in a flash of energy. Time seemed to slow as I stood, glancing over to Raven. He was still alive.

And it wasn't just through our bond, because I could sense every werewolf around us, too. Down to their beating hearts, and the blood pumping through their bodies. And, even more importantly, their souls. Like little balls of noxious black energy, each and every one of them was treacherous and hateful to their core, with Mav's being the darkest of them all. I shook my head with regret as I shifted to Mary, finding her soul as corrupted as the rest.

Now that Mav had sowed the seeds in them, they'd oppose Elka's rule until their dying breaths, I was sure of it. I gritted my teeth, steeling myself. There was a time to be softhearted, but this was not it. My father's words replayed in my mind. *A queen should act in the best interest of* all *her people.*

A tear dripped down my cheek as I focused in on each little swirl of energy. "You all were of the earth once. Return to it." I spoke not with power, not with anger, but sheer sorrow. They had been mine to care for once, mine to protect.

The power flowed out of me, enveloping every single one of them. Their bodies lit up with energy, bones glowing through their skin as if I had electrified them. Maverick roared, charging toward me, but Raven was there once again, intercepting him.

The other werewolves turned to dust, their remains dropping to the earth and sinking into the soil.

Gone.

As if they had never been.

But not Mav.

The magic I'd put into him flooded back to me all at once, and I turned to see him charging away, not even looking back. His fur was badly singed, and he ran with a clear limp, but he'd somehow managed to avoid the worst of it.

"I didn't focus enough of the magic on him. He's headed for the water." I took a step and Raven put his hand out, stopping me, pulling me into his arms. His body was shaking, muscles still spasming from what Maverick had put him through.

"No. Diana. Let him go."

Of all the things I thought would have come out of his mouth, that was not it. "What?"

"He...he has a part to play in all this yet. I don't know what, but he must live for now."

Behind us, the sun began to peek through the trees. Raven cupped my face and stared into my eyes. "Besides.

If we're going to die, let's not do it looking at that chick-enshit's scrawny ass."

My lips wobbled. "You think we're going to die?"

He shrugged. "Nah. I think the calvary is going to show up in three, two, one—"

The pounding of hooves and feet reached us as the sun crested across the horizon, and I knew it would be the last time I truly felt the sun's warmth.

But it was not the last thing I saw.

No, the last thing I saw was Lochlin as he threw a heavy blanket over our heads and tackled us to the ground.

The Ceremony was in full swing, and Elka had done us all proud, reciting the words and committing herself to be the new queen of our people.

As was tradition, she was crowned not in the keep, but in the valley of the black willows. Where our people, past and present, could see her, and hear her words. The night was blessedly free of rain or wind, and the darkness was absolute except for the single torch that Elka held.

As she turned to face the crowd, crown on her head, she lifted her one torch high. "Let the light of wisdom and hope continue to guide us to be better, stronger, and more resilient with every challenge we face."

The torches around the clearing all burst into flame and the crowd gasped. I saw Theo standing close to Myrr, rubbing his hands together. He'd made the suggestion, and I had to admit it was a nice addition. Not that I didn't think that Elka was capable, but the more we could do to help her...the better.

And a little show of magic for our tech driven people would go a long way.

Raven stood down with the others. A sultry smile slid over his face, and he gave me a slow wink.

Heat flushed through me, and I winked right back at him.

His smile widened, and an elbow was jabbed into my side. "That's enough, you two."

Myrr wobbled past me. "There are some that still don't believe, Diana. Some that need to be shown."

I blinked as she stuffed a cookie into her mouth. Where the hell had she—

She blinked up at me as she pulled a second cookie out of her pocket.

With a sigh, I made myself look out over the crowd. To see those who still had uncertainty on their faces, to see the subtle shake of their heads. The ceremony was done. She was queen, but our people had been so hurt, so betrayed...even by me at times.

"I would like to say something."

Elka turned and looked at me, everyone stopped what they were doing. "Diana?"

"A goodbye present," I murmured, thinking about how I'd been able to sense all the werewolves that had attached themselves to Maverick. I could again, I was sure, and if I could do that, and connect them all fully together....

"I was your queen, and my father was king before me, so you will always be my family. But perhaps somewhere in my efforts to protect you, I wasn't truthful enough. I lost your trust. I should've shared more, and I aim to do that now."

Frowns, the ripples of murmurs.

I opened myself to the shard, with as much calm and love as I could muster in my heart.

The power flowed through me once more, only this time I begged it to be gentle, to show them all how much they meant to me. How much being a part of their lives meant to me.

"Love is power, Diana, and you have great love for your people. Let it be done," the shard whispered through me.

Like a warm rain, the power flowed down on them. Giving them access to see the truth of my heart. How I'd fought for them, worried and worked for them, how I'd always tried to do best by them, even when it cost me my own wants or desires. That losing my wolf had cost me dearly.

That I ached for her still, even knowing that I would never see her again.

The women were openly weeping, and even some of the men as my heart was laid out for all of them to see.

"No matter that I've lost my wolf, no matter that I am no longer your leader, I will always love you all. And I leave you with the greatest gift I can—a queen who loves you as much as I do." The shard's power flowed down my arm, and I touched Elka gently on the cheek.

A tiny star appeared, white, strident lines streaking outward. And then Elka's heart was laid open to her people.

And they saw what I saw. How fierce she was in wanting the best for them all, the desire to protect and lift them up, and above all else, the deep and abiding love she had for each of them. The forgiveness she held for even those who had wronged her.

I drew back the power of the shard and slumped.

Raven caught me so I never hit the ground. "You did good, Frostbite." His voice was thick with emotion. "That was the most beautiful display of power I've ever seen."

He helped me stand and I turned to see my people—No, *Elka's* people—rush toward their new queen, ignoring customs.

Pressing her into their arms.

Re-committing themselves to her.

The shard whispered something I already understood. *They are more united than ever before. Seeing the hearts of their two queens allowed them to believe again.*

Raven slipped his arm around my waist. "Where to, my Queen?"

"You can't call me that anymore." I shook my head as I turned to face him.

"You will always be my queen, and I will always be yours to command." He pressed his mouth to the curve below my ear. "There is nowhere you would go that I wouldn't follow."

I wanted to look over my shoulder, to look back to my past one more time. But Raven was in front of me, and he was my future.

"What about a little treasure hunt?"

His eyebrows shot up. "As long as there are no big ass spiders involved, I'd be game. Are you thinking about something in particular?"

Again, I felt the pull of the shard, guiding me toward something I didn't fully understand. But I didn't *need* to understand. I just had to trust. And after seeing what my new power had enabled me to give to my people, trusting was easy.

"Yes. There's this book that was stolen. I think...I think it needs to be returned to its rightful owner."

Epilogue

Diana

The grimoire was a weight in the bag slung over my shoulder, the demon killing blade resting in a sheath next to it. Though the further I got from the Werewolf Territory, the lighter the bag seemed to be. Strange. When I'd first picked the book up, it had taken all my strength to lift it from its hiding place by the river.

"Fucking Maverick," I grumbled under my breath. To think that all along he'd been dabbling, tempting fate, carrying a curse...and I'd let him just walk into my life.

Gods, I felt like a fool, even now. Shame still burned me that I could be taken in by Maverick so many times. That I had been blind to his treacherous nature.

Worse, that he'd gotten away from us after the battle of the clans. Slipping away before he could be held accountable. Anger and shame warred within me, and I struggled to breathe past that deadly combination.

Through the bond with Raven, I felt his calm reach toward me. A flow of love that was so strong and solid I could have physically leaned into it. The shame faded some, and the anger slid away. "Thank you, love."

He knew how much I beat myself up about Maverick. No matter what he said, no matter how he tried to show me that it hadn't been my fault, I couldn't help but take the blame for all the deaths—deaths that Maverick had caused in an attempt to overthrow everything.

I blew out a breath and tried to focus on the world around me. This part of the forest skirted several borders. The river running down the length of our territories acted a bit like a natural border.

The forest of the wolves gave way to ethereal plants, gossamer leaves, and songbirds of such beauty that it took all I had to keep walking.

The fae would not bother me, as long as I stayed close to the river. Or at least, I hoped Cleona would hold to her word. Not that she was a liar but...I did not fully trust the fae queen. I wasn't sure I ever could with her fickle nature.

The river hustled along beside me, tumbling south.

I took a step and the weight in my bag suddenly redoubled.

"Damn." I tried turning to cross the river and the

same weight was there. Just as an experiment, I stepped backward, toward the werewolf territory. Same increase of weight. I turned left and the weight lessened.

Good enough for me.

I kept on moving, knowing that I was in a sort of no-man's land. There were these strange little pockets of neutrality here and there over the continent. Like Myrr's hut. The ruins. And, apparently, this witch's haven.

The forest was different here again. Darker, the branches of the trees sparser, dotted with long hanging moss, and rot. I sniffed the air. Rot and magic. They both lay heavy on the land here.

Other than Raven, no one knew I was here. Not that it mattered where I went any longer—I was no longer queen. Hell, I was a vampire in enemy territory no matter how I looked at it.

I shook my head. No, not enemy—allied territory. And that was what this was about. We needed all the allies we could muster to face Lilis. If this witch was as powerful as Maverick said, then it couldn't hurt to have someone like her on our side.

My brothers would have shit bricks if they knew I was coming here. We'd all been raised on the stories of witches ravishing the land, of them stealing children and destroying crops. Yet...I wondered if that was even true. The way Maverick's memories had played out, she hadn't seemed like that at all. She'd seemed reasonable at the worst, and, at the best, she'd seemed to have a true desire to help. I could only hope that that had not changed in her, that Maverick and the years since he'd seen her last had not hardened her.

The shard seemed to warm inside of me as I took a few steps into a small clearing. This was the space. The earth was soft beneath my feet, moss and loam sinking at my every step.

I pulled the bag around and held it up. "Lady of the forest, I bring something that belongs to you. A bastard named Maverick took it many years ago, and I would return it to you."

Around me the forest stilled. The bird song had faded. The light brightened and the ground below me shifted. I stumbled backward as a chimney and roof erupted from the ground, shooting upward, followed by a cottage of wood and beam, wrapped in deep green vines with even deeper red ruby flowers hanging like heavy droplets.

The door burst open, and a woman strode out. Her skin was as dark as Evangeline's, but her eyes were silver, rimmed in gold.

She was, in a word, stunning in her beauty. But it was her smile that caught me off guard.

"Diana. Huntress. Vampire. Werewolf. Queen." She tipped her head. "You carry the Veil well, young one."

Young?

A shiver went through me. "You know my name, but I do not know yours."

Her smile widened. "Yes, yes, I believe I can give you my name. Khalida."

Her name echoed between us, rippling with power. I tipped my head. "An honor to meet you, Khalida."

She motioned with her hand to enter her house, and it was my turn to smile. "I thank you for your generosity of your home and hearth, but I came only to return this."

We were close enough that when I held the bag out to her, she was able to take it, her long, tapered nails clacking. "You found my grimoire."

"Maverick hid it, at the river where I met him. I suppose it got too heavy at that point, and he could carry it no further." I grimaced. "He's a dick."

Khalida's head snapped up and she laughed. "He is that, isn't he? But why do you seem so...upset?"

Strangely I found myself spilling the truth. "He fooled me so many times. He caused so many deaths. I should have let that demon have him on the river all those years ago!"

She huffed as she flipped her grimoire open. "Regret is a strange thing."

"Do you regret giving him the blade?" I motioned at the bag. "I returned it as well."

"No. That was paid for. He stole only the book." She handed me the bag back. "The blade is yours now, princess."

I blinked. "Princess?"

"Are you not a child of the vampire king? You may no longer be queen, but you are still a princess." Her head tipped to one side. "What do you wish in return for the grimoire?"

I almost said we wanted her as an ally. To face down the dark goddess. But...I just couldn't.

"I was going to ask for you to be an ally to our cause but...I do not want to have an ally whose hand has been forced. You cannot trust them. Take the book as a boon. A righting of at least one wrong that Maverick caused." I took a step back.

Movement in the doorway drew my eyes. A second woman stood in the doorway. She had her mother's frame, but her skin was lighter, as if I'd caught the night sky just as the dawn approached. Her hair was lighter too, hints of gold and copper threaded through the long curls. But it was the shape of her eyes and mouth that had me staring. It couldn't be...she looked like *him*. Maverick.

"Yes. That is his daughter. And the only reason why I didn't kill him outright. A gift of a child is no small thing in our world, Diana. You know this." Khalida smiled fondly. "Perhaps one day you will know her name too, but today is not that day."

Her daughter straightened. "I am no longer a child, Mother. With her here, the signs are aligned."

Khalida sighed, her smile slipping. "You are not a child, my love."

I didn't understand exactly what was going on between them, but I felt the tension rising.

"It is time, Mother. I am ready to take my step in what the fates demand of me. You know that her arrival is a sign. When the lost queen returns that which was stolen, the stars wait for me to face my fate."

Khalida clasped her hands to her chest over the book. "Yes, that is as it was said at your birth."

Her daughter stepped out of the doorway; her smile fiercer than her mother's. "Then I go, and with my leaving I take the knowledge that my mother loves me. And that the world needs me to become the witch I am meant to be."

There was a crack in the air, like lightning, and Khalida's daughter was gone.

The witch's shoulders slumped. "She is headstrong. But her heart is good, Diana. Please remember that."

"You think she will cross paths with me?"

Khalida's smile trembled. "She will, I am sure of it. But not yet. Not yet."

A shudder passed through her, and she looked over me as if her only child had not just disappeared in front of us. "I hear the animals speak of you, Diana, of your loss."

I blinked at her, the change in direction throwing me off balance. "My father?"

"As devastating as that loss surely was, it is the natural order of things to lose a parent. This is deeper than that..." She shook her head with a sad smile. "Your wolf."

Pain lanced through me. "I–yes. It is perhaps the greatest loss of my life. She was my strength when I did not think I could continue. She taught me to be brave again, to be strong when I knew I was on the right path." I struggled to keep my words balanced and not full of tears. There would never be a day that passed, that I did not miss my wolf. Her strength. Her love. Her friendship. It wasn't like the love of a pet, or what I felt for Kevin the hell-hound. It had been like losing one half of a whole. My twin heart.

Khalida stepped back. "A gift then, from ally to ally." She rolled her wrist and sparks danced in the air between us, silvery white and blue. They hovered and then fell and when I looked up, Khalida was gone, as was her house.

I blinked and shook my head. "Good luck, Khalida, to you and your daughter."

A crack of twigs behind me had me tensing. I was close enough that a demon could have wandered this way —and, seeing as they would fight me, even now, with Gabe aligning with us...well, it was in their nature to kill first and never ask questions later.

I crouched and pulled the glowing blade free from its sheath. "Show yourself."

Another crack of twigs. A shadowy figure ghosting between the trees.

I stood up, chills sweeping through me. It couldn't be. I nearly dropped the blade, fumbling to get it back into its sheath.

White fur, high black socks, the black tipped ears, the black tipped tail. It could not be her and yet...there was no other with her coloring.

A name I'd never uttered out loud, one I'd barely allowed myself to *think* of slipped from my lips. "Eira?"

The wolf stopped and turned, frosted blue eyes staring into my soul. I dropped to my knees; certain I was seeing things. Either this was the cruelest of tricks or the greatest of gifts.

Eira stalked toward me, ears pricked, eyes on mine. She stopped only inches from me, the blast of her warm breath washing over my face, warming the tears that flowed down my cheeks.

My hand shook as I lifted it towards her, certain that I would encounter nothing but empty space, certain that I was seeing things. Yet the hope…the hope that bloomed in my chest was all I could hang onto.

Slowly, I pressed my hand to the side of her muzzle, *feeling* the warmth under my fingertips, the solid press of fur tickling against my skin.

"Eira."

I collapsed forward and she surged toward me at the same time, half catching me against her solid shoulder. Sobs wracked my body, as I clung to the other half of my soul, and I knew then that anything was possible.

That no matter the doubt and fears that plagued us as we faced down the darkest of goddesses, that perhaps, just perhaps, love was truly enough to see us through this.

Hope was enough. Faith in one another was enough.

I felt more than saw Lycan's presence, as if his hand rested on my shoulder. Even those who'd left us were still fighting from the other side, to help us through.

I blinked back tears as I sat back on my heels, my hands buried deep in the ruff around Eira's neck. Her eyes gazed deep into mine, sparkling with energy and the connection that she and I had always had.

She let out a soft huff of air and I grinned, knowing what she wanted as if she were still a part of me. "Yes. Let's run. And then let's go find our next key. We have a goddess to stop, Eira. Are you ready?"

Her lips rippled up over her teeth and she tipped back her head.

And howled defiance to the world.

* * *

Want more Alpha Territories? Here's a free Bonus just for you!

**DOWNLOAD
A FREE STORY**